THE UNCOMMON THREAD

Keeping secrets can be dangerous.
Telling them can be deadly.

LAURIE DOUGLASS

L. DOUGLASS BOOKS

For Tim, without whose encouragement,
love, and patience, this story
would have remained only a dream.

For Katherine, Abbie, Lauren, Maya, and Ari—
May your adventures, like Paddy's, bring you
the joy (and fun!) that comes from giving
of yourselves to others.

CONTENTS

I

LONGING

"ADVENTURE IS WORTHWHILE IN ITSELF."
-AMELIA EARHART

It was no ordinary storm. Even though Paddy was inside and several blocks away, he could hear the iron clasp clanging loudly against the flagpole as if it sounded an alarm. If only he could have realized it was a harbinger of the terrible events about to happen.

The nor'easter had been building in strength off the coast for days before it descended on the seaside village of Weymouth, pounding it without mercy. Swirling coal-colored clouds appeared to be ripped apart by lightning that was so close it made Paddy's hair stand on end.

Storms fueled Paddy's imagination, and the more violent, the better. He had hardly left the window seat for two days. His heart raced as he placed his hand on the vibrating window and listened to the shrieking winds. He closed his eyes, and he was sailing in first place in the America's Cup, heading into treacherous seas. He could almost feel the salt spray on his face.

The electricity periodically flickered, so the storm provided a welcome break from the monotony of cutting fabric, binding button-holes, and endless hand stitching. A rattle outside made Paddy's eyes dart up to the shop's sign, shaking him from his imaginary adventures. The wind whipped the sign so wildly one could scarcely read the gold lettering that read: Duncan and Sons—Tailoring, which reminded him of the reality of his predicament.

A cloud of foreboding had been growing in his mind about his future, and now that he'd graduated from high school, he could no longer avoid his dilemma. The swinging sign outside the shop was as irritating as his conscience, for it reminded him that "Duncan" was followed by "and Sons."

The shop had been built by Paddy's grandfather, William Duncan, when he came to America from Dundee, Scotland, in 1960. Paddy's father, Malcolm, took over the shop, and naturally, he expected his son to follow in his footsteps. Tailoring in the Duncan family dated back to 1775, so after 244 years, there was no little pressure on Paddy to continue the family legacy.

Paddy looked around at the tiny shop and imagined working there for the rest of his life. *How could Papa be content to spend every day in this tiny place? The most exciting thing that has happened in the past decade was getting a new sewing machine.* The prospect of staying four more years to get his journeyman's certificate left him feeling as though someone was holding him underwater. Finally, he was fed up with his indecision and decided he needed to talk to someone. He couldn't speak to Papa, and besides Grandpa, his friend David was the only other person he completely trusted to be honest with him. He had known David since seventh grade, and they had both been on track, wrestling, and sailing teams in high school.

Paddy spoke quietly into the phone so that Papa wouldn't hear. "Hey, David. What's going on?"

"I'm supposed to be filing college applications, but I can't decide where to apply."

"Same here," replied Paddy.

"I thought you were going to become a journeyman."

"I was . . . I am . . . ugh! That's my problem. I can't *stand* the idea of just staying here. I'm desperate to do something where I can travel, and I think I should get a degree first if I'm going to get the kind of job that lets me do that. But, if I say that to my dad, he might have a heart attack. He's been so sad since my mom died."

David listened and was quiet for a few moments before commenting. "You know, when my dad left for Afghanistan, I told him I wanted to be a Marine just like him. But he knew that I'm wired to be an engineer. Before he shipped out, he told me that each person has to find their own way. So, who knows? Maybe you aren't supposed to be a tailor. Maybe you should have a job where you travel for now. Then later, if you want to settle down, you might return to tailoring someday. If that's what you decide, hopefully, your dad will eventually understand."

Paddy was quiet as he let David's words soak in. He knew he had a long way to go to summon up the courage to tell Papa what he wanted.

"Thanks, man. I'll think about that. Hey, good luck with picking a college. Maybe you should just go with the one with the best track team."

"Ha! That makes the decision a lot easier!"

"Talk to you later, okay?"

"Okay. See ya around," replied David.

Paddy's thoughts drove him from the window seat to his bedroom upstairs. He moved his grandfather's latest cryptography challenge off his bed and flopped down. As he lay there, his eyes roamed over his many posters of faraway places like Finland, Brazil, and Australia. Finally, his gaze rested on the many pins covering the world map over his dresser. He swore he would visit all the marked countries someday. Dangerous thoughts he'd entertained over the past few weeks crept back into his mind. He imagined himself hitching a ride on one of the freighters that frequented the port of Boston or taking a walk and simply letting his feet keep going to see where his path might lead.

Though he knew it was silly, his desperation made him close his eyes and listen. He half hoped to hear some message in the storm that would guide him. The swirling wind as it shrieked against the clapboards of the shop seemed to be urging him to abandon the safety he knew and embrace the unknown. It was as if Nature herself agreed with the longing in his heart, and for a few moments, he thought he could faintly hear a chorus of voices carried on the wind, calling, "Be free!"

Papa calling interrupted his thoughts. "Paddy, come down. I've set up some oil lamps so we can keep working."

Paddy sighed, grabbed his thimble from his dresser, and descended the stairs slowly, the thud of his footsteps echoing his frustration.

As he entered the shop, Papa peered over his glasses and remarked, "Storms are no excuse not to meet deadlines. When the shop is yours one day, your reputation will depend on keeping your word." Papa went back to his stitching, his arthritic hands, and his hunched posture, making him appear twenty years older. He insisted on working in his suit and tie. He had an old-fashioned sense of propriety and said that wearing a suit put him in the mind frame to work hard.

"What were you doing upstairs? Reading again? You've read more books in your few years than most people have in a lifetime. If you devoted that time to tailoring . . ."

"Grandpa says it's good to have a thirsty soul."

"That sounds like him," he muttered. "What books have you read lately?"

Paddy hesitated. "*Les Misérables, Uncle Tom's Cabin*, a book called *De/Cipher*, about cryptanalysis . . ." He decided to stop with the last three rather than reinforce Papa's accusation.

Paddy settled into a chair and began hemming the sleeves of a morning coat for the mayor of Weymouth. His thoughts drifted to Grandpa's library in his cottage behind the shop. Paddy borrowed a book at least once or twice a week. He understood that the price for borrowing a book was to agree to quizzes from Grandpa on all sorts of details about its contents. To Grandpa, each work of literature was a work of art, not just to be read but to be experienced. He often bought new books on his business travels, so there was a constant supply.

Paddy couldn't say whether his desire to travel made him want to read about faraway places, or whether so much reading made him want to travel, but Grandpa loved his enthusiasm. He used Paddy's fascination with other countries to teach him foreign languages. As a result, Paddy could speak five fluently and two others reasonably well, though he never thought that his talent was extraordinary.

"Son," said Papa, "Go get your grandpa. It's probably safer if he stays here tonight rather than in that old cottage. This storm is getting worse."

"I checked on him earlier. He was napping in his chair. I think he was dreaming."

"Well, they won't be happy dreams if the storm rips his roof off. Honestly, we need to get someone to come to take a look at it. That roof has got to be well over fifty years old."

Paddy put on his raincoat and ran down the brick walkway to the cottage, the gale almost knocking him down several times. Wind and sleet whipped into his eyes, cutting his cheeks and stealing his breath. With a gasp, he pushed on the cottage door and lunged inside.

Grandpa was sleeping soundly in his old plaid recliner, his tall frame making the chair look too small for him. Paddy shook him gently by the shoulder. "Grandpa?"

"Hmm? What? Oh, it's you, Paddy."

"Papa says the storm is getting worse, and he wants you to stay in the big house tonight. He's worried about the roof of this old place."

"The roof? Nonsense. This place has weathered every Weymouth storm for . . . well, for many years. Besides, I replace the roof ridge every ten years. You tell him I'm fine right here." He closed his eyes again.

"Have you had supper?"

Grandpa peeked over his round glasses. "Oh, you are kind to ask, but I ate hours ago. Now you go on back to the house. Tell your papa not to worry. I'm snug as a bug."

Paddy stoked the fire and added some wood. It was the only heat source in the cottage, but Grandpa had built it well. It took up the entire corner of the living room, and the stones radiated heat long after the fire went out.

"Well, I'm coming back to check on you again before I go to bed, just to be sure."

"No need, but suit yourself. I'll be fine."

Paddy's eyes scanned the floor-to-ceiling bookshelves, and he thought if he couldn't go on a real adventure, at least by reading, he could sail away in his imagination.

"Do you mind if I borrow a book while I'm here?"

"You know the answer to that," Grandpa mumbled, with his eyes still closed. "I never mind."

Paddy ran his hand over the worn spines of the familiar books. Most of them were like old friends; he'd spent so much time with them. He found three he liked best and spent a few minutes trying to decide which one to borrow.

"Grandpa? Which of these do you recommend?"

"You haven't read *Travels* in some time. That would be my choice."

"*Gulliver's Travels* it is then." Grandpa called the book *Travels* because it was the first edition from 1724 which was then titled *Travels Into Several Remote Nations of the World*.

"So, have you decided whether you will be staying?" asked Grandpa as he straightened in his chair. He could tell Paddy had something on his mind.

Paddy sighed, flopped into a chair, and studied Grandpa's face for a clue to his thoughts. But Grandpa had already given his opinion—this was a decision Paddy had to make alone.

"No, I haven't. I'm stuck right where I was two weeks ago when you asked me."

"I tried on lots of lives before I chose this one," Grandpa said, with a faraway look in his eyes. "If you only think about the obstacles instead of what gives you a sense of purpose, you won't get very far. We don't know what we are capable of until we push past our fears. Your mama used to say, 'All good decisions are made from a balance between the wisdom of the mind and the passion of the heart.'"

***

THE STORM HAD ENTIRELY RETREATED BY MORNING. DESPITE THE raging gale, Weymouth awoke with barely a blade of grass out of place, so hardy was the village and its residents. Paddy was already working when Papa came down to the shop.

"Did Grandpa come to the house last night?"

"No, I checked on him before bed, and he insisted he was fine in the cottage. You know him," replied Paddy.

"It was pure nostalgia that made him recreate his dad's cottage—thatched roof and all. I doubt we can find anyone in the entire state of Massachusetts who knows how to work on a thatched roof."

"Maybe Weymouth is a lot like Dundee. Grandpa's roof seems to fare better in bad storms than the ones around us," observed Paddy.

Papa grumbled his disagreement and began cutting fabric for a vest.

"Good morning!" Grandpa said cheerfully as he entered the shop. His smile deepened the wrinkles at the corners of his eyes. Paddy thought he looked a bit like Abraham Lincoln with his high cheekbones and deeply set eyes. He still had thick red hair, though the speckles of gray increased with each passing year. The weathered skin of his broad forehead had wrinkles that Paddy could read like a map to know when he was deep in thought.

"Morning, Grandpa. How did you sleep?" asked Paddy.

"Like a baby!" he exclaimed, settling his tall, thin frame into a chair by the fireplace.

"Where are you going on your next trip?" asked Paddy.

"Oh, just a quick stop in Paris to see the new silk coming off the line, then I'll stop in Dublin on my way home."

"Papa, what do you think about my going along with Grandpa on his next trip? I could help him and learn about how he works with fabric vendors." It wasn't the first time Paddy had thought of going with Grandpa, but it was the first time he'd had enough courage to ask Papa about it.

Papa looked up from his sewing machine slowly. He looked over at Grandpa with an oddly stern expression for what seemed like several minutes and then fixed his eyes on Paddy. The tension in the room was palpable as Papa spoke slowly, "I'm going to say this only once. You will *never* go on a purchasing trip with your grandfather. It's *too dangerous*."

Papa closed his eyes for a moment as if he wished he could take back his words.

"What's dangerous about it?" Paddy expected some opposition, but he was not prepared for Papa to say it was dangerous. He felt his stomach tighten and his pulse quicken as he scrambled to think of what to say next. "I want to learn more about the purchasing side of the business, and it's a perfect time now that I've finished school . . ."

"I'll not discuss it further. I promised your mother I would keep

7

you safe . . ." His voice faded, and his expression looked as if he remembered something painful.

Paddy glanced at Grandpa, hoping for support, but Grandpa closed his eyes, put his head back against the armchair, and kept silent. Paddy stared down at his hemming, unable to keep working. Papa's tone made him feel punished, and he wanted to retreat to his room. He had agonized for weeks trying to find a way to say he didn't want to stay and run the shop, and traveling with Grandpa seemed the perfect answer. He had to try again.

He walked slowly across the room and put his hand on Papa's shoulder.

"Papa, I'll be fine. I'm eighteen now. I can help Grandpa with lifting the fabric boxes and keeping the purchase records. Wouldn't that be helpful? We might get home sooner with two people doing the scouting."

Papa dropped his handwork on the table and stood up, backing away from Paddy. His eyes opened wide, and his mouth twisted into a fearful grimace. He put up both hands as though he wanted to keep Paddy at a distance and froze where he stood for several moments.

"I *knew* this day would come." His voice trembled as he turned his eyes to look squarely at Grandpa. "Go ahead and tell him, but know this"—he waved his knobby finger at Grandpa as though scolding him —"I hold you responsible for his safety, and I will *never* forgive you if something happens to him." Papa stormed out of the shop and upstairs to his bedroom.

Paddy was angry at himself that he hadn't found a better way to present his plan. It hurt him that Papa still treated him like a child, but most of all, he was confused by Papa's angry response. He'd never heard his father that upset before. Paddy sat on the floor in front of Grandpa and silently waited. Grandpa seemed deep in thought as he sat looking at his old, worn hands.

Finally, he spoke. "Paddy, there is so much to tell you—about my trips, your mother, your heritage . . . but when I do, some of it will be hard to understand and maybe even harder to believe. I promise you that I will tell you everything as your papa has instructed, but it will take some time to explain it. Will you be patient and trust me?"

Paddy looked at him, still confused, and after several moments, he replied, "Of course, Grandpa."

"If you don't mind, we'll discuss it tomorrow evening after work. I have several phone calls and errands to run today."

"Grandpa, please. What's wrong with Papa? I don't think I can wait . . ."

Grandpa's deep-green eyes were full of understanding. He patted him on the shoulder and then rested his hand there for what seemed like a full minute. He whispered, "It's best, Son. Be patient; it'll all make sense soon." As he trudged out the back door to the cottage, his shadow on the garden wall cast an image of a much younger, stronger man. Paddy could tell by the lines on his forehead that he was troubled. It seemed a deep sadness had settled upon him, and Paddy was determined to find out why.

2

GONE

"MAY YOU LIVE ALL THE DAYS OF YOUR LIFE."
-JONATHAN SWIFT

The next morning Paddy rushed downstairs to begin work so he could finish early and talk to Grandpa. He was anxious to find out what Papa meant when he told Grandpa to tell him everything. Halfway down the stairs, the smell of warm cinnamon redirected his steps to the kitchen just as Clara put fresh hot cross buns on a tray with coffee for Paddy and Papa. Graham looked up from his newspaper. "Ah, Master Paddy, you are just in time. Get 'em while they're hot!"

"You-you-you'll l-l-like th-these; y-y-your f-f-favorite w-w-with extra cin-cinnamon," added Clara.

Paddy had learned from years of living with Clara to patiently wait for her to finish speaking and not to be distracted by her stutter. He inhaled deeply and closed his eyes, the warm cinnamon making him forget for a moment his rush to get downstairs. "Clara, you are the best!" he said, giving her a kiss on the cheek.

"T-today is l-l-laundry day. B-be s-s-sure everything is in the h-hamper," she reminded.

"It's all done. Graham, we're going to have to get you a tablet. No one reads newspapers anymore!" Paddy's voice trailed up as he descended the stairs carefully with the warm buns and coffee. He faintly heard Graham say, "No need teaching an old dog new tricks."

Clara and Graham were long-time family friends, and Papa employed them to help around the shop and take care of the house, especially since Mama had died. They were distantly related to Paddy's mother's side of the family and lived on the third floor of the shop. Clara did most of the housekeeping, and Graham did odd jobs like cleaning the shop, tending to the garden, and helping Papa with bookkeeping. Some chores were always left for Paddy because Papa insisted that he learn "self-sufficiency."

As Paddy began to work, he was so preoccupied with what Grandpa might tell him that he couldn't focus. *Why did Papa say Grandpa would be held responsible for my safety? Did that mean that maybe I would be allowed to go with Grandpa after all? Why did Papa seem so afraid? Had he gone with Grandpa on a purchasing trip before? Did something happen?* Paddy jumped at the sound of the door latch opening.

"Daydreaming won't get the work done. We have three jackets to complete by tomorrow." Papa's tone still carried frustration from the night before, and he looked as if he hadn't slept at all. Paddy tried to turn his attention to his work, but thoughts of yesterday's conversation with Papa made him feel anxious.

"Paddy, it's ten o'clock. Go see what's keeping your grandpa."

Paddy approached the cottage but stopped before he made it all the way. Something clearly wasn't right. The door sat partially open, and all the shades were down. A deep sense of dread filled Paddy's stomach. Rushing down the walkway, he quickly pushed open the front door and gasped as he stood frozen on the doorstep. The cottage looked like a tornado had ripped through it. Books, pictures, and overturned tables and chairs were all over the floor, and drawers were open as if someone had been looking for something. From where he stood, he could see into Grandpa's workroom where even jars of nails, screws, and bolts were strewn all over the floor.

"Grandpa! Grandpa!" Paddy searched the cottage, but Grandpa was gone. Sprinting back up the path, Paddy burst into the shop and yelled, "Papa! Come out here! Something terrible has happened!"

Paddy and Papa rushed out, with Graham following behind. They all stood in the open doorway, staring. Papa let out the most mournful sound as he held onto the doorframe to steady himself.

"Who would do this?" Paddy asked, horrified. "Where is Grandpa?" Paddy felt like someone had punched him, and waves of panic washed over him. He ran around to the back door, and then circled the cottage several times, looking in every direction, to no avail.

Papa couldn't contain his emotion, and he cried out, "Please, God, no!" his voice trailing off as he buried his face in Grandpa's raincoat, which hung by the door.

Paddy checked outside again for any signs of Grandpa, and upon reentering the cottage, he heard Papa whispering to Graham, "They know! Graham, it has to be them!" There was such anguish in Papa's voice that Paddy's throat tightened with emotion.

He repeated Papa's words in his mind and then asked, "Has to be whom? Who are you talking about?"

Papa just looked at him with his mouth partly open and said nothing.

"What is going on? What aren't you telling me?" he shouted.

"Graham, call the police," ordered Papa.

Papa spoke to Paddy as if trying to stay in control. "Go close the shop. Call our clients and tell them we have an emergency—that their jackets will be late, and that we are sorry."

"How can you be so calm? What happened to Grandpa?"

Papa slid to the floor in the middle of the destruction. Putting his face in his hands, he began to cry in huge, heaving sobs that wracked his frame. Paddy had not seen his father cry since Mama died, and he couldn't bear to watch him. Turning away, he ran back to the shop to call their customers. His voice trembled as he spoke, and he was sure they must have noticed.

As he waited in the window seat for the police, one question after another raced through his mind like cars on a speeding train. *Did someone break in? Did they steal anything? Was Grandpa hurt? Were they looking for something in particular?*

He pulled his legs up and rested his elbows on his knees, covering his face with his hands. He tried to apply logic to the situation. *Maybe*

Grandpa went on his purchasing trip a little early, or perhaps someone broke in after he left. He's probably fine. We'll probably get a call from him today.

Finally, he recalled again what Papa had whispered to Graham in the cottage. Paddy felt sure Papa knew what had happened. *But what was it, and how did he know? Don't they trust me? Do they think I'm too young to understand? How did Graham know? Was there someone who wanted to harm Grandpa?*

He was shaken from his thoughts by the police officer knocking at the door, calling, "Malcolm Duncan?" several times. Paddy opened the door, his face lacking any expression, and pointed toward the back exit.

"In the cottage in the backyard," he replied flatly.

Papa finished with the policeman about an hour later and returned to the shop. He slowly unlatched the door and sank into his chair by the fireplace. "The officer said there's nothing to report yet, but they'll let us know as soon as they find anything."

"What can I do to help?" asked Paddy, his clenched fist evidence of his agitation.

"Nothing for now," replied Papa softly.

Paddy looked at Papa for a long time. A leather-framed picture on the table of both of them taken three years earlier showed Papa with hair many shades darker, and the worry lines between his eyes were less visible than now.

"Papa," said Paddy. "I heard you speaking to Graham . . . you said, 'It has to be them,' and it sounded like you know something."

Papa finally spoke. "Paddy, I know you don't understand, but please believe that I didn't keep this from you because I don't trust you. I was trying to protect you." He took a deep breath and exhaled slowly.

"Please, tell me what's going on."

Then Papa began.

❀ 3 ❀

FLOCCINAUCINIHILIPILIFICATION

"I'D RATHER DO EVERYTHING FOR MYSELF, AND BE PERFECTLY INDEPENDENT." ~LOUISA MAY ALCOTT

"This will sound strange, even crazy, but there is a group of tailors who have done us much harm. It all began a very long time ago and continues to this day. That's why I reacted when you asked to go traveling with your grandpa. I promised your mom to keep you safe from them, and I felt . . . trapped. I wanted to keep my promise, but I couldn't bear to make you unhappy by forcing you to stay at home. I know I should have told you about this before, but I hoped it would all just stop; that they'd get tired after all this time and leave us alone. I'm sorry."

"You think these people would *harm me?*"

Papa's eyes brimmed with tears, and his chin quivered, making Paddy wonder which was harder—keeping a secret for so many years or finally having to tell it. Paddy couldn't bear to see Papa this way, so he changed the subject.

"Did the police say they had any ideas?" asked Paddy.

Papa rubbed his eyes and cleared his throat. "They have three teams of officers searching the neighborhood, the parks, and the woods. They'll be back in touch by five o'clock to give us an update. Paddy, I *don't* know for sure what happened to Grandpa. It's completely plausible that someone broke into the cottage last night looking for money, something to sell, or even food. But if my hunch is correct, he is in danger." He paused for what seemed like a full minute and then added quietly, "This is what I need to explain, and it's so hard to know where to start. How does one sum up seven generations of history?"

Paddy's eyes grew wide. "Seven generations? How have I never heard of this?"

"When I tell you, you'll understand. At least, I hope you will."

Paddy tried to be sensitive to Papa's reluctance, so he quoted one of Grandpa's favorite sayings, "It's always best to begin at the beginning." While he waited on Papa, a thought struck Paddy with such force he felt numb, and the hair on his neck bristled. Today was the thirteenth anniversary of Mama's death. He thought it best, under the circumstances, to keep it to himself.

Papa began again slowly. "It started a very long time ago; 1774, to be exact. Your grandpa's great-great-great-grandfather, Angus Duncan, was a very famous tailor. It was his pride in impeccable quality and attention to detail that built the legacy of the Duncan brand. Angus started the saying that has become our company slogan . . ."

Paddy finished his sentence, "'Perfection is our standard.'"

"Of course, you know it. Well, gradually, Angus started shops in other locations, and before long, Duncan Tailoring was in twelve other countries. What you probably don't know is that as the company grew, some tailors became jealous of Angus's success."

Paddy paced back and forth. "Papa? Not to be rude, but what does this have to do with Grandpa going missing?"

Papa waved his hand. "Just listen, and you'll understand. I'm telling you what Grandpa was going to say to you before he . . . Trust me, Paddy. There's no way you can understand without a full explanation.

"As I said, all this expansion by Angus made one group of tailors jealous. At around that same time, many tailors fell on hard times due to a terrible disease that was killing hundreds of sheep. The cost of wool became prohibitive, and the tailors who had opposed Angus petitioned the Guild to loosen its rules regarding wages paid to journeymen so they could pay them less. The Guild offered to assist these tailors financially with a temporary loan, but the tailors were too proud and didn't want to be indebted to the Guild. The schism was so deep that the dissenting tailors separated themselves. They formed another society called the Society of Master Independent Tailors, or SMITs for short."

Papa put his palms on his thighs and shook his head. "Things went from bad to worse as the SMITs began allowing their apprentices to perform the more difficult work of journeymen. Even though they were making garments at a much lower cost, they were selling them at rates only master tailors were permitted to charge.

"Some Duncan Tailoring clients tried using the services of these tailors, and they returned to Angus and showed him the quality of the work. It was not only shoddy work; the SMITs had misrepresented the fabrics as having come from the more expensive markets of India, China, and France. Then came the last straw for Angus.

"One of his regular clients, a Mr. James Watt, showed him a waist-coat made by one of the SMIT tailors. On the inner facing of the collar had been sewn a label that read 'Duncan Tailoring.' Even though the label was a poor counterfeit, the SMITs had put it in enough shoddy garments that the damage to our business took years to restore. Customers were upset at what the newspapers called 'the Duncan Disaster,' and the public, particularly more-affluent clientele, reported that they would take their business elsewhere. The SMITs' careful plan to discredit us worked—for a while. Ever since then, the SMITs have not stopped trying to sabotage our business."

"That's crazy! For over 200 years? Wait, you think someone from this group of tailors is responsible for Grandpa's disappearance? What do they want, a ransom? We aren't in the dark ages anymore. Why haven't we sued them, or gotten a protective order? Did you tell the police about this?"

Papa held up his hand. "No! We can't do that."

"Why not?"

"It's too dangerous. If you'll let me explain—"

Paddy growled under his breath. "Maybe another time. I've got to look for Grandpa, or at least for clues. We're wasting time," he said as he headed for the back door.

Paddy walked quickly out to the cottage before Papa could call him back. In the dirt on the little road that separated the cottage from the small field behind it, he could faintly see the outline of footprints. He examined them carefully. One was a type of tennis shoe, one was a heavy work boot, and one had the telltale "P&C" of Grandpa's bespoke Park and Croft oxfords, the only kind he wore. Paddy found five more sets of identical prints before they ended on the asphalt street.

Someone walked on either side of him. Did the police miss this? The tracks seemed to be heading toward the ocean, but there was no way to tell which way they went once they left the alley and reached the road.

Paddy scoured every street and yard between the cottage and the beach. When he reached the marina, he looked inside each sailboat, short of boarding them and looking below deck. There were at least thirty boats docked there, and he looked frantically for anything that might be a clue. Lastly, he checked around in the neighborhoods north and south of his own. It was seven thirty before he finished.

At least I have to let the police know about the footprints. Paddy turned his steps toward the town square and was within sight of the police station when he noticed Papa walking toward him from the direction of the station.

Papa stopped in front of him and put his hand on his shoulder. "Did you find anything else?"

"No, but I want to tell the police about the footprints."

"They saw them. They made a casting of the prints, but, Son, don't look to the police to solve this."

Paddy scowled and almost walked around Papa to go to the station anyway. "I don't understand you!"

Papa leaned close to his face, looking him in the eyes. "If you really want to help him, then trust me. We have another source of help we need to leverage, and they have capabilities the police don't. If you'll be patient and let me explain, you'll understand. You *need* to give me a chance."

❦ 4 ❦

NEWS

"IT IS AN UNFORTUNATE FACT THAT WE CAN
SECURE PEACE ONLY BY PREPARING FOR WAR."
~JOHN F. KENNEDY

Paddy and Papa were back inside the shop for only a minute when Graham burst through the door.

"Malcolm? Did you hear about this?" Graham set his radio on the table. The newscaster was speaking in a serious and urgent tone.

"Thank you for your time, General. Can you tell us any more about why the terrorist threat level is now high?"

"All we can share at this time is that we intercepted a communication indicating there may be an attempted attack against the United States."

"Do you know anything about the person or organization, sir?"

The general's voice crackled over the airwaves again. "Their leader has many aliases. He is a former Nazi spy who has eluded efforts to catch him since World War II. We believe he is working with a team of a dozen or so others."

"Do you have any information about what he may be planning or why?"

"We are trying to get more details, but it appears he may be planning to use a weapon of mass destruction. We have no information as to why, but we have intelligence that indicates he believes Germany would have won World War II if they had used this weapon. That's all I have at this time. We will keep everyone informed as we receive more information."

"Sir, just one more question?"

"I'm sorry; I have to attend a meeting with the Joint Chiefs at the Pentagon."

The announcer added, "One last note for our listeners—we just received notice that the United Nations is canceling their meeting scheduled for later today, and the president is flying back early from his meeting with the president of France. Everyone seems to be taking this threat very seriously." Graham switched off the radio.

"Graham, could you go through the pantry and check our stock of food, water, and candles? I'm not sure there's much else we can do," requested Papa.

Paddy's anxiety threatened to spin out of control. All he could think about was Grandpa, and he was so focused, not even the radio report could distract him.

❧ 5 ❧

DIE ANTWORT

"WAR DOES NOT DETERMINE WHO IS RIGHT,
ONLY WHO IS LEFT." -BERTRAND RUSSELL

The activity in the corridors of the Pentagon was evidence that the terrorist threat now eclipsed all other work. Staff hurried to carry out their part of the protocol for Homeland Security's threat level—Red. The Secret Service led the president to a door marked "No Admittance" and down a long corridor leading underground to a conference room.

"General Taylor, I understand your team intercepted several communications on this. What have you learned?"

"Mr. President, it appears they have at least ten engineers and a team of about thirty other workers. Satellite images of deliveries to a residential site outside Munich show some unusual items—chemical components of fuel, heat-resistant metals, and such. There's a reference to Calais also."

"Can we tell the size of it from the images?" asked the president.

"It doesn't appear they've assembled it yet, but they've been building the components. Enough supplies have been delivered that if they wanted to, it could pack a payload of twenty to thirty megatons, sir, but it's hard to be exact. They may be planning to assemble and launch it near Calais." There was silence around the table for several seconds.

"General Taylor, what do you recommend?" the president asked.

"I recommend we heighten satellite and air surveillance over Calais and this site near Munich. When you give the order, Mr. President, I think we should immediately ground all commercial and private aircraft, and that we scramble five F-22s and five F-35 fighters to shoot it down," offered General Taylor. "We should have another group ready to go if and when the first group runs low on fuel."

The president replied, "Any objections or concerns? Good. Let's do it. Tell the Coast Guard to issue a warning to every boat and ship they can reach. If we know the approximate path of this thing, anything in the vicinity should exit that area now. I want it destroyed before it gets anywhere near our shores. I assume NORTHCOM has been alerted?"

"Yes, sir."

"Let's get moving. We've trained for this."

"Commander Lanham, do we know why this man was never caught after the war?" the president asked.

"He is a master of disguises, sir. We believe that is his real name is Wilhelm Schattenlauerner. He reinvents himself every few months with a new identity and often in a new country. It is impossible to track him, but for the first time, we have several credible leads."

"He has to be in his nineties by now! Let's coordinate with the UK and France. I want to catch this guy once and for all." said the president.

"Sir, we just intercepted a communique that refers to the weapon as *Die Antwort*, 'The Answer.'"

"Thanks, Colonel Hatch."

As everyone was leaving, the head of the Defense Intelligence Agency, Colonel Tim Walker, called out, "Mr. President? May I have a quick word?"

"Yes, Tim? What is it?"

"Sir, I didn't want to mention it because, well, I may be tying threads that don't belong together, but I think you should know."

"We spent enough time in the Marines to know we should consider every angle. What is it?"

"There's an independent agent, whose code name is Scrydan. Amazing spy—did a lot for us. He worked undercover for the Allies during World War II. He's the only one we know from that period who hasn't retired. I tried to contact him this morning to see if he'd ever heard of Schattenlauerner, but I couldn't reach him. I tried again an hour ago and found an emergency contact for him in our file, a Douglass Duncan in Dublin, so I called him.

"And?"

"He said not to make it public, but he learned from Scrydan's family that someone kidnapped him a few days ago. Whoever did it ransacked his house as though they were looking for something."

🦋 6 🦋

SECRETS

"THE BEST WAY TO FIND YOURSELF IS TO
LOSE YOURSELF IN THE SERVICE OF OTHERS."
~MAHATMA GANDHI

With the radio report over, Paddy plopped down in a chair and sighed loudly. *I don't care if it's a nuclear warhead, we need to be looking for Grandpa!*

Papa turned to him reading his expression. "Paddy, we are doing everything we can at this moment to find Grandpa." He paused as he changed the thread in his sewing machine. "May I continue the story of Angus?"

Paddy again huffed loudly, his frustration audible. "If it will clue me in to why we aren't telling the police about these *wacko* tailors, then sure."

"Son, we have gone to the police. It's the first thing we did. We just aren't telling them something that will make them think we are nuts. A two-hundred-year-old feud with some tailors across the pond is hardly considered evidence. If the SMITs kidnapped Grandpa, and if I can't stop you from going to look for him, then you need to know more. But, if you'd prefer to do things your way, you can remain in the dark."

"Fine then," grumbled Paddy.

"Remember Angus's friend James Watt? He and Angus had spoken about what the SMITs were doing to damage Duncan Tailoring, and just before the next meeting of the Lunar Society, Angus received an invitation to attend."

"What was the Lunar Society?"

"It was a group of scientists that met to discuss their ideas about how their inventions might improve society. They met during the full moon, so traveling at night would be easier, hence the name. They mostly met in Birmingham, at Soho House, the home of Matthew Boulton. I could tell you much more about the Society, but you can look it up on your own. Now, I need to stay focused, and you need to listen very carefully."

Paddy sat leaning toward Papa, his muscles tense, desperate to piece together parts of the past to help Grandpa now.

"Angus went to the meeting and explained how the SMITs were destroying the reputation of Duncan Tailoring. The Lunar Society unanimously agreed to come up with a solution. Just before the meeting ended, they invited him to join the group in watching an experiment by James Keir. They went to the 'Demonstration Room,' where Keir began to test two metals he believed would combine into a useful alloy. About halfway through, there was a massive explosion. A giant fireball blew the roof off the building and stayed suspended in the air for some time. The vacuum created by the blast sucked up a large piece of lodestone into the fireball. A barrel of copper in the room burst apart and covered everyone in copper powder."

"Was anyone hurt?"

"Amazingly, no, but a spool of thread in Angus's pocket became coated in copper. That night, he put the spool on the bedside table, and in the morning, he noticed something curious. The thread was completely clean. Not a trace of copper remained, and even though he'd used almost all of the thread, the spool was now full. The thread was also no longer green, but white. Angus assumed the copper reacted with the dye in the thread and neutralized it somehow, but he couldn't understand why the spool was full.

"About a month later, Angus was invited again to the Lunar Society, and the members had a solution. They explained that Duncan Tailoring garments needed to have a distinguishing mark that, unlike a label, couldn't be reproduced. When clients saw it, they would recognize the garment as authentic. They proposed a seal, a sort of maker's mark, that Angus could sew into each garment."

"You mean that's how our seals started?"

"Exactly. The Society created a thousand seals to start with, and Angus shared them with other Duncan tailors. They also created fifty special seals with a miniature clockworks inside to be used for our most loyal clients. Both kinds of seals were incredibly ornate, and there was no way to reproduce them without a lot of expense. The SMITs were just as miserly as they are today, so they didn't even attempt it."

"Clockworks? Why?"

"It wasn't a real clock with a face to tell time. The top was an ornate seal and the back was glass so you could see the gears turning. It was to make them irreproducible."

Just then, there was a knock on the door. It was Sergeant Smith, who had stopped by with some items for Papa to identify. He laid them out on the table and asked, "Malcolm, have you ever seen any of these before?" The color drained from Papa's face as he reached for Grandpa's scarf. Grandma Agnes had knitted it years ago for him, and it was the only one he ever used.

"Do these other items belong to him?" Sergeant Smith asked, pointing to the items on the table. Papa picked them up one by one: Grandpa's pipe, a crumpled reminder on Duncan stationery that read, 'seam binding,' and a fountain pen that had Grandpa's name engraved on the barrel.

Papa nodded. "When and where did you find these?" he asked, his voice trembling.

"Around one o'clock, we found one every hundred yards or so heading down toward the docks. It looks like William was trying to show us the direction they took him, perhaps to a waiting boat. Malcolm, I don't mean to alarm you, but what I'm trying to say is that this has all the earmarks of a kidnapping."

I knew it! They took him for a ransom!

Papa slumped over, his face twisted in such painful sorrow. He drew all the items on the table toward him and put his head down onto Grandpa's scarf.

"I understand this must be difficult. Just know that we will not stop searching until we have exhausted every possible lead. We have notified the Marine Patrol, and they will search every boat they find. I have to ask you, though, is there anything else you have thought of that might help us find him?"

Papa looked up and stared at the sergeant for some time. Finally, he shook his head and sighed. "No, I can't think of anything. I wish I could."

"Thanks, Malcolm. I'll check back with you later and give you an update," replied Sergeant Smith as he left.

"Sergeant Smith is a good man, but he has no idea what he's up against," mumbled Papa as he held Grandpa's scarf.

"How could he know? You won't tell him." Paddy didn't usually speak to Papa that way, but his frustration was turning to anger.

Papa retorted, "Let's see, how would that sound? Our family has a war with the descendants of some tailors that got really angry with us in the late 1700s. They never got over it, so now they kill or kidnap a member of our family from time to time. They all are in the UK, but unfortunately, that's out of your jurisdiction. Oh, they also usually threaten that if we *involve the police*, they will kill the one they kidnapped!"

Paddy was taken aback. Papa never spoke sarcastically to him. "I'm sorry, Papa. Maybe you are right, but I'm just focusing on finding Grandpa, and it seems like we need help. I just need to *do something*. I do wish I had known about all of this before now."

"There is nothing in the world I hate more than talking about this."

"It's okay. I do need to know if you feel it will help me find Grandpa. You were telling me about the Lunar Society creating the seals. Did the seals stop the SMITs from using our name?"

"They did. But then somehow, the SMITs found out that there was something unique about our thread, and they began trying to find a way to steal it."

"But all our tailors use the thread now. Do they think it's just one spool?"

"I presume so. They've harmed enough people trying to get them to divulge the whereabouts of the thread. It's as if they think it's locked up in a safe somewhere."

"This makes no sense! They kidnap people to get a stupid spool of thread?"

"We aren't sure how much they know, but meanwhile, it keeps reproducing and hasn't run out for seven generations. Whoever has it *never* has to purchase thread again."

"Whoa! So that *must* be why they tore the cottage apart. They are still looking for it!"

Papa dropped his voice to a whisper. "Reproducing itself isn't its only unique quality. Angus soon realized that the thread also changed color *as he sewed* to match the color of the fabric."

"But ours does that too."

Papa waited for him to make the connection.

Suddenly, a look of understanding flashed across Paddy's face, and his eyes grew wide with realization. "We are using the very same thread, *the* thread that Angus had? I always thought ours changed color through some fancy chemical process." The hair stood up on his arms, and he was so excited that he went to the sewing table and picked up a spool to look at it through the lens of this new knowledge.

"Also, any garment made with it has never worn out."

"How is that possible? Wouldn't that be bad for business?"

"I don't know how it happens, but for over two hundred years, clients have been so impressed by how long our garments last that they assume that it's because of the quality of our work. Now, can you imagine what would happen if the SMITs knew all this? Rather than seeing it as a gift, they would exploit it. They'd probably try to sell pieces of the thread for hundreds of dollars. No, it falls to us to protect it from them."

Questions tumbled over and over in Paddy's mind. *Who else was harmed by the SMITs, and how? Where do we start to look for Grandpa?* Finally, he asked, "Papa, do you think that the SMITs had something to do with Mama's death?"

Papa stared at Paddy. He answered slowly, a sadness etching the lines in his face more deeply. He took a handkerchief trimmed with lace from the inner breast pocket of his jacket, and Paddy could see

Mama's initials embroidered in the corner. He held it as lovingly as he would have held her hand and replied haltingly, "Yes, I do. Your mama's kidnapping happened when she was on a trip to Ireland with Grandpa thirteen years ago. She wanted to see family, and he had business to take care of there, so she joined him. Once the SMITs took her, they sent us three messages . . ." He swallowed hard and winced. "They demanded the thread in exchange for her life.

"She and I had discussed many times the possibility that such a thing might happen, given our history, and she made me swear never to give in to them. But I broke my promise. I had to tell someone, so I hired an investigator. In their letters demanding the thread, the SMITs threatened that if we went to the authorities, they would immediately end her life, but I was so desperate to get her back. That's why I don't want to explain the truth to the police about your grandpa. When I hired the investigator, it's like I took Bridget's life myself." The agony in Papa's voice made it seem as if it had happened only yesterday.

"After nine months, the investigator closed the case and told me she probably had just left, but everyone knew it wasn't true. We held a funeral to have some closure, which you probably remember.

"I'm sorry that we didn't tell you what happened, but all this isn't something you can tell a five-year-old boy, and I haven't told you even half of it. Please try to understand that I did all I could." His eyes seemed to plead for forgiveness. Papa put his face in his hands. "I'm just waiting for the notes to start coming about your grandpa. It's all happening again."

Paddy couldn't contain himself any longer. "I'm going to find him and bring him home! And before you say 'no' again, remember that they have done this to me too! She was *my* mother, and he is *my* grandfather. I have every right to fight back!"

A panicked look crossed Papa's face. "I can't lose you too! Paddy, these men are ruthless." Papa's voice and hands were trembling.

"I've made up my mind. What if I get married when I'm older? Am I supposed to live in fear that something terrible will happen to my partner, my children? Someone has to put an end to this."

Papa was silent for several minutes. "If I can't stop you, perhaps I can at least prepare you."

"We don't have time for that. I have to go *now*." Paddy paced the floor.

"Son, you don't even know where to find them!" Papa caught himself and softened his tone. "And if you did, do you suppose they will just hand Grandpa over to you? Wouldn't you agree a *little* preparation and a plan is needed?"

Paddy's silence echoed his reluctant realization that Papa was right.

❧ 7 ❧

DÉJÀ VU

"TO SUBDUE THE ENEMY WITHOUT FIGHTING IS THE SUPREME ART OF WAR." ~SUN TZU

A small boat had ferried William and his captors to a large freighter waiting in the harbor. William's hands were tied to a pipe in a corner of the engine room. The rope cut sharply into his thin skin and held him in an awkward position so that his muscles cramped. The massive engine's turbines roared full throttle, making the room steaming hot. The lack of windows made it difficult to tell the difference between day and night, so William slept only a few hours at a time.

Aleksander and Filip, William's captors, assumed that he couldn't speak Polish, which gave him an advantage. So far, they'd revealed that the ship was bound for Denmark, after which they planned to take him to Germany by train to see their leader. Strangely, the men looked familiar, but William couldn't remember where, or if, he'd actually seen them before.

Initially, their assignment had been to confiscate an item from his cottage, and they seemed angry and afraid that they were returning without it. When they couldn't find it, they decided to bring William back rather than return empty-handed.

How did they ever find me? What do they want? No one connected with my undercover work has ever known my real name or found out where I live. As he slipped into a fitful sleep, he dreamed about an unforgettable mission in France in 1944.

THE CURFEW IMPOSED BY THE GERMAN OCCUPATION IN FRANCE gave the town of Rennes an ominous, foreboding feeling. Except for the sounds of rats and the rain trickling between the cobblestones, everything was silent. Bombs and gunfire had damaged most of the streetlamps that once lit this section of town, and the darkness heightened the feeling of danger that hung in the air.

As William walked up the hill to the outskirts of town, he felt sure someone was watching him. He passed a row house, and the curtains suddenly fell closed as he looked up. A dog barked and startled him, reminding William how uneasy he felt about this mission. He refocused and mentally walked through each step of his assignment. In his mind's eye, he could see the file presented to him only yesterday stamped, "Top Secret—Mission Critical."

The message he carried could easily have been sent from the Allies to the Resistance in code over the radio. Still, if it were intercepted and decrypted, the entire invasion at Normandy would be compromised. A message this sensitive had to be delivered by hand. His stomach tightened. Rennes was crawling with Germans and the *Milice française*—French paramilitary soldiers sympathetic to the German cause. Britain chose William because no one could get in and out of such a dangerous area more quickly and efficiently than he. Still, so much could go wrong.

A thick mist from the nearby river lay heavy over the city like a dark gray veil. Even the buildings seemed to exude a melancholy, hopeless feeling. He pulled his hat down and his collar up against the cold as he rehearsed what to say if the Nazis apprehended him. The Germans were increasingly stopping people on the street to see authorization papers, especially amid rumors of an imminent Allied invasion. William's papers were fake—good enough to fool an inattentive officer, but not convincing enough to save him if caught.

All he had was his contact's first name: Remy. He was a maquisard, a member of the French Resistance, most of whom hid in rural areas and sabotaged German efforts whenever possible. William slowed his pace. He was early, and he didn't want to raise suspicion by standing around once he reached the meeting place. A short man wearing a beret pulled down low over his eyes abruptly darted out of an alley and hurried toward him.

He said in broken English, "To subdue the enemy without fighting . . ."

William whispered in reply, "Is the supreme art of war."

Then Remy answered, "Abort! We are compromised. Do not go to the place of rendezvous!"

William's heart was pounding. There was too much at stake to miss this opportunity. As Remy started to cross the street, William grabbed his sleeve and pulled him back onto the sidewalk. He slipped the coded message into Remy's overcoat pocket, pressing it into his hand. Remy grasped it securely and quickly disappeared into another alley.

William didn't move. He breathed deeply, willing his pulse to return to normal. Finally, he looked at his watch to give the appearance of being calm, turned, and walked back in the direction from which he came. He walked quickly, but not so quickly as to draw suspicion, and soon he approached a cross street.

Just then, a woman wearing a black dress and gray raincoat came around the corner, heading toward him. With her gloved hands, she held a black leather handbag and a gray umbrella. Her dark hair was braided and tucked up into a small black hat adorned with a single red poppy. As they passed one another, they walked beneath a lantern hanging over a doorway. She averted her eyes, but he could easily see she was young, probably in her early to midtwenties.

As a trained tailor, William had developed a habit of noticing people's clothes. His father had taught him that often, what one wore was a reflection of one's character. Her choice of attire told him that she was probably highly organized and methodical, a quick thinker. William's "intuition," as he called it, also proved quite useful in his work as a spy.

The woman had walked about twenty-five yards past him when William reached a cross street and was about to turn left. Suddenly, heavy footsteps approached quickly from behind. He turned and saw two men running toward the woman. One pushed her hard with his forearm against her throat, pinning her to the wall of a building. Her hat fell onto the muddy sidewalk as the attacker muffled her scream with his other hand. His accomplice served as a lookout, while the first demanded information from her in Polish.

William slipped just around the corner and crouched behind a bush. A lamp in a street-level window behind where the woman stood cast enough light for William to see her take a small book from her pocket and slowly place it directly behind her on a windowsill. Somehow, neither of the men noticed; they just continued trying to force answers from her. From where William was, he only heard her repeatedly say in Polish that she "didn't know."

He desperately wanted to help her, but thousands of lives depended on him completing his mission. He tightened his jaw as the man questioning the woman became enraged. The man reached back as if preparing to strike her when a Nazi officer rounded the corner just feet from where William was hiding. Hearing the commotion, the officer drew his weapon and ran toward them, shouting at them to disperse. The attackers scattered in different directions.

"Your papers!" the officer demanded.

She fumbled with her purse and handed her papers over. When the officer examined her identification, he seemed to relax.

"Ah, I remember. You are from Hans's office. Miss, you should know not to be on the street at this time of night. What did those men want from you?"

"I don't know, sir. I'm sorry. I had to work late," she replied, her German as perfect as her Polish.

"Come, I'll walk you home," offered the officer. She turned and looked back over her shoulder at where she had laid the little book.

William stayed still until they were out of sight, all the while wondering why she had hidden the book. He reasoned that she was likely a spy, but for whom? The fact that a Nazi officer helped her probably meant she was working in some capacity for the Germans, so William thought the book might contain information valuable to the Allies.

His next contact was waiting for him not far away, to take him to his next rendezvous point, but his curiosity overcame his better judgment. He crossed the street and walked toward the window where the woman had placed the book. As he approached, the window swung open, knocking the book onto the pavement. William stopped and pressed himself against the wall of the building. Someone inside reached out the window and emptied an ashtray onto the sidewalk. William was no more than fifteen feet from the book. He bent down silently and pretended to tie his shoe, all the while eyeing the little book. He waited for the window to close, but after a few seconds, he could wait no longer.

He stepped forward, picked up the book, and, with one motion, tucked it directly under his hand into the sleeve of his coat. As William stood and walked away, he put his hands deep in his coat pockets, unzipped a hidden compartment inside his right pocket, and let the book slip inside. He zipped the compartment shut and tucked away the zipper tab to conceal access to the pocket, just in case.

William made his way through dark alleys and empty streets to the edge of town. He only knew this was the general vicinity of where he was to meet his contact, so his senses were hyperalert. He heard someone softly whistling a tune. He followed the sound and, peeking around the corner of a building, he could see a man sitting on top of a hay wagon.

After a few moments, William carefully approached and quietly said in French, "Looks like it might rain later on."

To which the man replied, "A little rain helps the turnips, but too much is bad for potatoes. Don't you agree?"

"Let's hope for the right amount then; for patriots need both turnips and potatoes."

Satisfied with William's answer, the man whispered, "I am Emile."

William nodded and replied, "They call me Scrydan. Thank you for the lift."

"There will be seven maquisards, radio operators, waiting for you at the farm. The Nazis are raiding transmitting stations, but so far, the farm has not drawn suspicion. Well, climb aboard and cover up with hay. We have to hope the Germans are not around tonight. It is well past curfew."

William took cover beneath the hay in the wagon, and about a mile outside of town, Emile pulled his large Belgian farm horse to a stop. William peeked out from beneath the hay.

"You really should take cover inside here to be safe," whispered Emile as he rapped his knuckles on the wood of the forward wall of the wagon. William looked where Emile had parted the hay and saw a trap door leading from the bed of the wagon into what was essentially a rectangular box beneath the driver's seat.

"There's not much room, but it's better than being found by the Nazis." William pushed his bag through the small doorway and carefully crawled inside.

On the way to the farm, Emile sang songs in French and interspersed the lyrics with phrases that informed William of the current state of the Maquis's resistance efforts. Anyone listening from a distance would have thought that either Emile didn't know all the words, or that he'd had too much to drink. William was grateful, though. Emile's singing helped to calm him, and he received a full update between song lyrics.

Suddenly, a convertible with three Nazi officers came abruptly face-to-face with the wagon, its lights scaring the horse. "Halt!" shouted an officer angrily as he stepped from the car and approached the wagon with his hand on his weapon. "What are you doing out at this time of night?"

"Good evening, Herr Kommandant!" Emile replied cheerfully. "My sincere apologies! You won't believe what happened today. My daughter fell out of the hayloft this morning and broke her leg. We had a terrible time finding a doctor to set it. So, I got a late start, and by the time I had delivered all the cheese and milk—well, just look at me! Out here on the road at this time of night! Never have I been out this late before. I could be shot as a combatant or some such nonsense when I'm trying to do my part to . . ."

The officer wasn't interested in Emile's excuse. He commanded his subordinates to check the wagon, and they commenced to thoroughly stabbing the hay with their bayonets. When they found nothing, the officer shouted at Emile, "You better hope you never find yourself out on the roads again at this time of night! Now get out of here!"

"Right away, Herr Kommandant!" Emile coaxed his Belgian around the car and down the road toward the farm as he breathed a sigh of relief. After a few minutes, he quietly began singing again. William wondered whose fears Emile was trying to calm—William's, the horse's, or his own.

When they reached the farm, William went to the barn behind the farmhouse. The Maquis hiding there offered him some bread and cheese and showed him the radio they used to transmit messages to the Allies. William checked the radio's components to be sure nothing was worn or broken, and then he quickly shut it off so the Germans couldn't trace it.

Pierre, one of the maquisards, spoke especially good English. "We are expecting a new shipment of radio parts, maps, and other supplies tonight. The airstrip is about an hour from here. Will you be returning home on the plane?"

"No, I've made other arrangements." When William didn't explain, the Maquis looked curiously at one another. William had visited this farm many times before to deliver messages and check radios, but his method of coming and going had always remained a mystery. Still, they always asked, hoping he would tell them.

He quickly changed the subject. "Is there any message you want me to take back to London?"

"We desperately need arms and ammunition, as always," offered Pierre.

William smiled. "It's coming. It's in my message to Remy. The OSS is sending them!"

Smiles spread across each face. The Maquis began to slap one another on the back and to quietly sing the refrain of "La Marseillaise," *Aux armes, citoyens!* (To arms, citizens!)

William smiled, but a bittersweet feeling came over him as he watched them singing quietly in the lamplight. He was glad to bring good news for a change, to reward their perseverance and courage with something tangible. At the same time, he didn't know how many would survive what was coming in the next few days and weeks. Of one thing he was sure: the men and women of the Resistance were some of the bravest people he'd ever met.

He thanked the Maquis for their help and reluctantly announced that he had to go. He pulled his scarf up over his head and ears and adjusted his hat, as the February temperature was almost freezing. He gave a salute as he headed out the back door of the barn.

"Where is it that he goes? I mean, how does he get home?" asked one of the maquisards.

"No one has ever figured it out. I tried to follow him once. It's as if he disappears. My father told me stories of a spy in the Great War they used to call the Shrouded One. Legend has it that he could disappear and go behind enemy lines to steal their codes. No one ever found out how he did it!"

"Scrydan is too young to have been in the Great War," added Pierre.

"Well, can you explain how he comes and goes?"

"Maybe he's the son of the Shrouded One?"

Another joked, "Jacques, unlike you, not all of us have spying passed down in our family as a formal occupation!" They all laughed heartily.

William climbed up the steep mountain behind the farm and stopped by a tall evergreen. He took a coat from his messenger bag, one that he called a "cover," and replaced it with the one he'd been wearing. Just before he slipped on the cover, he saw him.

About twenty-five paces away, hiding behind a rock, a rough-looking Frenchman had his rifle trained on him. His armband indicated he was part of the *Milice française*. William had heard French agents say that they had more fear of being caught by a *milicien* than being captured by a Nazi.

It was one of those moments in hindsight that plays out in slow motion. William's left arm was in the cover's sleeve, and as he slowly slid his right arm into the other, their eyes met. William stopped. Then he smiled and winked in the split second before he ducked behind the tree. The *milicien* pulled the trigger, but William was gone.

It was good to be back home in Dundee. William was overdue for a break, though he knew he would be back on an assignment before long. While he waited for his next mission, he worked day and night trying to decipher the black book but made little progress. There was no indication as to whom it belonged except for the initials "A. K." embossed on the leather cover. It was encoded using a combination of old and new techniques. It appeared to have been written by two or more people, and the authors took great pains to ensure it would be practically impossible to decrypt.

He surmised that the woman who left the book had written the text at the end, but the book's beginning was comprised of older types of encryption and written with a heavier hand. Stranger still, the middle of the book was coded using boustrophedon, with alternating lines having the text written in the opposite direction, and the characters were written as mirror images of the original characters.

As he was about to take a break and rest his eyes, he flipped the book's ribbon bookmark inside and shut the book. His eye caught something he hadn't noticed before. He opened the book again and examined the ribbon carefully. It was a crimson brocade, about three-eighths of an inch wide. He used his magnifying glass to look closer at the weave of the fabric.

"Unbelievable!" William exclaimed. Woven into the floral pattern of the fabric, down the length of the ribbon, was the word "Lygia." William was skilled in examining the weave of various kinds of cloth, and he knew that this type of detail was not easy to achieve because the letters were part of the intricate floral pattern. He began to wonder if Lygia might be a company name, such as the name of the company that made the book. Or, perhaps it was the name of the woman who hid the book, but it was an ancient name, so it seemed unlikely. He got up and paced the floor in his cottage, repeating "Lygia" to himself. He remembered he once read a book with a character named Lygia. He squeezed his eyes shut, willing his mind to recall the title of the book. It was as if the name of the book was coming slowly to him, like a ship sailing closer and closer through a fog.

Finally, he remembered. The character Lygia was in the epic work

Quo Vadis, by Polish author Henryk Sienkiewicz. The story is of a Roman patrician during the time of Nero, who fell in love with a Christian hostage. William heard the idea in his mind so loudly, it seemed audible; but as soon as he thought it, he dismissed it as impossible. Could the middle part of the book be a simple columnar transposition cipher? If so, what if *Quo Vadis* was the key?

There was only one way to find out. The text looked like row after row of indecipherable text with no spaces. It was the boustrophedon that made it appear complex. Using *Quo Vadis* as the key, it still took many more hours for William to decipher the book because it was so ingeniously encrypted.

He sat stunned as he read and reread the deciphered text. It described a method of transferring messages between Hitler and his generals via secret couriers. *But why would the German high command have risked sending communications by couriers? Did they realize that the Allies were intercepting and decrypting Enigma-coded messages?* Listed in the book were the names and locations of all the couriers used for exchanging messages throughout Hitler's highest ranks.

The book also described detailed plans to build a long-range missile the German's believed was capable of reaching the United States. Page after page gave instructions about everything from the tensile strength of the metals to the fuel components. As he sat looking at his notes, he knew he had to get this information to the Allies . . . quickly. He sent a coded message to London, saying only that he had intercepted an article that his contact needed to see right away.

❧

"MR. SCRYDAN, COLONEL GLASS WILL SEE YOU NOW," CALLED THE assistant. William was anxious to speak with Britain's chief intelligence officer.

"Mission accomplished, sir. I checked all radio posts in the area of Rennes. I left my full report with your assistant. Is there anything else I can do to help?"

"We're neck-deep in this war, Scrydan. There are a hundred areas to which we could assign you, given your talents, but I need to make sure *you* stay alive. Where do you think you could be of most help?" asked Colonel Glass.

"Well, sir, I do know how to keep radios in working order, but my strengths are in getting into and out of areas that most find difficult, and in cryptography. I've been working on ciphers for most of my life. My father taught me."

"If you're half as good as your father, that would be amazing, but you are still young."

"With all due respect, sir, seeing patterns in code is like speaking a second language to me."

"And, you speak six of them, I hear?"

"Seven. Sir, you knew my father?"

"Only by reputation. A reputation I imagine must be tough to follow."

"Yes, sir. Speaking of code, Colonel, I have something for you." William handed the black book to Colonel Glass, who flipped through the pages and gave him a questioning look.

"I recovered this book from someone in France, whom I believe to be a Polish spy, or she might be working for the Germans. She hid it to keep it from being discovered by men who were trying to force information from her. I decrypted it, sir. It outlines a top-secret system of communication using couriers for messages between Hitler and his top commanders, and it has plans for building a bomb."

Glass flipped through the book again, his brow furrowed deeply. "Are you sure? What kind of bomb? We know what they are using, and why would they risk using couriers?"

"I am sure. It even lists all the courier names and locations. The bomb appears to be large; I think it would do a lot of damage."

Colonel Glass was quiet for some time. Finally, he asked, "Bletchley Park has their way of assessing candidates, so this would break protocol, but are you open to my sending you there to work with them for the time being?"

"Of course."

"You can put your deciphering skills to work, and, no offense, but I'll need them to double-check your decryption of this book. Then, get a report to me ASAP on the contents so we can get it to our commanders."

"Colonel, secrecy is my business. My concern is whether they will agree to work with me without knowing my true identity, where I live, or anything about me. You know those are my conditions."

Colonel Glass wrote a note on a piece of paper and handed it to William. "Give this to the guard when you arrive." It read, "Cleared by Col. L. Glass. Call if questions—NO background check," followed by his signature.

"Thank you very much, sir."

William had almost reached the door when he heard, "Thank you, Son. Good luck to you."

William was taken straight away to Bletchley Park. He was excited to be working in the company of others who loved cryptography as much as he did. It wasn't long before news traveled around Bletchley about the newcomer with the strange name who was neither mathematician nor linguist nor crossword puzzle champion, as were most of the others. His daily routine was to go from hut to hut and help where he was most needed, and no one appreciated the challenges more than William himself. He was in his element.

On his last day, William finished his work and walked to where he was to find the car that would take him back to London. As he rounded the corner, he was surprised by the line of friends who had gathered around the car to say goodbye. He shook each person's hand and thanked them and wished them well.

The last person in the line, a young woman from Oxford who had become a good friend, handed him a small package wrapped in brown paper and tied with string. "Don't open it now, Scrydan. Wait until later, please." She added, whispering, "Actually, they'd have my head if they knew what it was."

"Thanks so much, Agnes." He shook her hand, and as he looked at her, he felt an overwhelming desire to stay. The driver honked the horn loudly. "Gotta go! Take care everyone," he said as he got in the car. He waved and took a mental snapshot of the moment. His time at Bletchley was the happiest he'd felt since before his father had died, and it kindled a renewed purpose in him. As the car made the hour-long trip to the Intelligence Office in London, he unwrapped the package. It was the little black book.

"Ho, ho! Now that's a souvenir!" he said to himself with a chuckle.

⚜

WILLIAM WAS JOLTED AWAKE BY SOMEONE CUTTING THE ROPE THAT tied his hands to the pipe in the engine room of the ship. "Wake up, old man! We are moving you upstairs!"

William had shown signs of illness, and the ship's medical officer observed symptoms that could indicate pneumonia. The engine room workers demanded that he be removed from the area so he wouldn't infect others. William was given a warm berth to himself, and though his hands were no longer tied, his door was locked from the outside.

The cook mercifully brought him three meals a day and seemed to take pity on him. "How are feeling today? Better, yes?" he would ask every morning in his rough English. William took the opportunity to ask when they expected to arrive in port.

"We arrive Denmark, Thursday. Two days more. Two."

It was so tempting to use the cover, but he had to find a way to thwart whatever was being planned. Otherwise, they would undoubtedly come after him again, and that could endanger Malcolm and Paddy.

❧ 8 ❧

THE RIDDLE

"PROGRESS IN EVERY AGE RESULTS ONLY
FROM THE FACT THAT THERE ARE SOME MEN
AND WOMEN WHO REFUSE TO BELIEVE THAT
WHAT THEY KNOW TO BE RIGHT CANNOT BE
DONE." -RUSSELL DAVENPORT

P addy awoke to a sky as dark as his mood. Other than the footprints and the few items the police had found, they had made no progress toward finding Grandpa. He dressed quickly and started to go downstairs. When he opened his bedroom door, he could hear a commotion of voices and rushing footsteps.

"W-w-will we n-need to e-evacuate?" Clara asked anxiously.

"Sweetheart, we are just preparing as a precaution. We'll wait for further instructions before we do anything else," replied Graham.

"Graham, let's make sure we have plenty of wood and batteries," Papa shouted from the shop.

"What's going on?" asked Paddy.

"The president has ordered everyone on the Eastern Seaboard to prepare for possible power outages and water shortages. They believe an attack may be imminent. Let's pray they are wrong," replied Papa as he taped a big X on each window.

Paddy rubbed his eyes. He had to admit, as desperate as they were to find Grandpa, it was good that Papa and Graham had been listening to the radio. By noon, they finished all preparations that could be made.

"Work is the best remedy for worry. I'm going to finish Colonel

Brandywine's suit. He's supposed to come by today to pick it up, though with everything going on, I'm not sure he'll show. Either way, I want to have it done. Paddy, why don't you keep going through the cottage and see if you can find any clues left by the kidnappers. I'll come out later."

"Papa, where are the SMITs? I mean, do they have a shop somewhere?" asked Paddy cautiously.

"Yes, in Dublin. They have a warehouse where they churn out clothing assembly-line fashion. It's an embarrassment to our profession. They call it the Manufactory."

"Most likely, that's where they took Grandpa."

Papa replied, "Sergeant Smith says that there was a freighter bound for Denmark that left the bay shortly after Grandpa disappeared."

"Can we get more information on that ship? Maybe the authorities can search the ship when it arrives?"

"The police are working on it," answered Papa.

Paddy couldn't think of anything else to suggest. "All right, I'm going to look around in the cottage."

When he reached the cottage, he opened the door slowly. Seeing the chaos and destruction made Paddy's stomach roil with anger and fear for Grandpa's safety. So many of Grandpa's treasures lay broken on the floor: a native mask from Cameroon, a book on Chinese writing on handmade parchment, a brass replica of an ancient Siamese warship from Thailand, a statue of a Moai god from Easter Island, to name a few. The intruders had thrown most of the books from their shelves, obviously looking for something.

As Paddy reshelved the books, he noticed *The Call of the Wild* tossed into the corner. He flipped through the pages, and images flashed in his memory like an old home movie. He'd read it when he was around ten, and he remembered that when he'd finished it, Grandpa gave him a coded message to decipher from the text, with a set of numbers corresponding to letters. Once Paddy had looked up all the letters, he wrote them out and put the Roman alphabet above it. He smiled, remembering how much fun it was. *I wonder if . . .*

Paddy flipped to the back of the book. Inside the dust jacket was a folded paper with Paddy's decryption that Grandpa had saved. The simple message, "Jmq stax jl et elx vthl zdl dblkh?" translated, read: "Why don't we go get some ice cream?" Paddy could feel a lump forming in his throat. He loved Grandpa more than life. *Why would anyone want to harm him?* Just the thought made his chest tighten and his heart race. *Ugh! I need to stay focused! He needs me to figure this out.*

Of Mice and Men lay beneath the coffee table. As he picked it up, he noticed a place where Grandpa had made a handwritten note. He often made notes in his books, but this note wasn't in English, or in any other language that Paddy recognized. It read "daeirln-4591." Paddy sat down and scoured the entire page and those before and after to discern its meaning—without success.

He had picked up almost all the books when he reached for one of his favorites, *Ivanhoe*. He casually flipped through to look at the pictures and stopped when he noticed another note that read, "daopln-8391." Again, he read the surrounding text, but couldn't understand the meaning. As he closed the book, his eye caught the page number—21. He looked back at the notation in *Of Mice and Men*. It also was written on page 21.

Paddy began to pull books back off the shelves and check them —*Farewell to Arms* read, "asursi-2991," *Brave New World* read, "ywonra-0491," *The Man Who Would Be King* read, "yaitl-6591," and *Ben-Hur* read, "yargemn-0491"—each written on page 21. He made as many words as he could from "asursi" until he spelled out "Russia." *Maybe he bought this on a trip to Russia?* Grandpa usually brought home a new book when he traveled.

He followed the same unscrambling pattern for each notation and made a chart showing which book was matched to each country. Paddy put both hands on his head and whispered, "This is so like *you*, Grandpa!" Still, he wondered what was so important that the country names were in code, and what did the numbers mean?

He arranged the books around himself on the floor. Each set of numbers following the country name ended in "91" and each contained four digits. Paddy wrote each group of numbers on a piece of paper side by side. In reverse order, they all began with 19. *Could these be years?* If so, the year that matched Russia was 1992; Ireland was 1954; Germany was 1944, and so on. When he wrote 1944 beside Germany, he paused. *Was he in Germany during World War II?* He would ask Papa to confirm whether the years corresponded with when, and if, Grandpa had traveled to these countries.

By two thirty, when Papa arrived to help, Paddy had found over fifty books with the same kind of note in the margin of page 21. Interestingly, he found multiple books with the same country noted, but with different years. Papa looked around at all the books on the floor surrounding Paddy. "Not making much progress, are we?"

"You'll never guess what I found!" As Paddy began to explain, he noticed that Papa seemed distracted.

"Did you know about this already?"

Papa put his finger to his lips to signal Paddy to be quiet and motioned him to come with him outside. "We can't risk discussing this in the cottage. It is possible that they bugged it," he whispered. "Let's take a walk down to the pier."

"You think someone bugged the cottage? Are the SMITs that sophisticated?"

Papa was quiet for some time as they walked. Finally, he spoke. "There is no easy way to say this . . ." He stopped and faced Paddy. Papa looked as if he'd rather be anywhere but there, at that moment. "I have dreaded this day your entire life, but there's no way to keep it from you any longer. Your grandfather is, well, your grandfather is a spy." Paddy was so stunned, he didn't move or speak.

Papa continued, "He has been a spy all of his adult life. He works independently, and only the highest-level operatives know his code name. Your grandpa specializes in carrying messages into places most spies cannot go."

"A spy? He's a *real* spy?"

"Keep your voice down. Let's keep walking."

Paddy was silent for a long time. *Why didn't Grandpa tell me?* It was hard for him to process how he felt, but it was much like feeling left out; like your best friend had kept a secret from you. Finally, he asked, "So all the trips to search for fabrics were really spy missions?"

"Sometimes no, but mostly yes, and sometimes both."

"If he's a spy, wouldn't it be more likely that he was kidnapped for information rather than taken by the SMITs?"

"It's certainly possible, but I don't think so."

"How did he become a spy, and why would he want to do that?"

"You have it reversed. You have to understand the why before you can understand how. This may sound old-fashioned to you, but there is a pride that has been passed down through our family tree—a pride in what our ancestors have done for others. Our history is more than something we recite that happened long ago. It's what flows in our veins and gives us purpose to live this life not just for ourselves, but so we make a difference in this world. That's the reason your Grandpa became a spy and why he risks his life for other people. He is trying to make things better for people, companies, and even entire nations."

"How can one person do all that?"

"What if the great men and women who sacrificed to make America a free nation had just kept to themselves or believed that change couldn't happen if only a few people spoke up?"

"We'd still be under British rule," replied Paddy.

"In our home country of Scotland, people created symbols to remind themselves and others of what they stood for. These symbols often became part of their crest, motto, or coat of arms. The unusual coat of arms you've seen hanging in Grandpa's living room is for our branch of the Duncan Clan. It shows a knight riding a horse into a storm while holding the earth in his hand. The earth is shown partially torn in two, symbolizing what evil can do when left unchecked. The earth is like a garment that is in the process of being sewn together with a needle and thread. The knight has a horn tied to his saddle for calling others to come and help those affected by distressing times. His sword hangs at his side, but its tip is broken, signifying that in fighting wrong, we do not rely on deadly force, we use our wits. The knight is missing the backplate of his armor, which means that he takes on battles intending to win or die. He never retreats.

"The whole image is bordered by a belt, upon which are the words of our motto, *Orbis Terrarum Relevetur ut Unum ad Tempus Consuo*. It roughly translates to: 'Healing the Land, One Stitch at a Time,' and refers to doing one good deed at a time. If you put all these symbols together, you have a message, a core belief that we are to find those in distress and do the most good possible in the time we have, not counting the cost.

Paddy, we are to be givers, not takers." There was a solemnness in Papa's voice as he spoke as though he were echoing his ancestors.

"Wow. It's sad that there aren't more courageous people like that in the world."

"Courage begins with the belief that right *matters*. It is developed gradually over time before the event requiring it ever happens." Papa had a far-off look as he spoke, and Paddy had a feeling that he was quoting someone.

Paddy thought about all Papa had said for a long time before he spoke. "Um, Papa?" He paused and waited for Papa's attention. "You've told me the 'why,' but how did he *become* a spy?"

"I'll let Grandpa tell you that story when he returns. I have to believe that he will return, and I hope it will be soon."

Paddy walked the rest of the way to the pier with Papa in silence, remembering story after story Grandpa had told him. Each story followed a pattern. Each one had a theme of helping someone in trouble. *What if they weren't just stories?*

At the pier, Papa looked for any sign of Grandpa that the police might have missed, but he found nothing. "Let's go back to the house and get the car. There's one last place we haven't checked."

THEY DROVE TO THE UNITED FIRST PARISH CHURCH IN QUINCY, not far from Weymouth. Paddy followed Papa inside and saw that no one else was in the church. Papa went to pew number 54 and sat down. He reached beneath the pew as if he expected to find something. Then, he removed a rolled piece of paper that had been taped to the bottom of the pew and slipped it into his pocket. He motioned to Paddy to join him in walking back to the car.

"What is that? How did you know something would be there?"

"Shhh . . ."

As soon as they were in the car, Paddy began asking questions again.

"Son, please wait until we get home."

When they reached home, Papa immediately went to his chair to open the note. It had a small green wax seal, which he removed, along with the heavier outer paper that wrapped it. Inside, there was a smaller red seal, which Papa carefully opened before unrolling a small note. He held out the message for Paddy to decipher. Once Paddy finished, he gave it back and Papa read it aloud:

Have recently learned new information. If I'm gone, know that it's time to enter the lion's den. Have courage. Dare to set him free. If you do, this will aid his journey:

Fear not! To Bhaile Átha Cliath come,
Across the swift An Bhóinn.
Where aflame was kept the light,
And some did pay the final price.
Their guide is silent, its face doth fade,
Among the servants who once obeyed.
In its heart is a treasure sown,
With ample pow'r to heal thine own.

At the very bottom, this was added hastily:

Tossed between duty and passion,
Unsure of where he belongs,
Never was there a more True Son,
So brave and daring and strong.

*Trust he will find helps in the Sanctuary. **Remember, always do what you are afraid to do. - R.W.E.

"Sanctuary? Does he mean inside the church?" Paddy asked.

"No. Your grandpa always refers to his cottage as his sanctuary."

"I've looked for clues in the cottage. The only thing I found that seemed like a clue was the coding system in Grandpa's books."

"We have to keep looking." Papa sounded frustrated as he reread the note. "Maybe he had an idea that they, whoever they are, would come for him, or that he'd be gone for some other reason. Before you ask, I don't know what it means, but I know this kind of riddle. In my experience, it usually directs one to find something."

"Your experience?" asked Paddy.

"Of course. He taught riddles and ciphers to me too when I was growing up. I just never caught on quite like you."

Paddy read over the note again. "What is Baile Átha Cliath and An Bhóinn? I can't even pronounce them."

"Baile Átha Cliath is pronounced sort of like, 'Blocklia,' and is the Irish word for Dublin. An Bhóinn, is pronounced a bit like, 'On Wonnan,' and refers to the River Boyne north of Dublin."

Paddy replied, "This note is written to you, since you are the only one who could have known where to find it. Is Grandpa referring to me when he wrote, 'Dare to set him free?'"

"Yes. As to whether I have the courage, I doubt it. I was . . . I *am* afraid, and I have a right to be."

❧ 9 ❧

DISCOVERY

"THE REAL VOYAGE OF DISCOVERY CONSISTS
NOT IN SEEKING NEW LANDSCAPES, BUT IN
HAVING NEW EYES." -MARCEL PROUST

Paddy went back out to the cottage just as another storm began to blow in from off the coast. *What does the note mean? Did Grandpa know something would happen to him? Should I leave now and find the SMIT tailors in Dublin? What could I leverage to get them to let Grandpa go free? What if he's not with the SMITs? What if an enemy spy organization took him?*

He reread the last part of the riddle: *"Tossed between duty and passion, Unsure of where he belongs, Never was there a more True Son, So brave and daring and strong."*

Why did he capitalize True Son? He ran his hand along the spines of the books he reshelved earlier: *Silas Marner, Les Misérables, The Raven, Oliver Twist, The Count of Monte Cristo, The Light in the Forest* . . . He stopped. Grabbing Grandpa's note, he looked again at the riddle at the bottom. *True Son is the name of the main character in* The Light in the Forest! In the story, True Son needs to make a choice between living with his adopted Native American family and living with his wealthy birth family. Paddy took the book from the shelf and flipped the pages forward and backward, looking for a notation or something hidden in the book but found nothing. It wasn't until he started to replace the book that he saw it.

On the wall behind the book was an almost undetectable small panel. Paddy slid it to the side, revealing an opening about the size of his fist, with a numeric keypad inside. *Is this for opening a safe?* He began to rack his brain to think what code Grandpa would most likely have used. He looked again at the note and tried various codes he derived from the text. He tried the date Grandpa came to America, he converted the word "sanctuary" into different code sequences, and he tried several other memorable words and dates, all to no avail. Frustrated, he left and joined Papa for dinner and told him what he found.

Afterward, he slowly climbed the stairs to his bedroom. He couldn't stop thinking about his discovery, so he returned to the cottage and took *The Light in the Forest* from the shelf again. Flipping again through the pages, he found nothing, but tucked deep inside the back flap of the dust jacket was a paper showing Paddy's deciphering of another cryptography challenge. There, penciled in his twelve-year-old handwriting, was the solution. Six steps were required to locate all the letters through different types of ciphers. The answer was "Lenape," and the corresponding code was 7-1-9-6-4-3. *Could it be?*

He slowly punched in the numbers on the keypad and waited. Then, he heard a low rumbling, like the grinding of an engine starting up. The rug in the living room began to slide sideways at the same time a panel in the floor opened. He gasped as a stone staircase gradually came into view beneath the floor. He thought about running to get Papa but changed his mind. After all, it could merely be a root cellar or a storm shelter. Then again, if that were true, Grandpa would have told him about it. As often as Paddy had spent time with Grandpa in the cottage, he had never known that there was a basement. *Could this be a secret hideout for Grandpa's spy work?*

Paddy looked around before going down the stairs. He felt sure Grandpa had meant to keep this secret, so he reasoned that it was his duty to protect it. He pulled the shades down on all the windows and locked the front and back doors.

Satisfied that he had done all he could, he took Grandpa's flashlight from beside the front door and slowly started down the steps. The opening was so narrow that he had to turn sideways a little, and his shoulders almost touched the sides. Rather than a basement, he found himself in a tunnel about four feet wide and six feet tall. It was well-built, with the entire floor, walls, and ceiling made of perfectly placed stones.

He guessed that the tunnel ceiling must be about six feet under-ground, and he wondered why and when Grandpa had built it. As he inched farther into the tunnel, he noticed the passageway was remark-ably clean, and he guessed that Grandpa used it frequently. There were several twists and turns, to the point that Paddy lost his bearings. He knew there was a small field behind the cottage, so he guessed that he must be well into the area beneath it by now.

Finally, the tunnel ended at an arched door. Paddy was both excited and scared as he stood before it. He tried the door, but it was locked. The doorknob and lock were quite old.

Frustrated, he started to head back to the cottage to look for the key when he remembered a Scottish legend Grandpa had shared with him when he was little. It was about a man who lived underground in a cozy home he entered through a hole in a huge oak tree. A staircase led down to a tunnel that ended at a door. The man didn't get many visi-tors, but with those who were welcome, he shared a secret. Written on the door was a riddle, which, when answered, led the visitor to the key. "That way," Grandpa said, "the man was sure that all his visitors were wise and capable of intelligent conversation."

Paddy shined the flashlight back and forth slowly over the door doubting he'd find anything. He sucked in and held his breath when he saw it. There, on the bottom right corner, was the following: "DWYC, WWYG, WYA. - S.B.W."

Paddy thought for a few minutes and was about to give up when he focused on the last three letters, obviously initials. "Could it be?" he asked himself as he remembered a quote Grandpa often used to admonish him. It was by Squire Bill Widener from the autobiography of Theodore Roosevelt. He looked at each letter as he recited from memory, "Do what you can, with what you've got, where you are." He searched the walls for a loose stone and felt the lintel above the door, without luck.

He closed his eyes in frustration. Finally, he asked, "What do I have, Grandpa?" In his thoughts, he heard Grandpa answer, "*Your mind, of course!*" He remembered reading Roosevelt's autobiography and taking the test Grandpa had made to check his memory. He'd only missed one question—the published date.

"Whoever looks at that?" Paddy had asked, frustrated that he'd missed the question. Grandpa wanted to teach him to develop the ability to remember what he had seen, even if he didn't realize he'd seen it. He asked Paddy to "flip back the pages of his mind" and find it. After what seemed like an eternity, he did see it: "Publish Date: 1920." That was the first of many times Paddy would practice developing "memory pictures," as Grandpa called them.

"See?" Grandpa had declared proudly, "Now you'll never forget it."

Any time numbers were involved, Grandpa would turn them into a code, or a map, or a clue of some kind. Not knowing what else to do, Paddy counted the stones, beginning at different starting places, and counted one down, nine right, and two down, but none of the stones would move. He tried several more scenarios, and after over an hour, he was ready to give up.

Ugh! I can't read your mind, Grandpa. He tried one last time, by counting from the stone on the floor directly beneath the doorknob. He counted one back, nine to the right, and two back. He felt around the edges of the stone. It was loose! He used the end of the flashlight as a lever to help him remove it. There, wrapped in a piece of old cloth, was a key.

Suddenly, the fact that Grandpa was a spy started to seem not only real but scary. *What sort of things did he do as a spy? Didn't spies do things that were sometimes on the edge of the law? Who hired him for missions?*

I should get Papa and see what he thinks. Maybe it's just a hurricane shelter. He turned to go back, putting the key in his pocket, but as he did, he felt the note from Grandpa. In the pale light cast by the flashlight, he silently read again, *"Trust he will find helps in the Sanctuary." Grandpa means for me to do this alone.*

He faced the door again. Fierce resolve rose in his heart as he thought of all the Duncans who chose to do what was good and right over what was safe or easy. He remembered Mama's courage, telling Papa that, no matter what happened to her, he was not to give the thread to the SMITs. Paddy stood before the door as if passing through it would induct him into what it really meant to be a Duncan. His skin tingled from the conviction that he felt, and he searched for the words to fix this moment upon his memory. It began as a whisper and grew louder as he felt the depth of his commitment rising within him.

"I solemnly swear, by the lives of my forefathers, to commit my life to find those in distress, and to do all the good that I can in the time given to me—not counting the cost." He added, "I pledge my soul and all that I am to it." At that moment, Paddy felt as though he'd passed from his old life to a new way of thinking about the world, others, and even himself.

He turned the key in the lock and slowly pushed the heavy door open. The space beyond the door was pitch dark, but Paddy had an eerie feeling that what lay within would change the very fabric of who he was—forever.

He remembered his flashlight and soon found an oil lamp and matches on a small table close to the door. As his eyes adjusted to the lamplight, he saw that the room was quite large, and the ceiling was higher than that of the tunnel. Against one wall, there was an enormous postman's desk with tiny cubbyholes full of neatly folded papers. Next to it, there was a large rack of shelves full of long rolled-up documents, each tied with a tagged string. He peered into the end of one and saw that it appeared to be a map.

On one wall, there was a portrait of Paddy's grandmother Agnes, taken when she was a young woman. She wore a corsage—a single gardenia. On a bureau beneath her picture was a small box. Opening it, Paddy could see that it held mementos, letters to Grandpa, a necklace, and some photographs. Lying on top of the contents was a pressed bloom of a gardenia.

Along the far wall, there was a bookcase filled with volumes of classic literature. Several steamer trunks lay about the room, and a map of India was lying open upon a table in the center of the room. A wooden marker marked the city of Jaipur. Paddy remembered that Grandpa had just visited their satellite office in Jaipur recently.

Looking around at the room, he was sure that this had to be where Grandpa planned his missions. An old grandfather clock in the corner of the room chimed four o'clock. He was so caught up in the wonder of discovering Grandpa's "Cave," as Paddy had dubbed it, that hours had passed in what seemed like no time at all. The realization hit him that if Papa came to the cottage, he would wonder why the doors were locked.

He took one last look around, and something strange caught his attention. He noticed that the wall with the doorway was around sixteen feet long, but when he looked at the far wall, it was substantially shorter—about eleven or twelve feet long. At first, he thought it was an optical illusion. If this room had been dug out by hand, the measurements might be off a bit, but not by that much. He found a ball of twine in the desk and measured the walls to be sure. *This room is a trapezoid! Grandpa would never have built it this way unless there was a reason.*

The walls were coffered mahogany paneling with matching support beams on the ceiling. On a hunch, Paddy began to knock on the paneling as he walked toward the far end of the room. When he was halfway to the opposite end, the sound of his knocking began to change. He continued farther until he had almost reached the end of the wall, and the change in the sound was unmistakable. There was a hollow space behind the wall.

He looked for what might be a door or a latch, but he couldn't find anything. *Darn it! I have to get back in case Papa comes.* He left everything as he'd found it and went back up the stairs into the cottage just as Papa came to look for him.

When Papa entered the cottage and saw the shades closed, he asked, "Did you find something?"

Paddy only smiled as he reopened the passageway to the tunnel. Papa's astonished expression was evidence that he didn't know about Grandpa's secret either. He walked over to the opening and looked down.

"How did you find this?"

Paddy put his finger to his lips, remembering Papa's comment about the possibility of the cottage being bugged, and motioned for him to follow him down into the tunnel. When they reached the door,

Paddy said, "Wait until you see this! It's like a cave with all his spy stuff!"

As Papa entered, he kept saying, "Oh my!" and "I never knew . . ." Paddy was so distracted by telling Papa what he'd discovered that it was a few minutes before he noticed Papa had stopped in front of the portrait of Agnes, his mother. He cleared his throat. "I always wondered how he could spend so much time in this tiny cottage, and all along, he had this! There must be decades of history stored here. Good job, Son. Brilliant work." Paddy felt a flush of pride.

৩৯৩

AFTER DINNER, PADDY WENT STRAIGHT UP TO HIS ROOM. HE GOT A large piece of butcher paper from Clara and taped it to his bedroom wall so he could visually lay out a timeline of the events since right before Grandpa's disappearance. There were the clues the police had found on the road to the pier, the message hidden at the church, the notes in the books in Grandpa's library, and now, the Cave. He looked over Grandpa's message again. "Trust he will find helps in the Sanctuary." It was clear that Grandpa meant for him to find the Cave. He just had no idea why.

Paddy went to bed and fell into a light sleep. As he slept, it was as if his mind was flipping through images of things he'd seen in the Cave. At about two o'clock in the morning, Paddy woke and sat bolt upright in bed. Something was peculiar about one of his mental pictures. He remembered seeing a basket hanging from the ceiling that held various office supplies. It wasn't what was in the basket that drew his attention, but rather how it hung from the ceiling. There was no hook. Instead, the basket hung from a rope that had been fed down through a hole, which seemed odd. That thought, coupled with the odd shape of the room and Paddy's certainty that there must be a hidden compartment behind the wall, eliminated any chance that he could go back to sleep.

He tiptoed downstairs and out to the cottage and reopened the tunnel. As he reached the bottom step, his hand brushed against a switch on the wall. He flipped it, and the panel in the floor above him began to close. Paddy smiled. Grandpa had attached the rug to the floor panel so that when it closed, the rug moved perfectly back into position. *Grandpa, you are a genius!*

Walking quickly through the tunnel, he unlocked the door once more and lit the lamp. His memory was correct. The rope descended from a hole in the ceiling. He stood on a stool to get a closer look and shined his flashlight past the rope up into the space above. He pulled the rope to the side of the hole to make more room for him to see, and, as he did, a panel on the wall slid open a few inches. It so startled him that he almost fell off the stool. He pulled again on the rope, and the panel opened farther. His heart was pounding as he imagined what he would find in the compartment behind the little door.

The panel uncovered a small triangular-shaped space, just big enough for someone to lie down on the floor and for a few additional items. In the space, there was a pillow and blanket, a small trunk that contained a worn world map, some tins of food, a can opener, spoon, bowl, and two bottles of water. There was also an oil lamp and a flashlight with spare batteries. He stood puzzled for some time, looking around the small space. He noticed a handle on the inside of the sliding panel, which he took and slowly slid the doorway closed. He watched the basket through the remaining opening lift back up to its original height. *Perhaps something important was hidden here? Could this be a hiding place for Grandpa in case his enemies found the tunnel?*

Paddy yawned, realizing how much sleep he'd missed already. He started to go back to the shop and reached to open the compartment door. As he did, he dropped the flashlight, and it bounced on the floor and flipped over, then the base of it tapped against the outer wall of the compartment. He picked up the flashlight and used it to knock against the wall. He held his breath as he continued to tap high and low and to either side. The wall sounded hollow, just as the paneling on the inside wall of the compartment. *There has to be a room on the other side!* He searched for some way to open the panel, but it wouldn't slide, and there was no visible keyhole or latch.

He sat down again and studied the tiny space, shining his flashlight up and down the walls. It was roughly finished with the studs exposed, but, oddly, every inch of wood had been sanded and finished until it gleamed. *Why would he do that?*

Then he noticed a small portion of one stud about two inches high and three inches wide that looked like a tiny door at the bottom of the wall next to the floor. He slid it open, revealing a small lever in a recessed area. He pushed it to the side and heard a click, but nothing happened. He stood and searched up and down the walls for anything similar and found seven more hidden levers and a dial, somewhat like a combination lock.

It all reminded him of the puzzle boxes Grandpa would use to challenge Paddy when he was young. Grandpa had a collection of them from several countries. Some of them required up to forty-six steps, moving a series of sliding panels, levers, and knobs to open them. It was then that it hit him. This whole compartment *was* a puzzle box, and he was *inside it!* Paddy's heart raced with excitement. *But how do I figure out the order of the steps?* He began trying different sequences. On about the twentieth time, a small portion of the outer wall of the compartment popped away from the wall, forming a simple revolving door that rotated on a center pin. He pushed it and stepped through, finding himself in another room, this one smaller than the Cave.

On one wall was a small desk, and, in two of the corners, there were large, ornate matching bookshelves filled with books protected by etched-glass doors. There was an oil lamp on the desk, which Paddy lit and held up to get a better view of the whole room. Unlike the other, this room had stone walls and a rough wood-plank floor. Between the bookshelves sat a trunk, which he opened carefully, and saw that it held boxes of old letters. He took the top letter in the box closest to him and read:

William,

I hope I have shown by my actions how much I repudiate the actions of my family against the Duncans. I thank you for your willingness to believe me, for I don't know if I would be able to do so were our roles reversed. From the beginning, Angus behaved honorably, and the Society did nothing but betray that honor, and so it continues to this day. I hope that you will grant my request and allow me to offer my services to your family and company so that in some small way, I may repay the enormous debt my family owes to you.

Yours in humble service,

Richard B. Falmouth (former SMIT)

Former SMIT? The guy defected? Gosh! He continued looking through the trunk and found a transit, several compasses of different sizes, a spyglass, an odd-looking astrolabe, and some books that appeared to be military message-decoding field manuals. Stacked in one corner of the trunk were about twenty or so journals filled with Grandpa's handwriting, but it was all in code.

There was a world map tacked to a bulletin board hanging on one wall. Red, yellow, and green colored pins marked numerous locations all over the world. A handwritten legend in the corner read, "Red— three months ago; Yellow—two months ago; Green—within last month."

"Grandpa must be going to several countries at a time when he travels. So that's why his trips take so long," he said aloud as he ran his hand gently over the colored pins.

Everything in the room was dusty, as though Grandpa didn't use this room often, but Paddy could see footprints in the dust that led from the compartment to a massive armoire. *How did he ever get this in here?* He tried to open the doors, but it was locked. He tried a key he found in a small drawer of the desk to no avail.

He felt up and down the walls of the armoire until he reached a section of ornamental scrollwork in the wood. On a hunch, he slid it to the side and, like a puzzle box, it revealed another lever which led to another. Finally, a tiny compartment opened in which was the key. He opened the door, revealing a large number of similar-looking brand-new coats with tags. Upon closer examination, he noticed that the tags had an odd series of letters, which he recognized as the same ones written on page 21 of so many books upstairs. One read, "Asursi," which stood for Russia; another read, "Daeirln," which he remembered was the scrambling of the word Ireland.

As he held the lantern closer to the Ireland coat, he could see the detail of the stitching where the lining met the outer wool fabric.

Paddy gasped. It had the most beautiful hand-stitching he had ever seen. He examined the finished seams, covered buttons, bound button-holes, and tabbed cuffs. The exquisite lining was pure silk, not the synthetic blends used now. He traced the hemline with his fingers, but stopped when he noticed something vaguely familiar. It looked like a button—somewhat like the seals they currently used, but it was larger and much more ornate. It was also in the wrong place. Duncan Tailoring sewed their seals into the inside breast pocket, not on the hemline.

Then, he remembered. Goosebumps covered his neck and arms as he recalled Papa's words. *This can't be one of the seals the Lunar Society made for Angus!* It had ornate copper filigree on the top, with porcelain beneath and a piece of amber in the center. The seal was attached to the hem by looping thread through tiny rings attached to either side, which allowed the seal to be flipped over. He recalled Papa explaining that John Whitehurst, the clockmaker, had collaborated with other Lunar Society members to make fifty special seals with clockworks inside. Paddy turned the seal over, and what he saw took his breath away. He watched through the glass on the back of the seal as gears turned, moving in perfect synchrony. He stared at it for a long time in disbelief—for it was beyond anything possible. He checked the other coats. Each had the same type of seal, and all the seals' gears were still turning.

Paddy ran his hand along the sleeves of several coats and whis-pered, "What if Angus made all of these?" He began to feel as if he were touching something sacred, something that should be in a museum because if he was right, these coats were well over two hundred years old. *So, how are the clock parts still moving?*

There must have been over twenty coats altogether. He closed the armoire and started to go back to the shop to tell Papa, when he turned and reopened it once more to look at the coats. It was as if they were alive, with a tiny heart beating in each one.

He was lost in the wonder of it all when an idea came to him. *What would be so wrong about putting one of the coats on—just for a minute?* He took one off its hanger and held it in front of him. It would be a little like going back in time. Just holding the coat made Paddy feel as if he were reaching through time, as if the coat were a touch point connecting him to Angus.

He carefully put his arm into the left sleeve. He looked at how the lapel lay on his chest, and he ran his hand slowly over the stitching. His heart began to beat faster, and he sensed a tiny electric shock deep in his chest. Then he put his right arm in the other sleeve.

Suddenly, he felt like he was jerked up inside a tornado! He plunged into darkness and sensed that strong wind was spinning his body uncontrollably so that he began to feel nauseous within seconds. When he could manage to barely open his eyes, he could see tiny flashes of light here and there, but it was impossible to keep his eyes open. He couldn't move his arms or legs because of the enormous pressure of the wind against his body. The loud, whooshing sound rushing past his ears was deafening and completely muffled the sounds of his screaming. The last thing he remembered was the sensation that hundreds, maybe millions, of tiny objects were softly touching the exposed skin of his face and hands. Finally, he got so dizzy that he blacked out.

When he regained consciousness, he was lying in what seemed like a coffin. He panicked, shouting, "Help!" several times and pounded the sides with his fists. He soon realized it was not a coffin because he could sit up. Still, Paddy was sure he had died. He was so confused and afraid, he felt for his pulse, and his pounding heartbeat confirmed that he was very much alive. Because of the darkness, he could only explore his surroundings by touch, and it seemed as if he'd landed in a box filled with different types of fabrics.

After a few moments, his fear turned to sheer terror. Paddy pounded on the walls while shouting, "Let me out!" over and over until his voice began to fail. Finally, he slumped against one wall. He opened his eyes wide and tried to see his hands, but the thick darkness was so complete, it seemed he and the world had disappeared. Hopelessness and confusion closed in around his mind, and his terror made his chest tighten so that it was hard for him to breathe. He closed his eyes, trying to steady his nerves, and one thought pressed upon his mind. *What would Grandpa do?*

IN ÉIRE

"A SHIP IN HARBOR IS SAFE, BUT THAT IS NOT
WHAT SHIPS ARE BUILT FOR." -JOHN SHEDD

A crack of light appeared and gradually grew larger. Paddy could now see a weathered hand holding the edge of what seemed to be a door to the darkness that held him.

"Hello? Papa? What . . . what happened? Where am I?" he asked, his hoarse voice trembling. His eyes had grown so accustomed to the dark, he now had to shade them from the light. Gradually, the opening grew wider, and Paddy could see he was in a closet. The door was being opened by a short, older man with a wizened face that appeared very angry.

"*Cé tusa?*" he demanded.

"I'm sorry? I don't know what happened. Where am I?"

The man stared at him silently.

"Do you speak English?" asked Paddy timidly.

"Who are you?" came the angry reply in a thick Irish brogue.

"My . . . my name is Patrick Duncan, but I go by Paddy."

The man stared at Paddy with a knitted brow and a deepening frown. Finally, Paddy slowly eased himself out of the closet. The edge of a coat in the closet was stuck to the hem of Paddy's coat, as though from static electricity. Paddy tried to jerk the coat away from the other one. Before he knew what was happening, the man grabbed Paddy's coat by the shoulders from behind and pulled it off him in one swift motion.

"Hey! Give that back to me! That's my coat!" yelled Paddy.

"It is not! I suspect that before today, you'd never seen that coat before. Well, well, well. From the looks of things, you just had quite a surprise." The man stood scratching his chin and looking at Paddy.

From where he was standing, Paddy could see through a doorway into what was a small tailor's shop in one section of the house. "Look, I'm sorry to have intruded into your privacy. I meant no harm. My father has a tailoring shop too. I'm his apprentice. Perhaps you know my grandfather, William Duncan of Duncan Tailoring?" Paddy thought he saw the man's eyes soften in recognition when he mentioned Grandpa's name. "May I know your name, sir?"

The tailor's response was cold. "Iain Callum. Can you prove you are this, Paddy Duncan?"

Paddy felt his back pocket for his wallet but realized that he was still in his pajamas. "I, I wasn't . . . I didn't know I would be going anywhere. I left my wallet at home."

"A likely story. Leave! Now!" came the stern reply.

"Sir, I don't know where I am or how I got here! Won't you help me? May I use your phone to call my father?" asked Paddy, now in full panic.

The tailor pushed Paddy out into the shop and through the front door, shutting and locking it quickly behind him. Paddy knocked and pleaded that if he could just explain, but he wasn't sure what more he could say.

Paddy began to wonder if the old fellow was senile, or perhaps he thought Paddy was a thief who had been hiding in his closet. Paddy walked away from the house down a little lane, which led to a wider dirt road. He didn't recognize any landmarks at all. He walked about a hundred yards down the road and came upon a sign that read, "Bhaile Átha Cliath è 10 km." The color drained from Paddy's face, and he suddenly felt dizzy. "Th-this has to be a dream," he stammered. He touched the sign to be sure it was real. He felt queasy and sat down on a fallen tree beside the road and breathed into his cupped hands.

He thought through the sequence of events, searching for a logical explanation. He looked up at the sign again. *Ten kilometers to Dublin? What language was the old tailor speaking?* He realized that it was afternoon by the position of the sun. *What happened to the intervening hours?* He needed answers, and other than a few cottages dotted here and there between rolling fields, there wasn't any civilization in sight.

Paddy looked back down the road to the old tailor's shop. *He doesn't care about helping me, and he stole Grandpa's coat!*

Meanwhile, Iain placed a phone call. "Hey Malcolm, are you missing a son?"

"What are you talking about?" asked Malcolm.

"I do believe Paddy found William's armoire of covers because he just passaged and showed up here in my closet."

"Oh! I'm sorry, Iain! Are you sure?"

"I haven't let him know that I'm sure, but I wanted to see if you knew first. I do believe I'll give him a bit of a hard time for not letting you know what he was up to!"

"Oh, Iain, he's eighteen now and he's stretching his wings. I've been telling him some things, but I'm going to have to fill him in on it all soon. Feel free to explain things to him while he's there. He'll probably receive it better from you. I'll send a ticket to fly him home."

"Okay, but act surprised when he calls you to tell you what happened."

Malcolm sighed. "It's a wonder I don't have more gray hair. Well, one thing's for sure, he inherited his genius from his mother, not me! Poor guy. I bet that was quite a shock! Thanks for letting me know."

"Sure thing. Actually, it's a nice surprise to see him. I'll try not to be too hard on him," said Iain. "Hey, any more news about William?"

"Nothing yet. I promise I'll call as soon as we learn anything at all."

"Same here. We've got all ears to the ground. Well, I'm sure Paddy will be calling you soon." They both chuckled.

As Paddy looked back toward the tailor's cottage, he noticed an old sign close to the side of the road beside his driveway. The wording was obscured by dust from cars passing by on the dirt road. Paddy wiped the accumulated dust away and read it aloud as he made out the lettering: "Iain C. Duncan - Tailoring and Cobblery Shoppe - Perfection is Our Standard."

Iain Callum indeed! If this man's name is Duncan, why didn't he say so? It's no coincidence he has our motto on his sign!

He ran back to the shop and around to the back door hoping it was unlocked. He burst through into the kitchen, where the tailor was seated. "You lied to me! You are Iain Duncan! Right? Tell me now!" shouted Paddy.

Iain acted startled and replied feigning fear, "Y-yes, I-I am . . . I am Iain Duncan."

"Why did you lie to me?" Paddy shouted.

"I did *not* lie. I am Iain Callum, Iain Callum Duncan. How do I know you're not an imposter!"

"You have my family's saying on your sign out there. That's not a coincidence!"

Iain spoke in a quiet voice, "How can I believe you are Paddy? Besides, Malcolm would have told me you were coming—that is if you told him."

"You know my father?"

"If you are who you say."

"He didn't call you because he doesn't know I'm here! I don't even know where I am . . . or how I got here."

"You are in Ireland, the outskirts of Dublin, to be specific."

"What? How . . . ? Was I in a coma? Did someone bring me here? What day is it? Ask me anything. I'll prove who I am. I am Patrick Duncan. I live in Weymouth, Massachusetts. Let me call my dad and he can prove it. Won't you please help me?"

"I have a cousin named William. If you are who you say, you might be his grandson, but I don't know. Can you recite the motto?"

"What motto?"

"If you knew it, you wouldn't have to ask," retorted Iain flatly.

"*Orbis Terrarum Relevetur ut Unum ad Tempus Consuo.*" Paddy had made a mnemonic as soon as Papa had told him the motto, so he wouldn't forget it.

Iain looked up slowly at Paddy but kept silent.

"What will it take for you to believe me?" Paddy pleaded.

Iain squinted at him and declared, "A test of wits. If William is your grandfather, you shouldn't have any trouble. There have been many imposters who claimed to be Duncans to get information, or to get something else. I need to be sure I can trust you. You put the heart crossways in me, showing up as you did.

"If you are Paddy Duncan, your grandpa would have had you reading books since you were a tyke. So, I will give you a quote, and you reply with any sentence that uses the last name of the author."

"This is crazy! Why can't I just tell you the author?" asked Paddy.

"This is how it's done." Paddy thought it was stupid to waste time on a game like this, but there was no escaping it.

Iain began, "'But, especially he loved to run in the dim twilight of the summer midnights, listening to the subdued and sleepy murmurs of the forest, reading signs and sounds as a man may read a book, and seeking for the mysterious something that called—called, waking or sleeping, at all times, for him to come.'"

Paddy was ready before Iain finished the quote and replied, referencing Jack London's *The Call of the Wild*, "I think after I leave here, I will travel to *London* and meet the queen."

"Beginner's luck," retorted Iain. Paddy rolled his eyes.

He offered another. "'We all live with the objective of being happy; our lives are all different and yet the same.'"

"Let me be *frank*; I need to know how I got here," Paddy replied sarcastically. "Everyone knows that quote from *The Diary of Anne Frank*."

Iain scowled. He thought for a while, trying to find a more difficult challenge, and then continued:

The best thing for disturbances of the spirit is to learn. That is the only thing that never fails. You may grow old and trembling in your anatomies, you may lie awake at night listening to the disorder of your veins, you may miss your only love and lose your moneys to a monster, you may see the world about you devastated by evil lunatics, or know your honor trampled in the sewers of baser minds. There is only one thing for it then—to learn. Learn why the world wags and what wags it. That is the only thing which the poor mind can never exhaust, never alienate, never be tortured by, never fear or distrust, and never dream of regretting.

Paddy thought about the last time he had read T. H. White's *The Sword in the Stone*. He decided that if Iain needed to test him, perhaps he should also test Iain. So, he replied with a quote that would answer Iain's quiz and see just how much Iain knew. "'And I have by me, for my comfort, two strange *white* flowers—shriveled now, and brown and flat and brittle—to witness that even when mind and strength had gone, gratitude and a mutual tenderness still lived on in the heart of men.'"

"Ha! That's a fret! One of my favorites—H. G. Wells's *The Time Machine*. You are not only well-read, you're a swift thinker. Well, there is no doubt that you know your way around the classics, but now to check your knowledge of family history. To whom do we credit the secrets and the science our family has discovered, and why?"

"Angus Duncan, my grandfather five generations removed, because he dedicated himself to fair business practices and to helping others. He believed that he should do the most good for those in distress in the time he had—not counting the cost to himself." There was a tone of respect and pride in Paddy's voice, and he squared his shoulders as he spoke.

Iain couldn't help but smile. "It's good to see you again, Son. It's been a long time. I'm sorry I was so inhospitable when you arrived. I had to be sure you weren't an imposter."

"Are you related to my grandpa?" asked Paddy.

"We are cousins. William's Aunt Katherine is my mother."

The mention of Grandpa brought Paddy back to the reality of his abduction. "Do you know anything about where Grandpa might be? We think the SMITs kidnapped him."

"No, Son. We heard about the kidnapping. Malcolm called Douglass, William's brother who lives nearby, the day it happened. We also heard from someone at the NSA. We've notified all the satellite offices."

"NSA? Wow, maybe they wanted him to do a mission. The police found some things he dropped near the beach, so they think the kidnappers took him by boat."

"I know you are worried about him. We all are."

"May I borrow your phone? My dad will be so worried."

"Of course! There, on the wall. Be sure to dial the country code, zero, zero, then one and the number."

Papa answered on the first ring and feigned relief at hearing Paddy was all right. "I'll get a plane ticket to you. Give Iain my thanks for putting you up."

"All okay now?" asked Iain.

"Yes. He's sending a ticket for a flight home."

"That's good because we don't have a Weymouth cover here at the moment."

"What do you mean when you say *cover*? And, why does Papa understand how I got here? What happened to me?"

Iain smiled kindly, understanding Paddy's confusion.

"I realize this all must be quite a shock for you, but I do believe you are the first one in history to have traveled through a passage without realizing it, except for Angus, of course." He threw back his head and laughed at the thought. "My boy, you have some more surprises yet! Why don't we have a wee snack and we can talk by the fire? These old bones don't hold the warmth they used to. I'll wet the tea. I believe there are some fresh biscuits in the press. You go on in and get warm. Put on that jumper by the door! Looks like you left home in your pajamas."

Iain prepared some strong tea and set it on a tray with a beautifully embroidered napkin covering assorted butter cookies.

"Impressive handwork," noted Paddy as Iain laid the tray on the table.

"My wife, Eliza, God rest her sweet soul, she could embroider like no one else."

Iain returned to the issue of Grandpa. "So, what makes you think the SMITs kidnapped your grandpa?"

"Papa is sure. He said it feels like when my mom . . ."

"Ah, so you do know the real story about your ma. Paddy, you were born into a family with a heavy burden to bear. Part of that burden lies in keeping secrets."

"I couldn't find anything in the cottage that seemed like a clue about who took him or why."

"Well, you are to be commended for having the insight to find your grandpa's office downstairs. That must have taken some serious problem-solving!"

"Oh, you know, one thing just led to another." Paddy was proud of all he'd discovered, but he wasn't ready to share with anyone how he did it.

"Now, let me tell you how you got here, although the chances you'll believe me are like hen's teeth.

"Covers are what we call the coats you saw in your grandpa's office. We call using a cover for transport 'passaging' because . . . Well, the simple explanation is that when you put one on, you go through an electromagnetic passage to get to the cover's twin. Each cover has a special seal sewn to the hem, as you've seen. All the coats work in pairs, and the magnets of each pair *want* to be together. When we put on a cover, the tiny bit of electricity from our bodies works like a jumper cable and boosts the electrons in the seal's magnetic field to connect with the earth's magnetic field. We travel in the earth's magnetic field until the seal's magnet reaches its match."

Paddy's eyes grew wide. "It was the coat?"

"Yes. William has a pair for each country in our tailoring network, and he uses the covers to travel between them."

"How in the world can a coat transport a person somewhere else? I mean, how does your body travel?"

"Do you know about the thread Angus had in his pocket during the explosion at the Lunar Society?"

"Yes, Papa told me about that, and that it has special properties. I've known for years that our thread changes color to match the fabric. I asked Papa about it when I was younger. He just explained that it was supposed to do that. I guess I never questioned it, odd as that sounds. I mean, ladies today have makeup that changes color to match their skin, right? So, why not have a thread that changes color?" He smiled slightly, but Iain didn't return the smile.

"This is serious stuff, Paddy. There are theories, but so far, we are stewards of a phenomenon that we don't fully understand. Angus's diary records that when he received the fifty special seals from John Whitehurst, he decided to thank him by making him a morning coat. He attached one of Whitehurst's special seals onto the hem using the thread. When he finished, since he was about the same size as White-hurst, Angus tried on the coat to see if anything needed adjusting. The next moment, he found himself in another room, where he had left the box containing the remaining seals. The seal in the coat was stuck fast to a seal in the box as if by magnetic attraction. You can imagine how shocked he was."

"Wait! That's what happened to me! My coat was sticking to the coat in your closet when I got here, remember? But, how was he carried to the other room by the seal?" Paddy's eyes were wide, as he waited for Iain to continue.

"Angus's initial observation was that the magnets in these special seals must be unusually strong, but he knew there had to be more to it than that. So, he investigated further. He wondered why the seal in the jacket only sought out one *particular* seal in the box, and, like you, he also wondered how he was physically carried from one room to another in an instant. He questioned why the seal only reacted when he put the coat on, and he wanted to test to see how far the morning coat and the second seal needed to be separated before the attraction would be too weak to work.

"He experimented by separating the two seals by longer and longer distances. One day, he took the second seal and traveled to the shop of his cousin, Daniel Duncan, in Perth, over twenty miles from Dundee. When he tied his horse behind the shop, he hid the seal in the barn. He told Daniel he would leave his horse overnight and return for him the next day. Then, he traveled home by coach. The following day, he put on the coat, and in an instant, he was standing in his cousin's barn in Perth."

"Whoa! Can you imagine?"

Iain laughed. "Why do you sound surprised? You just crossed the Atlantic by the same force! You see, the seals only work this way when at least one of them is sewn into a garment with the *benysoun*, that's what we call the thread. It means 'blessing.' The thread is heavily saturated with a type of inert copper that makes it act like a circuit wire. The human body is the last connection that needs to be present for the jump to the earth's magnetic field. Your papa told you about the explosion, correct?"

"Yes, but not about the coats."

"Covers, Paddy, covers," corrected Iain. "Teach yourself to never speak of them as coats. Everything we've protected for generations depends on it."

"Sorry."

"Angus theorized that tiny fragments of the lodestone that blew up in the explosion remained suspended in the earth's magnetic field. When a person puts on a cover with one of the special seals, it uses the particles still in the atmosphere as a kind of cosmic highway to reach its twin."

"Is that possible?"

"No one knows . . . yet. When the Lunar Society made the fifty special seals, they used pieces from the remaining lodestone left over from the explosion. Each seal has a magnetic rod that passes through the middle of each one, and the north south axes within the rod are what keep the clockworks moving. Angus thought that each piece they chipped off could have had a unique memory, of sorts, of the crystalline structure of the piece that was next to it within the stone. He postulated that if the pieces weren't stable or complete without the other, that might be why each seal's magnet seeks its partner."

"What exactly happened during the explosion? Did Angus record any details?"

"We have his diaries. Angus recorded that, when he opened his eyes, he could see a huge fiery ball in the sky that had blown through the roof of the building. When it rose, it created a vacuum that drew the contents of Keir's experiment along with several other items, including the lodestone, up into the air. Angus wrote that after some time had passed, the fiery cloud dissipated, and the lodestone, the half that remained, fell back into Boulton's Demonstration Room glowing from the heat. Angus believed that the lodestone's chemical formula changed when it combined with some of the chemicals used in Keir's experiment. I think it's safe to say that if the reaction had occurred in the Demonstration Room instead of up in the sky, they would have all died, and neither you nor I would be here today."

"That's intense!"

"As Angus gained a better grasp of the power of the seals, he thought about what could happen if they fell into the wrong hands. Someone could commit a horrible crime and then effectively disappear. He also reasoned that they could be useful for doing good. He began volunteering to help the military with its most dangerous assignments, and he was so successful that, well, the rest is, as they say, history.

"When the SMITs' scheme to use our name failed, they began threatening our tailors with terrible things. Angus suggested that those who were able should move to countries where we purchased fabric and set up shop there. That way we'd have one of our own to build relationships with local fabric vendors. Twelve tailors did this, and that's how Duncan Tailoring expanded into a worldwide company. Angus took these tailors into confidence about the thread and the covers, and they began helping him arrange secret missions. He made a pair of covers for each country, and he always took the cover for Dundee with him so he could return home."

"This is unbelievable! We expanded into a worldwide company because of a rock?"

Iain burst out laughing. "You are my cousin's grandson all right. I've never quite heard it described that way!

"Well, not long after that, Angus decided that it was too dangerous to have the covers in the same city as the SMITs, so he moved everything here to Dublin. Within a year, the SMITs bought the Manufactory and moved here also. Angus realized that it didn't matter where he moved, the SMITs were determined to put Duncan Tailoring out of business. When we began to build a worldwide reputation, they stepped up their efforts to sabotage us and our satellite offices."

"Each of the tailors that moved to other countries kept one of the covers and Angus kept the other. Is that how he'd travel to each office?"

"Yes."

"Is that what Grandpa still does?"

"Exactly. That armoire where you found the cover contains all the matching covers for each country. The duty of Master Keeper has passed to the next generation five times."

"Master Keeper?"

"That's what we call the one in charge of keeping all the partner covers and the works of literature we use as cipher keys. So, there you have it."

"I want to get this straight. You are saying that my body traveled along the earth's magnetic field to get here because the seal in the cover for Ireland wanted to be with the seal of the matching cover you have here?"

"That's a simple way of putting it," replied Iain as he eyed the lingering doubt on Paddy's face with frustration. "Follow me." He led Paddy to the back room and unlocked the door to the closet. "Now, you see, the seals are not together, right? Here, put the cover back on."

Paddy did so and instantly found himself pushed up against the closet. When he opened his eyes, he could see that the seals were magnetized together. Iain held up the seals to allow Paddy to examine them more closely. The clockworks inside were spinning so fast that Paddy couldn't even see the separate gears within the seal. He gently took off the coat, and the seals fell away from one another.

"Can you understand now why that small group of tailors agreed to support Angus in his spy work? They believed that this secret is a gift, and that they were its stewards. It's never been just about keeping the thread from the SMITs. It's about using the covers to change the world!"

"Wow, this is a lot to take in."

Iain sighed and looked at Paddy.

"What? You look like you were going to say something else? Did I interrupt you?"

"No, no. I just want to give you this information gently. It is, as you say, a lot to take in."

"There's more?"

"Yes."

Paddy took a deep breath. "Okay, go ahead. I can take it," he said with a nervous smile.

"Through the use of a device, William can disappear."

"I know. You told me. You put on the cover and you are transported."

"I mean he can disappear while still being here."

"What? No way!"

"Sean Duncan, Angus's son, made only two devices. They work by using spinning electrons to move the matter attached to it—the atoms in your body—into a different state. You are technically present, except that you move to an overlapping layer of parallel time. You can see what's happening around you, but you can't change anything. You can't open a door, for example. You just walk through it. Well, you don't actually walk, your mind wills you to move in a direction and you sort of float."

"Well, that's a heck of a way for parents to spy on their kids. Uncle Ian, is this a joke?"

"No, Paddy. I'm telling you the honest truth."

Paddy was quiet for a long time. "That sounds crazy scary. So, if he moves to another layer of time, does that mean he is traveling through time? How is that even possible?"

"Ah, Paddy, the question to ask is not about time *travel*, but *what is time?*"

"I reported on something similar as part of my physics class. According to Einstein, time and space are relative and flexible to accommodate the constant speed of light, or basically the fabric of space/time is bent."

"Exactly! That stretching of the invisible fabric of space/time is known as the 'geodetic effect.' For example, the planets orbit the sun, not because of the sun's gravitational pull, but because they travel in the deformation in the grid, or fabric, of space/time caused by the sun. All *we* had to do was harness the spinning electrons properly to make ourselves 'heavy' enough to bend time and space enough to move to a different layer for our purposes."

"What are our purposes?"

"Well, for example, during World War II, your grandpa used the NOVA to get information about how Germany coded their messages and then he shared it with the Allies. In some cases, it allowed the Allies to counterattack in time to save whole cities from being decimated. A few times, he walked right into German camps and transmitted messages that purposely gave away the key to decrypting that day's messages. I'll admit it was a bit reckless, but he considered it to be doing his part since he couldn't fight in the war."

"Why couldn't he fight?"

Iain looked surprised that Paddy didn't know. "William was born with a hole in his heart. The doctors thought that, like most babies, it would heal as he grew, but that didn't happen. Back then, they didn't have the surgical techniques available now, so he just lived with it. When we were boys, William would get out of breath easily when he would run, so he didn't participate in sports. I suppose that's how he got so interested in reading books and doing his experiments because he had to stay inside so much."

"What does the NOVA look like?"

"It looks like a cross between a compass and a watch. It's worn on a chain around the neck, so it's positioned close to the heart. It's called a NOVA, a scrambled derivative from the latin word *evanesco*, to vanish."

"Why didn't Papa tell me?" Paddy asked, sounding frustrated. "How has all this gone on around me my whole life, and no one told me? Don't they trust me?"

"Think about it, Son. Your dad lost your mom because of SMITs' stupid jealousy. Isn't it reasonable that he would want to keep you as far away from all of this as possible?"

"I guess so. I just don't like feeling left out. I mean, this is part of my family heritage. It's my responsibility to know about it and protect it too."

"Son, I have a feeling there is a good reason you have come to Ireland."

II

ANNA

"YOU ARE BRAVER THAN YOU BELIEVE,
STRONGER THAN YOU SEEM, AND SMARTER
THAN YOU THINK." -WINNIE THE POOH

William looked out the window above his berth. Today they would arrive in Denmark. He decided to take a nap before the cook brought him dinner. He was still catching up from the sleep he'd missed in the first part of the trip when he was tied in the engine room. Thankfully, the better accommodations were helping him recover from his cold.

As he drifted off to sleep, he once again began to dream of France. He dreamed of a personal trip he took to Rennes seven years after the war was over. He remembered chiding himself as he packed for the trip that it would be a waste of time. Still, he'd felt compelled to go. It was this trip that was becoming a recurring dream as if there was something he needed to remember.

☙❦❧

NOTHING WAS RECOGNIZABLE AS WILLIAM WALKED THE STREETS OF Rennes. He wasn't even sure he was in the right part of town. When he was here during the war, the city looked weary, as though it were heaving its last gasp of life. Now it seemed reborn. New buildings were everywhere, businesses were thriving, and the people seemed full of hope. All this change made it hard for William, relying only on his memory, to find the place that still haunted his mind with so many questions. It seemed silly even to him, but he wanted to retrace his steps from that night when Remy had met him, and he had found the little black book.

He studied countless streets, trying to imagine them during the bleakness of the war, but none fit the picture in his mind. Finally, he turned a corner, and he knew. This was the street, the very corner where he had watched the woman hide the book. It was surreal to stand in the same place he'd stood in such danger, with the fever of war raging, compared to now. Instead of the darkness of oppression and terror, the sun shined on children playing and couples walking hand in hand. The very same window where the woman had left the book was open, and lace curtains fluttered in the summer breeze. He strolled up and down the street several times as his mind replayed every detail of that night.

He was drawn from his thoughts by the smell of fresh galettes and coffee, and the tempting aroma led him to a small cafe nearby. He sat at a table outside and took in the sights and sounds around him. Flowers were everywhere—spilling over the edges of window boxes, sold by street vendors—all of which filled the air with the light, sweet scent of lavender.

The outdoor area of the cafe was filled with couples and families enjoying the beautiful day. He was lucky to have arrived just as a couple was leaving, or he wouldn't have gotten a table. As he waited for the server, he noticed that a woman sat alone in the far corner of the outdoor area. Her table was close to the window of the cafe, and she was facing away from the street. From her reflection, he guessed she was in her early thirties. *A shame she's alone on such a beautiful day.*

A waitress stopped at his table and asked for his order. He replied with a smile, "Can you bring me whatever smells so wonderful?" She returned the smile, and within moments brought him a cappuccino and a fresh apple custard galette. From where he was seated and how the sun was shining, he could see into the apartments over the shops across the street.

In one apartment, the door was open, letting in the breeze, and he could see a grandmother rocking an infant while a toddler played at her feet. In the next apartment, he noticed an older man standing in an upstairs window who appeared to be looking down at the street as if he were waiting for someone. William looked back at the woman sitting alone, this time seeing her and the entire street's reflection in the tinted window.

In the reflection he saw a flash, like the sun reflecting off metal. William looked back at the apartment where the man had been standing and saw the curtains close. He started to look away when a hand pushed back one of the curtains, and William could see up the barrel of a rifle to a mounted scope. He spilled his cappuccino as his body tightened, and his mind raced into action. It appeared the weapon was pointed directly at the woman sitting alone.

William shouted, "He has a gun!" and leaped to his feet, bounding toward where the woman was seated. She stood and turned, and he quickly moved between her and the gunman to shield her. A shot rang out and shattered the glass table where the woman had been seated. Customers screamed, and everyone tried to rush inside the cafe all at once. Two more shots were fired, and the cafe window shattered.

"This way!" William guided her toward a side door into the cafe. They crowded inside with the other customers until the police arrived.

As the police began questioning the customers closest to the front of the cafe, the woman whispered to William, "I must leave. I cannot stay here."

"It's not safe for you out there!"

"I can't explain. I must go."

William couldn't let her go outside alone. He followed her to the back of the cafe, trying to convince her to stay, but she refused. William had a sinking feeling as he wrestled with whether to go with her or stay. He imagined hearing about her death on the news and decided to try to go with her, at least until she was somewhere safe. No one noticed in the commotion as they quietly exited the back door.

He kept asking her questions. "Don't you think you'd be safer with the police? Do you know who might be trying to harm you? Has this ever happened to you before?" The woman didn't answer as she walked quickly away from the cafe before slowing her pace. William was beginning to feel he'd made the wrong choice in coming with her.

Finally, he asked, "Ma'am, are you in any trouble?" She remained silent until they came to the river, La Vilaine.

"Thank you for helping me, but you should go now."

"May I at least know your name?"

She hesitated.

"I mean you no harm," he added with a gentle smile. William felt sure there was little chance that she would give her real name.

"My name is Anna, Anna Kumiega."

Even though he wasn't on a mission, he used his undercover name since he knew nothing about her. "My name is Scrydan."

William's curiosity began to war within him. Part of his mind involuntarily toyed with the idea that she could be the same "A. K.," whose initials were on the black book's cover, while his logic, like a mental schoolmaster, reprimanded him for the absurdity of the thought. So much about her seemed to fit the image in his memory.

She found a place between two trees and stood silently, looking out over the river. As he stood with her, William's thoughts drifted to the book, the complexity of the code, and the secrets it held. The one thing in the book he didn't understand was the mention of the Deuxième Bureau, the French intelligence service. The Germans had allowed the group to continue working during the occupation, not realizing that the Bureau was loyal to the Allies.

"You need to leave, Mr. Scrydan. You are not safe if you are with me."

"Why don't you go someplace more secluded. Anyone can see you out here."

"The river will provide ample cover."

"Surely, you are not thinking of . . ."

"You wouldn't understand. Please! Go!"

"I can't just leave you here."

She was crying as she spoke, and William realized she was seriously thinking about ending her life. "I'm so tired of running from them. They tracked me to Argentina, to Russia, even to Australia. I cannot run anymore."

"What do they want?"

"It doesn't matter anymore. It's something that was given to me by my father and brother. People during the war lost their lives trying to keep it safe, and I lost it!" She put her face in her hands, and huge sobs shook her frame.

William's curiosity got the better of him. He reasoned that if she was referring to the book, he could relieve her of her suffering. If she wasn't, he could apologize for the misunderstanding. He decided to take a chance.

"Why were you carrying it that night?"

Anna slowly looked up. "What?"

"Why were you carrying it when it could so easily have fallen into the hands of the Nazis. There must have been a reason."

The look of pain on her face turned to anger. She assumed William was the enemy and had deceived her. "Who are you?" she demanded. She didn't wait for an answer but turned and began to walk quickly away from him, mumbling to herself in Polish that she was not worthy of living. Anna turned, wanting to be free from years of torment and spoke with a tone as if nothing mattered anymore.

"I was taking it to the head of the Alliance, to Hérisson."

"The famous spy?"

"Yes, her real name was Marie-Madeleine Fourcade."

"Those men who stopped you . . ."

She looked at him in disbelief. "How did you know? Oh well, it doesn't matter. They were Polish turncoats who sold their souls to the Nazis. I tried to hide it, but when I returned to search for it later, it was gone." She looked dazed and wrung out like someone exhausted from overmuch sorrow.

"There! Are you satisfied? I don't know why you all still want it, but I *don't* have it! Can't you even leave me to die alone?" She turned again and walked away from him, moving closer to the edge of the river. William heard her say to herself, "I was supposed to get it to her. I was supposed to stop the couriers. So many died . . ."

William had rehearsed in his mind a thousand questions he wanted to ask if he ever got the chance to meet her. Now, faced with the opportunity, he had stupidly scared her away.

He replied to her gently in Polish as she walked away, "Oh, Anna, you didn't lose it. You hid it to keep it safe on the windowsill; you kept it out of the hands of the enemy! I took it to London for you. The Allies got all the information, all the names, all the locations. They broke up the entire network—all because you were brave, all because of your courage."

She stopped walking.

He continued, "You didn't fail, Anna. I came back here today to celebrate the day I found your masterpiece. I never dreamed I would find you and have the honor of returning it to you." He reached in his pocket and unzipped the secret compartment and withdrew the book, which was now much more worn than when he'd found it. He held the book out toward her, hoping she would come back.

She turned. Tears filled her eyes, and she had a look of utter disbelief. She cupped her hands over her mouth, and the look in her eyes was like someone reunited with a long, lost child. She ran to him, took the book, and pressed it to her heart as she closed her eyes. She sat down on a nearby bench and flipped through the pages, fingering them lovingly. William stood next to her and kept watch for anyone who looked suspicious.

"Can this be true?" she whispered to herself over and over.

"Anna, seven years ago, you were on that street not far from the coffee shop when those men stopped you. I was about to come over to help you when the Nazi officer ran up to you, and the men ran away. I heard him say he would walk you home, so I assumed you were safe, well, at least for that night. I always wanted to know the story behind the book. It truly is the best cryptography I have ever seen."

She had a faraway look in her eyes. "That officer recognized me from the Deuxième Bureau, where I worked. It was under the Vichy government then. They thought we were ridding France of communists, but we were giving information to the Allies. Wait . . . why were you there that night?"

"I was delivering a message to the Resistance from London."

Anna held up the book, fresh tears in her eyes. "Isn't this something that belongs to your government now? How can you give it to me?"

"Normally, you'd be correct, but I think even they'd agree that a treasure like that belongs to the one who created it."

Fresh tears spilled down her cheeks. "This book was started by my father. My brother added the information he secretly obtained about a weapon, and then I added what I learned about the couriers. Despite the contents, the methods represent a chronology of my family's cryptographic knowledge and how it evolved. Cryptography was something we all loved and shared." She fingered the pages again. "Not to mention, it's all I have left to remind me of my father. He ended up in Dachau, where he died two days before liberation."

"Words could never express how sorry I am for all that you've been through."

"It seems like another lifetime ago now. The Nazi courier network was called Operation Hermes. We worked with the Alliance to have spies infiltrate the network. That's how we learned so much about it. Toward the end of the war, one of our team turned double agent and leaked information about our book. There is still a group that thinks they need my book, though I have no idea why. I suspect they sent that gunman to scare me today. I'm not much good to them if I'm dead. I don't know why they are so fixated on keeping their old secrets hidden. It seems a bit late for that!" She smiled faintly.

"Countries always have secrets to keep. The greatest secret of all is their method of keeping secrets," he said with a laugh. "I am curious; do you know if Germany ever built the bomb described in your book?"

"I don't know, but the plans were made right before the Normandy invasion. I think by then, with America joining the war, the Germans had to turn their attention to bigger things." She looked across the river. "I was going to end it all here today." She held up the book and smiled. "I guess you saved my life twice today. How can I ever repay you?"

"On the contrary. I and many others owe you a great debt for the brave work that you and your family did. Does your family live here?"

"My brother lives with his wife and children in Poland. I have a little flat near where they live. It's all the family I have left."

William noticed a tiny red poppy on the hat she held in her hand. "Do you wear the poppy in memory of someone?"

She touched the flower. "Oh, yes—for my grandfather. He died in the Great War. He is the reason I became involved, to do what I could in his memory."

"He must have been a special man."

"Yes, very special."

"Anna, we should get you somewhere safe. I may have done you a disservice by returning the book to you since someone out there may still be looking for it. My car is not far from here. I could drive you to Paris and take you to the Polish embassy. Would that be helpful?"

She started to refuse and decided to accept. "That would be wonderful."

"It's the least I can do."

They talked about many things as they made the four-and-a-half-hour drive to Paris, their unique connection dissolving the rigid cautiousness observed by the best of spies. They had many things in common. They both had a gift for cryptanalysis, and their fathers had trained them in espionage. William wondered if he would ever stop long enough to settle down and have a family. Once begun, the life of a spy was a difficult one to change.

"The embassy is just up ahead on the right," instructed Anna.

"It looks like we'll have to park on the other side of the street and cross the courtyard. The road is blocked off, so cars can't get right up to the gate." William had an uneasy sense of the situation. He parked, grabbed his bag, and began to walk Anna to the embassy gate. Suddenly, they both heard a gunshot, but couldn't tell from which direction it came. William took Anna's arm, and they both began to run toward the gate.

"Open the gate!" they both repeatedly shouted in Polish.

They heard another shot, and William felt a searing heat pass through his lower right leg, knocking him down onto the brick street. Anna stopped to help him up.

"Go! Go! Anna, don't stop! Please, go! I beg you to go!" She ran to the gate, and soldiers took her safely inside behind the wall that surrounded the embassy.

As they closed the gate behind her, she turned and shouted to the soldiers, "Go help him! Please!" The soldiers stood at their posts inside the entrance, unable to leave, as they had no jurisdiction outside the embassy grounds.

Suddenly, a dark gray Mercedes raced up the street that fronted the embassy and skidded to a stop beside William. Two men jumped out of the backseat and dragged William inside the car, which quickly sped off. Once inside the vehicle, William felt a sharp blow to the side of his head with what felt like the butt of a gun. The force of the strike was so violent that William's vision blurred. Then everything went dark. The car stopped just as he slowly regained consciousness. He had no idea where he was or how long he'd been in the car. The men led him into an abandoned building, then into a room that was bare, except for a table and a few folding chairs.

The man giving the orders had a severe limp, and he steadied himself with an ornate black cane with a silver handle. Though he spoke English, his accent gave away that he was German. He sat down in the corner, staring at William with cold, lifeless eyes. The other two men questioned William for almost an hour. Most of all, they wanted to know what he had done with the black book.

Finally, the leader instructed one of the men to call someone named Franco from the next room. William could hear heavy footsteps as the man approached. Franco had to duck his head to enter the room, and he looked at William with a vacant expression. One look and William knew that Franco's expertise lay in extracting confessions by force. He looked like a street fighter. He had a collection of scars, and his size was enough to intimidate anyone. William had a terrible headache from the blow to his head, but he willed his mind to work on an escape plan. He noticed one of the men had used a toilet that was inside a small wooden cubicle in the corner of the room. Thankfully, it had a door.

"May I?" he asked as he directed his eyes toward the toilet. The leader nodded and motioned to Franco to wait. Franco cracked his knuckles and flexed his muscles in preparation. The men began talking among themselves, ignoring William for a few moments. His messenger bag had been searched and thrown over to the wall, close to where the toilet was, so William silently scooped it up as he entered the small bathroom. Once inside, he exchanged his coat with the one in his bag. In a split second, William disappeared.

⚜

ONCE HE REMOVED THE COVER, WILLIAM SAT GINGERLY IN HIS OLD leather armchair, exhausted from his ordeal. He wasn't sure which hurt the most, his headache, or the stabbing pain from the bullet wound. Thankfully, the bullet had gone straight through his calf, and the tissue damage was minimal. He disinfected it thoroughly and wrapped his leg. It certainly wasn't the first bullet wound he'd gotten.

A storm was brewing off the coast of Dundee, and the wind made the unlatched front gate bang against the post. William limped outside to close it and stopped to close his eyes as the blustery wind swirled around him. He smiled. *What were the chances I'd meet her? The book—that treasure—is back where it belongs. How I will miss it. Thank goodness I made a copy! I hope Anna isn't in more danger now.*

He returned inside, built a fire, and made some tea. Then, he sighed and chuckled to himself. *I bet they are still wondering how I flushed myself down that toilet!*

⚜

WILLIAM AWOKE WITH A JOLT AS HE HEARD LOUD ENGINE NOISES and someone unlocking the door to his tiny berth. As the fog of his deep sleep lifted, the reality of his predicament elicited an audible moan. He realized he'd been dreaming again about the trip to Rennes when he'd returned the book to Anna. *Why do I keep having the same dream?*

He stood, his clothes disheveled from wearing them for so many days. William recognized the sailor who opened his door as an engine room worker he'd seen when he first boarded the ship. He had a severely disfigured face from a burn, probably from an on-the-job accident.

"You will come with me. We are docking now," he said in a raspy voice. He grabbed William's hands, tieing them firmly together with rough rope. William spun around and quickly grabbed his cover from the bed to bring with him. The sailor pushed him into the hallway and toward the stairs leading up to the main deck. There, he handed William off to a short man named Filip. Out in the frosty air, William could see they'd arrived at the port in Denmark.

Filip turned and draped William's cover over his hands to hide the rope, and led him down the gangway into the busy port. Aleksander joined them, and they made their way to the train station. As they walked, William remembered many of the times he'd evaded death or capture, and he wondered if he was finally going to meet his end this time.

❧ 12 ❧

REVENGE

"VENGEANCE AND RETRIBUTION REQUIRE A
LONG TIME; IT IS THE RULE."
-CHARLES DICKENS, A TALE OF TWO CITIES

I t was evident that Filip and Aleksander didn't have much money.
Once they boarded the train, a worker directed them to the
freight car, where they tied a rope to William's hands and
connected it to a metal ring, which was presumably for tying livestock.
The rope was long enough to allow him to sit. The men lay down on a
pile of empty feed sacks and promptly fell asleep.

Almost twelve hours later, they arrived and were driven by a chauf-
feured car to a mansion surrounded by a black gate. The home was of
white stucco and looked to be very old. William was led to an ornate
bedroom.

Aleksander said, "We'll come for you early in the morning, so get
some sleep. Don't think of doing anything stupid. The windows are all
wired into the alarm, and several tigers are guarding the property." To
William's surprise, Aleksander didn't lock the door.

William slept for what seemed like only a couple hours when Filip
opened his door and woke him. "Get up, old man. You are going to
meet Wilhelm. Wash your face and put this shirt on," he barked as he
threw a clean white shirt on the bed. "You need to look your best if
you want to try and stay alive. I'll be back to get you in a few minutes."

Stay alive? Who are these people, and what do I have that they want? No matter how hard he tried to remember past missions, nothing came to him that would answer his questions.

Half an hour passed, and Aleksander hadn't returned. William opened the bedroom door and took a step into the hall. Almost immediately, he heard a fierce growl so loud he could feel it in his chest. An enormous tiger came bounding down the hall toward him. William ducked into the bedroom and pressed his shoulder to the door as he flipped the bolt to the locked position just in time. He heard the tiger sniff at the bottom of the door.

"Rudolph! Leave!" yelled Aleksander. William unlocked the door and stood back. Aleksander opened the door and ordered, "Let's go." They walked down a marble staircase and into a vast room that appeared to be a study. There were at least ten animal trophy heads arranged on the walls. Behind the desk sat an older man leaning back in his chair. A cane was propped against the desk beside him with an ornate silver handle.

"So, we meet again," hissed Wilhelm.

The jolt of William's memory connecting with his present reality sent a shockwave through his body, almost making him nauseous. This was the same man who he'd escaped from when he was captured in France on the trip when he met Anna. *This was the reason for the dreams. These thugs are still looking for the black book! But why?*

"What do you want with me?" William asked, purposefully keeping his tone and expression firm.

"I want what I wanted the last time we met, and I will have it. We've been following you for years, and we can wait no longer."

"If you've been following me that closely, you'd know I no longer have it."

"I know you love cryptography, and you'd never let it go without keeping a copy." Wilhelm's voice was shaky but determined.

It seemed to William that Wilhelm was the type who had people killed with the wave of a hand. William saw their conversation as a chess game. It was his play and he had to think fast if he was to come out of this alive. His next move was, by far, the riskiest one of his life.

"Well, why didn't they just ask me? If I'd known what was needed, and that a simple copy would suffice, I could have provided it before they destroyed my house!" William tried to inject a note of cheerful confidence in his tone.

Wilhelm glared at his assistants. They stood quietly off to the side, looking down, trying to avoid Wilhelm's eyes. "Where is it?" he shouted, startling everyone.

"Oh, I keep it in my sugar canister in my kitchen. I never use sugar, so the canister is a perfect place to store little mementos."

Wilhelm turned to Filip. "You will fly this time, and you have three days. If you don't return with it, you should take your life to save me the trouble. Go!"

Wilhelm ordered Aleksander to return William to his room. William assumed he'd be summoned at least by the time Filip returned, but a week went by, and another, and another—until he lost count. Meals were brought to William's room, but no one would tell him anything.

Finally, after what seemed like at least eight weeks, Wilhelm came to see William. He entered the bedroom with a tiger by his side. "I have your copy of the instructions, and I've had my engineers build the missile components. We are launching it in two days, but my engineers say that something in the algorithms is missing, and they can't get the fuel injectors to work properly. William knew this moment would come.

"What will you do with the missile?"

Wilhelm sneered as he limped around the room, leaning on his cane. "What should have been done with it when the design was conceived! I will provide it as a gift to the Americans to show them that Germany is the true victor of the war!"

"Haven't enough people died? Didn't we all learn valuable lessons from that war?"

"Now, they will learn how stout is the heart of Germany! That no matter how long we have to wait, the superior race always wins."

William was silent. Wilhelm looked as if he'd said more than he wanted to. *Clearly, you didn't learn anything from the war.*

"Follow me," commanded Wilhelm. "Come, Rudolph." William took care not to follow the tiger too closely. They exited the mansion on a side William hadn't seen before. About fifty yards away was an enormous building with sliding doors. Through the open doors, he could see men welding, and he assumed this was where the missile was being constructed. Several men wore white coats. *Those must be the engineers.*

"You will help them get this fixed, or you will never see your Malcolm again." William shuddered at the thought of what Filip might have done to find out Malcolm's name and relationship to him. He walked over to one of the engineers who was wringing his hands as he read the copy of the missile instructions. *Why did I ever keep a copy?*

"Hello. Is there anything I can do to help?"

"Who are you?"

"Who I am isn't important, but that is my copy of the original document you are trying to understand. Do you need help?" asked William again, trying to sound respectful and hide his anger.

The engineer spoke broken English, so William asked him to continue in German. "The algorithms cannot be correct!" he whispered, looking over his shoulder. "I have been working night and day, and he says he will kill my family if we don't find a way to make it work! Did anyone ever build a working version of this?"

"Look, if you help me, I will give you the missing algorithms. He plans to harm my family also."

"You have them?" the engineer almost shouted, drawing the momentary attention of nearby workers.

"Shhh! Yes, but you must help me too. I must keep this missile from reaching America. If I help you assure it launches, will you do me a favor?"

"I will do anything to save my family."

"Can I trust you?" William had learned over many years that when asked this question, people answered mostly with their body language. An overly assuring response was usually a lie. Averted eyes often signaled no capacity for loyalty.

The engineer looked him straight in the eye and, with tears, answered, "Yes."

"Do you know where he intends to launch it?"

"Calais; he wants us to transport the components in large trucks and assemble it there."

William thought hard, testing each possible move of his chess pieces. He took a pencil and paper and began to write out the algorithms the engineer needed. The engineer's eyes lit up when he saw the correction of the problem.

"Thank you! Thank you!" he repeated. "Now, what can I do for you?"

"I need you to . . ." and William proceeded to tell Paul, the engineer, his plan.

Three days later, the trek began for Calais with six massive trucks. It was a long and tiring trip with each truck crossing the border into France separately, not to draw suspicion. When they reached a vacant lot just outside Calais, the workers began to assemble the missile.

This was designed over seventy years ago. There's no way this can reach the US, but I can't take any chances.

When the missile was assembled, Wilhelm was beside himself with excitement. William looked over at Paul and gave him a slight nod.

Paul addressed Wilhelm. "You know this American will not keep this quiet if you let him go. He will give our identities to American and international police. I think we should give him a free ride home, don't you?" he asked as he pointed to the missile. A worker was preparing to rivet and weld the last panel in place. Wilhelm cackled with glee, slapping Paul on the back for such a good idea.

Suddenly, William felt a gun at his back. He moved toward the missile with his cover in hand, ascended the ladder, and climbed into the space within the missile accessed by the panel. The worker closed it up, and soon, he felt the engines start. He knew he had to work quickly to disable the rocket, but not before it successfully launched. Still, he had to do it before being burned by the excessive heat.

He put one arm into the cover with difficulty as he only had one little ledge to stand on. From his pocket where he'd hidden them, he withdrew a pair of wire cutters. The missile launched, and the heat began to build until William was drenched in sweat and his skin was red. He counted to ten and began cutting every wire he could reach. He was about to cut another when the wire cutters dropped out of his hands and fell below him. William wasn't far from the computer panel, so he jumped to the next ledge and used all his strength to tear off the heat shield. He noticed a lever that was hanging. It's only purpose had been to ease the missile sections together. Using the lever, he smashed the panel with all his might until he was about to pass out from the heat.

Finally, with his last ounce of strength, he put his other arm into the cover and disappeared.

⚜

"Hello, Nandini."

"William! Oh my gosh, we've all been so worried! Abel, come. It's William!"

Abel rushed to the kitchen. "William! You look terrible. Where have you been? Are you all right?"

"Oh, you know, I could smell Nandini's cooking all the way from Dublin."

Nandini replied, "Normally, I'd take it as a compliment, but you are not all right. Your skin is as red as my roasted curry."

Abel took his arm. "Come, my brother, lie down on the couch and cool off. Sweetheart, can you bring some ice packs?"

Once William felt better, he told them the story.

"You *gave them the plans* to build a bomb?" asked Nandini incredulously.

"Let him finish, dear. You know William had a plan. He always has a plan."

William smiled. "Would you all mind if I stick around for a few days here?"

Nandini's beautiful eyes lit up. "Oh, I have so many things I can cook for you!"

Abel replied, "We both would be honored, William. And you should know you never have to ask. Now, do you mind if I send a quick radio signal to the Base? I think they and all the portals will lift a glass tonight that you are safe and sound."

Nandini added, "Yes, and I think you should write a book about this latest escapade of yours. It will be a best seller!" They all laughed.

✣ 13 ✣

TULLYALLEN

"WHEN ONE DOOR CLOSES, ANOTHER DOOR
OPENS; BUT WE OFTEN LOOK SO LONG AND SO
REGRETFULLY UPON THE CLOSED DOOR THAT
WE DO NOT SEE THE ONES WHICH OPEN FOR
US." -ALEXANDER GRAHAM BELL

The next day, Iain called Paddy to the kitchen and asked him to sit down. "We've heard from your grandpa."

"Oh! Thank God!" cried Paddy. "Is he all right? What happened?"

Iain held up his hand. "Whoa now, let me fill you in. He said two spies, not SMITs, tracked him down. They took him to Denmark, then Germany, and then to France. He'll fill us in more later, but he did say he was able to disarm a missile headed for the US. Luckily, when the spies made William leave home, he asked if he could bring his coat. It was the cover to Jaipur. He put on the cover and passaged there, so he's safe now. It looks like the SMITs didn't have anything to do with his disappearance, after all."

"When I left home, there was a big scare that someone planned to launch a weapon of mass destruction against the US. We heard it on the radio. That has to be the one Grandpa disarmed! May I call Papa and tell him?"

"It's already done, Son."

"Why did Grandpa wait so long to use the cover, I wonder?" pondered Paddy aloud.

"I believe he wanted to stay long enough to see if he could sabotage

94

what they were planning, especially since they were using his information to build the missile."

"What? . . . No way!"

"It's true. Apparently, the instructions for the bomb came from an old document William had from World War II. The spies were searching for it in your grandpa's cottage. That's why the place was such a mess. When they couldn't find it, they kidnapped him. He took a huge risk and told them where the instructions were hidden—in his sugar canister, no less!"

"So, they went back to find the plans?"

"They did. William knew once they'd found him the first time, they would never stop trying to find the plans, and that would put you and your papa at risk. So, he told them where they could find a copy and let them build the missile, knowing he'd have to sabotage it. Wisely, he left the algorithms out of his copy of the plans, so the engineers had to rely on him to provide them. I'm not sure how he sabotaged the missile, but I'm sure he'll fill us in when we see him. The good news is that the missile is now somewhere at the bottom of the Atlantic. He took one of the engineers into his confidence and had him call an old friend at MI6. The agents were in Calais shortly after the missile launched, and they arrested the leader, Wilhelm, with French police support. He's in jail now."

"When will we get to see him?"

"Soon. I think it was stressful for him to be their prisoner for all this time. He wants to lay low and get some things done in Jaipur for a week or so."

Paddy sat down, speechless. The full weight of the emotion he'd held inside hit him, and he put his face in his hands.

"There's something else. A message just came in that none of us could decode. I expect it's for you." He pulled a paper from his pocket and gave it to Paddy. Paddy smiled, recognizing the code that he and Grandpa had created years ago.

A few minutes later, he'd deciphered it. It read: "Paddy, I've waited a long time for you to see my world. Sorry for my little detour and for causing worry. Please follow my instructions in the note—a life urgently depends on it. See you soon. - Grandpa."

"All this time, I thought Grandpa expected me to find him, but it seems he wants me to go help someone else." Paddy handed Iain the deciphered message.

Iain replied, "I believe you are right. Where is this other note he mentions?" asked Iain.

"Oh, I almost forgot! Papa found a note at the church in Quincy from Grandpa."

"Let's see it then . . ." Iain sat down at the kitchen table and put on his glasses. Paddy waited as Iain read the deciphered note to himself and then out loud.

When he finished, Paddy said, "I figured out the last part. It refers to *The Light in the Forest,* a book Grandpa wanted me to find."

Iain looked at him solemnly, his deep-green eyes reflecting the weight of his thoughts. "Son, I don't know what's working behind this odd sequence of events and how you just happened to choose the Ireland cover, but this note proves that William intended for you to choose the cover to come to this portal. I may be able to help a little, but I suspect he's given you the tools to figure out this riddle."

"I've never had to solve a riddle where someone's life depended on it. Hey, what do you mean by a portal?"

"Just as we call the coats 'covers,' so we call the tailors in different countries 'portals,' and all the portals together form our network, called Proteus. I'm the portal for Ireland, for example. In this business, we can't be too careful. Now, let's see here. It says, 'Where aflame was kept the light, and some did pay the final price . . .'"

"Maybe he's referring to an area where there is a lighthouse . . . perhaps where a battle took place?" guessed Paddy.

"That's a good thought. Let's see . . . there's Rockabill Lighthouse, but that's too far south. There are Dundalk and Haulbowline, but both are a bit out into the water. I doubt it would have to do with them. Read the rest of it."

Paddy read slowly, "'Their guide lies silent, its face doth fade, Among the servants who once obeyed.' It sounds like it's describing someone who has died, yet when he was alive, he was a master or lord of some kind."

Paddy continued, "'In its heart is a treasure sown, with ample pow'r to heal thine own.'"

Iain sighed, taking off his glasses and rubbing his temples through his gray hair.

Paddy added, "I don't see why he couldn't write exactly what he wanted to say in code instead of enciphering a riddle. We'd decipher it in no time and move on to the next thing. It seems dangerous to guess at something this important."

"You know your grandpa. He is a master at disguising the truth to keep it from those not worthy of it."

"What did you say? Disguising the truth?" Paddy slapped the table. "That's it! People don't pay the final price for *visible* light. They lay down their lives for their beliefs—the light is the light of truth. 'There aflame was kept the light,' refers not to a lighthouse, but the defending of truth. We need to find a place where people fought for what they believed and defended it to the death!" Paddy looked with expectation at Iain, desperately hoping that such a place would come to his mind.

Iain looked at the note silently for a few moments and finally looked and Paddy. "Well now, that's a place to start. There are few places where truth was more defended than the old churches and monasteries around Ireland."

Just then, a motorcycle arrived in front of the cottage. Without knocking, a young woman walked briskly through the door. She took off her helmet, letting a cascade of shiny auburn hair fall around her shoulders. She looked to be no more than eighteen and wore blue jeans tucked into leather riding boots. She had on a leather jacket and a red scarf tied tightly around her neck. She dropped a messenger bag beside the door as she walked in. She spoke directly to Iain. "*Conas atá tu?*"

"Doing well, thanks," replied Iain, nodding toward Paddy. "Corryne, this is Paddy Duncan, William's grandson, who is visiting from America."

Corryne glanced at Paddy and replied, "Pleased," with no change in affect.

"Paddy, Corryne is my niece and my counterpart in stirring up trouble now and then." He grinned.

Corryne turned to Iain. "I've checked on the order. It will be ready on Friday. Will you be home so we can examine it then?"

"Yes, that will be fine."

Corryne replied, "Then we'll decide what's next. I'll come around on Friday at three o'clock." She glanced back at Paddy as she turned to leave, nodded slightly, and then left as quickly as she'd come.

Iain glanced at Paddy. "Corryne and I are doing a bit of undercover work to gather information from the Manufactory."

"That's the SMITs shop, right? Papa told me a little."

"Pfft! A tailoring shop it is *not*. Workers in their warehouse receive low wages to make inferior garments on an assembly line, and they have the gall to call it tailoring. It's a betrayal of everything that good tailoring stands for. They treat their workers like slaves. They have dormitories where some sleep, and they work twelve hours a day. Sometimes apprentices go there to learn, and they soon leave disillusioned to work for real tailors. We have learned a lot from having to retrain those who've worked there. Now, let's focus on deciphering this note."

Paddy ventured another question. "Um . . . so, what kind of information are you trying to gather about the SMITs?"

"A few days ago, Corryne disguised herself and pretended to be the representative of a wealthy foreigner who wants to have a suit made for an upcoming event. We both crafted the order and made it so complex that we are sure the SMITs won't have the skill to make it. The only way they can pull this off is if they have a master tailor working for them. I'm sure they didn't want to turn down the order because of how much we offered to pay."

"Do you think that they have one of *our* tailors there?"

"Not willingly, of course. SMITs find tailors around the world and use various tactics to put them out of business. It's not unusual for them to set up shop near another tailor and gradually steal business by charging less and selling shoddy work. Often tailors have little choice but to work for them. They're like a kind of mafia. There have been three other disappearances over the years. We want to know if they are holding one of our tailors, and I think William's note to you confirms that."

Paddy was stunned. "How will you know one of our tailors made the suit?"

"The workmanship, of course, and the initials. You know all our tailors sign their work, so we'll check the breast pocket and see if there are initials inside. If the SMITs don't allow the tailor to put his initials in it, we'll still know. You know the marks of our work—double binding where seams cross, the signature triple knot of the thread in every hem, double-sewn bound buttonholes. It's a telltale code."

"Of course!"

"If it is Duncan-made, then we'll know on Friday, and we'll need a plan to get into the Manufactory. Now, let's get to deciphering William's note. Where were we?"

"You suggested we should look for monasteries or churches."

"There are few places more famous than Mellifont Abbey. There is also a cemetery at the Abbey of Kells, and an impressive old tower the monks used for protection. I think we should take a ride up there. It's not that far. Let's ask Luke and Clyde to come along and help. They support your grandpa in his missions too. The more eyes, the better, right?"

"Sure."

"You know, why don't we all pay a visit to my sister in Tullyallen tonight? It's not too far from the abbeys. We can explore both places starting early tomorrow. Let me give her a ring . . ."

Iain's tone was cheerful as he greeted her. "Rebekah! How are you? Oh, fine, just fine. Got a blow in from America; thought I'd show him the north country. Okay with you if we come 'round? Do you mind if we bring Luke and Clyde? Good! How about tonight? Yes, by seven, I'd say. Thanks ever so much! See you soon."

Iain dialed another number. "Luke? How would you like to come along to help me with a project up near Tullyallen? Bring Clyde along and grab an overnight sack. We'll leave within the hour. Thanks!"

Forty minutes later, a pickup truck arrived. Luke and Clyde entered the kitchen.

"Ah, here you are," observed Iain. "Come in, come in!"

"Luke, Clyde, this is Paddy, William's grandson from America."

"Nice to meet you," replied Luke, reaching to shake Paddy's hand.

"Hey," replied Clyde, burying his hands in the pockets of his jeans.

"Paddy has a note from William with a bit of a riddle he needs to solve. We think what we are looking for may be at one of the abbeys and we could use your help in finding it," Iain explained. "Clyde, can you make some *sambos*? Then we'll hit the road."

"Sambos?" asked Paddy.

Clyde rolled his eyes.

Iain smiled and shook his head. "Americans! You are going to have to learn the way we talk over here! A sambo is a sandwich. Paddy, why don't you help Clyde? There's ham in the cooler and bread in the press."

Paddy found the bread in the cupboard. *A cupboard is a 'press'?*

Iain packed a rucksack with clothes and a toothbrush for Paddy. "Pretty sure these clothes will fit you," he noted as he put everything in the car. Glancing at Paddy, he added with a chuckle, "Don't worry, they aren't old guy's clothes. They are my nephew Kirk's—jeans, T-shirts, and a couple of hoodies."

Paddy replied, "Thanks!" *Thank goodness!*

Clyde and Luke waited in the car for Iain and Paddy. "I don't see why Iain is devoting all his time to this wet-behind-the-ears kid; I don't care if he is Uncle William's grandson. I heard he didn't even know about the covers and only ended up here because he was snooping around where he shouldn't have been," grumbled Clyde.

"He's not a kid. He's our age. Now quit acting the maggot," replied Luke.

"We've got real work to do, and we have to stop and help this greenhorn out." Clyde's dislike of Paddy was more than evident.

"You were a greenhorn once," Luke observed.

"Oh, so I suppose you are on his side."

"I don't take sides, Clyde, and you shouldn't either. Now shut up. Here they come; stop being childish."

The four of them ate as they drove to Tullyallen, and Iain explained his thoughts about the riddle.

Paddy reread the quote at the bottom of the note to himself silently. "*Always do what you are afraid to do. - R.W.E.*" *Grandpa's favorite Emerson quote.* Paddy thought about how he had discovered the Cave, the secret compartment in the wall, the inner room, and the covers. Grandpa may have shrouded these instructions with a riddle, but he knew Paddy's abilities.

Paddy looked at Iain curiously as he remembered the notations of encrypted country names and years in Grandpa's library. "What book is the code key for Ireland?"

"*Gulliver's Travels*. Apropos, don't you think?"

"Oh, of course. Jonathan Swift was Irish. Say, do you guys use symmetric key algorithms?"

Clyde muttered, "Show-off" under his breath.

Iain replied, "There's a slight transformation on my end; a character shift by two or more spaces, depending on the day and the month, of course."

Iain knew more about codes than Paddy thought.

"How do you know which publishing year to use? I mean, some of those old books were reprinted many times, which might change the page numbering."

"William is the Master Keeper. Whenever he decides on a book that will serve as a key for a country, he buys two identical ones and leaves one with the portal. We change keys every year or so, or more often if there's a risk."

"So, Grandpa's library has the code keys for everyone? I thought you meant that he was called the Master Keeper because he keeps the covers."

Iain replied, "He is the keeper of everything. The rest of us keep a cover or two and a key for decryption. William assumes more risk than all of us put together. Without him, everything stops."

Luke asked, "Hey, Paddy, did you know there are two villages in Ireland that might not be there if it were not for your grandfather?"

"Really, why?"

"Well, during World War II, in what we call the 'Emergency,' he intercepted a message that a couple of villages were about to be hit by German air raids."

"I thought Ireland was neutral during World War II."

"Well, unfortunately, that didn't stop the bombs—whether by mistake or on purpose. But your grandpa decoded the Nazi's message and went straight to those villages and made sure everyone safely evacuated. Since he used the covers, no one could find him afterward. People here say it was an angel that warned them."

"Oh, wow. An angel? I like that."

Iain added, "You ponder all those stories he told you growing up. I suspect they were accounts of actual missions, though I'm sure he changed a few names."

Paddy's heart warmed with pride.

"You know, Son. He's done great things his entire life without any recognition. I suppose it doesn't matter, though. That's not why he does it. I guess that saying is true, 'Life can only be understood backwards, but it must be lived forwards.'"

Paddy smiled and whispered, "Søren Kierkegaard."

❦

THE SUNSET WAS FADING IN RAYS OF SOFT ROSE AND AMBER AS THEY neared Tullyallen. Rich green pastures surrounded them, neatly divided here and there by ancient stone walls strung together by white wooden gates. The houses were small and scrupulously well-kept. Paddy had a sense that the people here were hardworking, and there was no doubt they took pride in their land.

Rebekah's home was the epitome of a quaint country cottage, with a rose garden in front and a vegetable garden in the back. Its thatched roof and ivy-covered garden wall made the home look like it could easily have been a postcard scene. As they headed up the stone walkway, Iain called out, "Sister?" He knocked but let himself in before hearing a reply.

"Iain! It's been too long!" They hugged one another tightly, and their affection made Paddy smile. Rebekah was tall and appeared strong as if she was used to hard work.

"Rebekah! Aren't you a sight for sore eyes! Oh, it smells like your famous pork and cabbage. You shouldn't have gone to the trouble! We had some sambos in the car."

"No trouble at all. Oh, I can't tell you how glad I am to see you all!"

"Sis, this is Paddy, grandson of William, the Troublemaker! What a lucky surprise to have him visit from America." Iain chuckled and winked at Paddy as he spoke.

"Very pleased to meet you, ma'am," replied Paddy politely.

"Oh, come here and let me hug you! I am so glad you came! Goodness, last time I saw a picture, you were only a little tyke! Now, all of you, pull up a chair and have a little of this stew. No one beds down in my house without a hot meal on board—house rule."

Rebekah had a pleasant, singsongy way of talking that made Paddy feel welcome. Her eyes were a soft china blue, set against milky skin. She had light-blond hair with some gray here and there, and her smile started first in her eyes and radiated a bittersweet joy—the kind that comes from having weathered many trials.

"How long will you be in Ireland?" asked Rebekah as she took a loaf of soda bread from the oven.

Paddy paused, glancing at Iain. "Not too long ma'am. Thanks for letting me stay here."

"Such a polite young man! Now, don't you ruin him, Iain," she mocked with a hearty laugh. They finished eating, and Rebekah suggested they bring their things in from the car before the rain started.

The last couple of days had taken their toll, and Paddy suddenly felt overcome with exhaustion. "I don't mean to be rude, but would it be okay if I went to bed early?"

Clyde scoffed, "Wimp. It figures." Luke shot him a stern glare.

"Of course, of course! A trip from America can knock the stuffings out! I've got you all set up in the back bedroom, where there's a fire. You'll be warm there. The jacks is down the hall." Paddy walked down the hall and could see that the cottage was much bigger than it looked. An addition to the back enlarged the home, adding several rooms. As soon as he got settled into bed, he was asleep in minutes.

The next morning, Paddy followed a delicious smell to the kitchen. Rebekah had risen early and made a feast of rashers, eggs, black pudding, fruit, homemade bread, jams, juice, and tea. Paddy ate as if he were starving and kept apologizing for doing so.

"Being asked for a second helping is the best compliment of all," Rebekah said with a kind smile.

"Don't let her fool you, Paddy. She's known far and wide as the best cook in all County Louth. Her bread and jams win the first prize every year."

"Don't exaggerate, Brother."

Luke and Clyde joined the group and served themselves.

"Thank you for this feast, Sis! It will keep us through the long day ahead," offered Iain.

"This was the best breakfast I have ever had. I appreciate all your hard work," added Paddy.

"You are sweet to say so, Paddy. You may not remember, but your mother was a wonderful cook, God rest her soul. Did you know she was my pen pal when we were just girls?"

"I didn't know you knew her," Paddy answered awkwardly.

"She was the closest friend I've ever had, and she brought me much comfort in some very dark times. I can tell you have her kind heart." Rebekah began to get teary, and the mention of Mama by someone who knew her well touched Paddy.

"Thank you, ma'am. It was wonderful to see you." Paddy joined Iain, Luke, and Clyde, who were already waiting by the door.

Traffic was heavy, making the drive over an hour long, but Paddy was glad for the time to review what they had discussed about Grandpa's note. "Grandpa often refers to truth and light in allegory in his stories. Remember the story about Diogenes roaming the streets of Athens with a lamp, saying that he was trying to find an honest man? The lamp was symbolic of truth."

"Sheesh! I haven't heard that story in donkey's years. Okay, here we are. I thought we'd start with the Abbey of Kells since it's furthest away. Then, if we need to, we'll go to Mellifont Abbey. Let's split up and have a look around. I'll check out the cemetery, and you three start by going around the perimeter and work your way toward the tower. We'll meet there at eleven."

At eleven, Paddy found Iain, Luke, and Clyde standing at the base of the tower.

"Find anything?" questioned Paddy.

"Unfortunately, nothing that looks relevant," offered Luke.

"Well, I may have," noted Paddy.

"Of course you did," grumbled Clyde with a smirk. Iain heard him and shot him a stern look. Clyde wandered off a few steps and pretended to look interested in the tower.

Paddy led them to the remains of a building that had three faces carved in relief over a doorway.

"Grandpa's note says, 'Their guide lies silent, its face doth fade, Among the servants who once obeyed . . . ' If one of these is considered the 'guide,' maybe the other two are the 'servants,' or perhaps the servants are people buried here."

Iain took the note and read it quietly to himself. "Hmm, let's keep looking around this area."

❦

TWO HOURS LATER, THEY HAD RUN OUT OF IDEAS.

"Paddy, I think we should move on to Mellifont Abbey. We can always come back." Iain took a pocket watch from his jacket pocket and opened both the front and back. He held it to his eye and looked through the center and pointed it toward the carved faces. He pushed the button at the end of the stem and closed the two sides. "Ready to go?"

"What did you just do with that watch?" asked Paddy curiously.

"Oh, this? It keeps terrible time, so I use it as a camera."

Paddy looked at Iain, wondering if he had a few screws loose, but noticed that he was smiling.

"I thought maybe a photo might help us later," he explained, chuckling.

Paddy started to ask about the camera, but instead said, "I guess this whole spy business is the real deal."

They started for Tullyallen but had only gone a few miles when Iain hit his fist against the steering wheel. "Ah! Why didn't I think of it before? My old age is creeping up on me! I know the place we should check."

"Where?"

"Monasterboice, of course! If we hurry, we still have time to check it out before sunset." Paddy resolved to remain skeptical this time rather than get his hopes up and risk disappointment.

"What is this place, Monaster . . ."

"Monasterboice was a monastery founded in the late fifth century similar to the Abbey of Kells. It has ruins of a settlement, a tower, and some beautiful high crosses."

"Fifth century! And I thought Weymouth was old."

Iain had barely stopped the car when Paddy opened the door and began walking toward the cross called Muiredach's High Cross. Iain, Luke, and Clyde spread out to look in other areas. Paddy walked over to the West Cross and studied the scenes meticulously carved into the sandstone.

His attention then turned to a tall rectangular stone pillar within the iron fence enclosure that surrounded the North Cross. It had a hole in it a few inches from the top, and there were faint lines of markings radiating away from the hole, ending at an arc that suggested a circle. He could make out another circle below the top one, and another one below the second. The markings had faded from weather and age. While the two circles below the top one seemed to be ornamental, the top one was clearly a vertical sundial even though the gnomon was missing. Paddy guessed that the times marked must have been for when the monks stopped their work to gather for prayer or meals.

Paddy walked to another area while he read Grandpa's note aloud softly. He tried to hear it as though it were the first time. "'Their guide lies silent, its face doth fade . . .' Who was their guide whose face is now faded?" He had barely said the words to himself when he almost shouted, "Oh my gosh!" He ran so fast he was standing in front of the sundial in seconds. "It's not a who, but a what! A sundial is a guide, and it has a face! And, here it lies among the servants, the monks, who obeyed it daily."

Iain and Luke approached. Iain quickly picked up on what Paddy was thinking. "Ah, the sundial. Good job, Paddy. That is certainly a possibility."

"Yes, but a sundial doesn't have a heart," added Clyde as he sauntered up.

Paddy and Iain looked at each other as if a thought came to both of them simultaneously. Iain spoke first. "Luke, you are the tallest. Can you reach up and see if you feel anything inside the hole? If this sundial has a heart, it has to be where the gnomon belongs."

"Aren't we going to get in trouble?" whispered Paddy, looking around nervously. "This is an ancient relic, and it has a fence around it for a reason."

"We aren't going to harm it. Would you like to leave without even checking if something is in there?" asked Iain.

Luke waited for a visitor to walk to the other side of the tower. He quickly reached up and placed his finger in the hole. Everyone watched his face intently. He gasped.

"What do you feel?" whispered Paddy.

Luke drew out a tightly rolled piece of parchment and handed it to Iain.

Iain put the note in his pocket. "Okay, gentlemen, let's get back to the car," he whispered.

Iain drove a couple of kilometers and pulled the car over. He removed the parchment from his coat pocket. A ribbon and a wax seal held it closed. Iain looked at the note and then at Paddy. A smile slowly lit up his face, and his eyes twinkled.

"This is William's seal. Paddy, you did it!"

"It looks like the seal that was on the note Papa found at the church."

Iain nodded and handed it to Paddy. "What do you see written on the bottom of the seal?"

"It looks like, 'A.D. 1776.'"

"A.D. is for Angus Duncan, and 1776 was the year he discovered the properties of the thread and the covers. It was the year this whole adventure began. Go ahead, open it!"

Paddy held his breath as he carefully lifted the seal away from the ribbon and unrolled the outer paper. Then, like the other note, there was a second seal on the note inside. He unrolled the parchment, which was about six inches wide and ten inches long. There, in exquisite detail, was what appeared to be a blueprint of several buildings in a compound. Rooms were labeled, as was each floor of every building. A fence with a large gate surrounded the perimeter.

Iain looked at the document, and his expression changed to dread. Luke and Clyde looked at the blueprint over Paddy's shoulder. Iain got out of the car and walked across a field, then back to the car, then back across the field again. Paddy watched him intently and was growing increasingly uneasy, given Iain's reaction.

He looked back at the blueprint. The word "Dormitory" was written over one building, and one room showed what appeared to be beds lined up along the walls. Everything was labeled—lavatories, stairs, exits, kitchens, workrooms, even sheds outside. Paddy had a hunch that this was the Manufactory, and he remembered that Corryne would be going there on Friday to pick up the suit she and Iain had ordered. He glanced back at the first note with the riddle. He'd forgotten about the text at the top, "It's time to enter the lion's den."

Iain returned to the car, looking exhausted.

"Is this a blueprint of the Manufactory?" Paddy asked, half whispering.

Iain, Luke, and Clyde all replied in unison, "Yes."

Iain's face was expressionless. "I'm getting way too old for this," he muttered.

It was late when they returned to Tullyallen, and they all decided to return to Iain's right away to discuss the blueprint.

On the way home, Iain finally spoke. "The Manufactory is dangerous, Paddy. Even if we found a way inside, there's no guarantee we'd ever get out if they caught us."

Paddy desperately wanted to know more, but given how stressed Iain appeared, he decided to be quiet and wait. Of one thing he was sure, if Grandpa wanted him to help rescue someone being held at the Manufactory, there had to be a way . . . without getting caught.

❧ 14 ❧

MESSAGE REVEALED

"TO RESTRAIN [EVIL MEN] BY THEIR SENSE OF
HUMANITY IS THE SAME AS TO STOP A
RUNAWAY HORSE WITH A BRIDLE OF SILK
THREAD." ~SIR WALTER SCOTT

The next morning, Paddy found Iain at the kitchen table, staring into his tea with a troubled look on his face. He looked like someone who knew what he had to do but dreaded doing it. He nervously rubbed his fingers over the flowers on his teacup. "Good morning," he offered, feigning a slight smile.

"Morning, Uncle."

"There's no way around it. Somehow, we need to figure out a plan to get in the Manufactory . . ." Iain shuddered as he heard his own words. "Communications from the other portals around the world indicate that the SMITs have been busy lately."

"Doing what?"

"There have been strange things happening—thefts, equipment broken without explanation—they think it's sabotage. Sean Geelan has declared that he will find the thread within the year."

"Uncle, may I speak my mind?"

Iain nodded warily.

"I've been thinking. First, either the blueprints somehow came into Grandpa's possession, or he drew them from a firsthand account. Second, this blueprint may be helpful, but it's not enough."

"What do you mean?" asked Iain.

"It's too vague. We can't exactly walk in and inspect every building, can we? I know Grandpa pretty well, and this is not his way. There has to be more. Is there any way there is some code embedded in the wording on the blueprint—perhaps in the labels of the buildings?"

Iain looked again at the blueprint and shook his head. "I don't think so."

Paddy looked again. He couldn't see anything that stood out to him.

"Wait . . ." Iain went to his desk and took a flat piece of metal about six inches square from the drawer and brought it over to the kitchen table.

"What is that?"

"It's a magnet. I know this is a long shot, but a long time ago, Angus's grandson Owen created a virtually invisible magnetic ink by charging certain particles . . . Oh, never mind how he did it. The ink contains fine metallic dust that you cannot see with the naked eye. If you hold a magnet beneath the paper, the particles attract toward the magnet, and what you see looks like reverse embossing." He flipped the blueprint over and rubbed it lightly with a slightly damp cloth. "Moisture softens the paper and enhances the effect," he said as he held the magnet underneath.

"Oh my gosh!" Paddy leaned in over Iain's shoulder. "What does it say?"

"These are numbers. It's a message in code. Hang on; let me get my key." Iain retrieved his copy of *Gulliver's Travels*, and Paddy helped him decode the message from Grandpa's telltale modified quinate code. The deciphered message read:

"4 Ds held. Urgent—1 sick, retrieve first. Others later. Find her in workhouse, station 27; Women's Dorm, bed 5; or in clinic."

Iain read it aloud, his voice trembling as if he were afraid of what it might say. "There are *four* Duncans being held! He says one is ill. He wants us to focus on getting her out first. Then we are to go back for the other three." Iain paused and looked at Paddy. "Who could they be?"

"What does the rest say?" urged Paddy.

"She works at station twenty-seven in the workhouse and sleeps in bed five in the women's dormitory. If we don't find her, she might be in the clinic building. See?" He turned the note over to examine the blueprint. "Here's the clinic across the compound from the dormitories."

"Why can't we just call the police?"

"That would be completely logical if Sean Geelan hadn't bribed them to turn a blind eye to reports about the Manufactory. No, sir, they not only won't help us, but they will also tell Sean that we reported them."

"I hate them!" Paddy's anger seethed as he tried to think of a workable plan.

"Have you thought about what might happen if you do get into the Manufactory and the SMITs recognize you?" asked Iain.

"How would they know me? I've never even been to Ireland before."

"Son, I don't mean to scare you, but they have likely been watching your home since you were born. You live and work in the same shop as William. Trust me, they know you. In many ways, you'd be a special prize for them. That's why it's so dangerous for you to go there—even for you to be here in Ireland."

Paddy was silent. It never occurred to him that the SMITs would know him.

"If you do find a way to go in the Manufactory, we would have to have Corryne disguise you."

"Disguise me? How?"

Iain chuckled. "I'll call her to come over, and you'll see. She can give you a sample of her work." Iain went to his bedroom and phoned Corryne and returned to the kitchen.

"She says she'll try to stop over when she can."

Paddy sat at the kitchen table, holding the note. He ran his fingers over the numbers coded on the back and thought of Grandpa. He remembered so many fun afternoons tinkering with him in his workshop in the cottage. He would say, "Come, Paddy! There's a mystery, and I need you to solve it!" His childlike excitement belied the depth of scientific knowledge he'd amassed from years of personal study. Then, there was his love of literature. Sometimes, he would read a passage from a book and then close his eyes as if he were savoring a fine wine or listening to a symphony. But what Paddy treasured most of all was what Grandpa's eyes spoke when he looked at him. It was like looking in a mirror, but rather than seeing himself, Paddy saw all the good things he hoped to be.

"I hope Grandpa comes back soon."

"We all do, Son. He gave us a scare, for sure. Thank goodness he's safe."

"So, what is it that Corryne does? I mean, does she have a job or is she in college?"

"She is a sales representative for her father's notions-and-fabric company for the Dublin area, and she's also training to be a tailoress. I'd say she is about where you are in your training."

"Seriously?"

"She was raised in it, like you. Why do you sound surprised?"

"I don't know any women tailors, that's all. More power to her, I say. Good for her." Paddy was startled by a loud knock at the door.

"Could you get that?" asked Iain as he rose to go down the hall to his bedroom.

When Paddy opened the door, an elderly lady greeted him. "Good day! Iain Duncan—is he home today?" Her voice trembled, and her frail, wrinkled hand shook as she leaned on her cane. Paddy instinctively reached for her arm to steady her as he invited her inside and helped her to a chair.

Paddy asked, "May I give him your name?"

"Marion, just Marion. He knows me well," she replied in her high-pitched, cheery voice.

Paddy called toward Iain's bedroom. "Uncle Iain, you have company. Miss Marion is here."

When Iain didn't respond, Paddy went to his bedroom and found him with his face buried in a pillow, his body shaking as if he were crying. Paddy took him gently by the shoulders and asked, "Uncle, are you all right? There's someone here . . ." Iain sat up. His face was beet red. He was laughing so hard he was almost breathless. All he could do was point back toward the kitchen as he mouthed words that Paddy couldn't make out. Confused, Paddy went back into the kitchen, with Iain following behind, doubled over with laughter.

Corryne was seated in the kitchen with a smile of satisfaction on her face. Beside her on the table were the accoutrements of her disguise that had created Marion.

"Okay, okay, you fooled me," Paddy admitted, feeling embarrassed. Iain and Corryne laughed hysterically until finally, Paddy interrupted. "Since you are so good at disguises, Corryne, do you have one for me? I'm going to the Manufactory." His mention of the Manufactory was enough to dispel the jolly mood.

Corryne scowled and drummed her fingers on the table. "Explain," she demanded.

Iain recounted how they had followed the clues in the riddle to find the blueprint and how they had decoded the message. Corryne seemed troubled about the note indicating there were four Duncans at the Manufactory.

"Well, you are not going by yourself," declared Corryne.

"Why not?" asked Paddy.

"Besides other obvious reasons, there are the minor little details such as your having never driven on the right side of a vehicle or the left side of the road, and you don't have your driver's license with you."

"Well, then you can be the chauffeur," replied Paddy, with a wry smile. Corryne scowled.

"Where did you learn how to do this?" asked Paddy, pointing to the pile of disguise clothes on the table.

"I learned it from my mom."

"Uncle Iain says the SMITs might know what I look like, so maybe you could disguise me somehow?"

Corryne softened and looked at him through squinted eyes. "Let's see now, who shall I turn you into?"

"Corryne has a lot of experience," offered Iain, looking at her cautiously. He winked at Paddy and patted him on the shoulder. "I can't wait to see who you will become!"

"'For what do we live, but to make sport for our neighbors, and laugh at them in our turn?'" quoted Corryne, a tiny smile of satisfaction lifting the corners of her mouth.

"Jane Austen! I didn't know you were a reader, Corryne."

Iain looked at Paddy and smiled, shaking his head. "Get used to it lad. She's got a mind quicker than lightning, that one, and you never know what she'll come up with."

Corryne flipped her long red hair behind her and scooped up her disguise as she headed for the door.

She stopped and turned just before leaving, to say, "Oh, I picked up the suit from the Manufactory today. There's no need even for me to bring it over. It was as we suspected. Double-bound seams, telltale Duncan knots, and the initials 'K. D.' inside the breast pocket."

Iain's heart sank. "I was hoping it wouldn't be true."

"What will you do with the suit?" asked Paddy.

"I'm going to give it back to him when we get him out of there. Who knows, maybe it will fit him."

Iain added, "That confirms we are on the right track to go in there and get them out."

"We'll begin making our plan tomorrow morning at six o'clock," announced Corryne confidently. "You all better go to bed early."

Iain smiled and shook his head as he walked back to his bedroom. "I dunno if ever a fellow will be able to ask for her hand. T'would be like lassoing a tornado! A very smart and capable tornado!"

✵ 15 ✵

TRESPASSER

"BAD MEN NEED NOTHING MORE TO COMPASS THEIR ENDS, THAN THAT GOOD MEN SHOULD LOOK ON AND DO NOTHING."
-JOHN STUART MILL

A blanket of dense, misty fog suffocated the morning sunlight. Iain couldn't see anything out the window as he sipped his Assam tea and listened for Paddy to wake up. The tinkling of sheep bells and short, punctuated whistles told him that across the lane, Ernie was moving his sheep to the lower pasture with Jennah, his border collie. Rivulets of condensation rolled down the kitchen windows from the heat of the oven.

"He's slept long enough," Iain whispered to himself. "Paddy, come get it while it's hot!"

Paddy stumbled in from his bedroom, still in pajamas. "What is that wonderful smell? Ooh, bread! How did you become such a great baker, Uncle?"

"I used to help Eliza. She was a patient teacher. She always reminded me of Beckett's saying, 'Ever tried, ever failed, no matter. Try again, fail again, fail better.' It took me years to learn the feel of the dough when it's had enough kneading. Now I can do it with my eyes closed."

Paddy inhaled deeply and closed his eyes. "It smells so . . . familiar."

"That's because it's your mama's recipe. I bet it's the one Clara uses at your house. The tiniest bit of cinnamon. That's the secret. Your mama was close to my Eliza. She used to come here to visit us every year. How she could light up a room with that smile."

Corryne burst into the kitchen at precisely six o'clock. "So! We ready then?"

"Now, you sit for just a moment and have some of this bread. You need a good start to your day."

Corryne picked up a slice of warm bread and held it in her mouth while she hoisted herself to sit on the counter. She wore her usual jeans tucked into her riding boots and an untucked flannel shirt over a T-shirt. Around her neck was her trademark red scarf.

"So, any ideas?" Corryne was laser-focused on the agenda.

"I have a thought that we could maybe build on," replied Paddy.

"Let's hear it then," directed Iain.

"Why don't we do something to create a big enough distraction so that we can blend into the chaos. You know, like . . . an explosion or maybe a fire."

Corryne raised her eyebrows. "Not the master of subtlety, are we?"

"Whoa, laddie! We want to rescue not kill or maim," Iain added with a chuckle.

"No, no. We need something that *looks* dangerous, but isn't. I'm talking about something where outsiders would come to help—like firefighters and ambulances. We could blend in with the rescuers and go in with them and find this lady."

"May I see the note from Uncle William?" asked Corryne. "I want to see if the blueprint is accurate."

"Accurate? How would you know?" snapped Paddy defensively. "If Grandpa did it, it has to be right."

"You haven't told him," Corryne observed, looking at Iain. Iain sighed and sat down at the table.

"Sweetheart, I've tried to wipe the memory of that awful time out of my mind. My blood pressure goes up just thinking about it." Turning to Paddy, he explained, "Corryne was taken by the SMITs when she was just fifteen and was held there for six months. So, she's been inside the Manufactory and has seen it firsthand. Sean kidnapped her to coerce her father into divulging the location of the thread. Idiots! They still don't know that *all of us* have it. You see, a rumor started after they took your mom, that to protect it, William must have moved it from tailor to tailor to try and keep its whereabouts unknown. That assumption led them to harass and intimidate many within Proteus."

"You escaped?"

Corryne nodded.

Iain continued, "Corryne knows their daily routine, when the workers get breaks, and where the clinic is. You two will need to work together closely for this to succeed."

Paddy was quiet for several minutes. Finally, he asked Corryne, "Does anyone know which Duncans are there?"

"No, but the conditions are horrible. I can't imagine what it's like for this lady who is sick. It's hard, even for a healthy person to hold up. The 'convicts,' those they hold against their will, never get to leave, so I doubt they've sent her for any medical treatment."

A little bell rang, indicating the post had arrived. Iain glanced through the letters. "Paddy, your dad sent your plane ticket and your driver's license. You have thirty days before the ticket expires."

Paddy took a deep breath. "We'd better get this done." Paddy tried to sound brave, but the deadline troubled him.

At just that moment, the seed cup attached to the inside of a decorative birdcage hanging in the corner of the kitchen began to light up and flash with a red light. Paddy hadn't noticed the little birdcage until now.

"Sensors picked up something," whispered Iain warily.

"What sensors?" asked Paddy.

"Shh!" rebuked Corryne.

The shades on the windows began to lower automatically, and the locks on the doors flipped into the locked position.

"My bike is out there, Uncle. If anyone touches it . . . they'll get a lesson they won't soon forget."

"You will not go out that door, young lady," Iain commanded in a loud whisper. "Everyone—take a position."

"A position? What's happening?" Paddy was confused and growing more worried by the moment.

"Uncle? You didn't tell him?" whispered Corryne, sounding angry.

Iain scowled. "I haven't had time to tell him *everything*."

Corryne went to a window. "Paddy, get over here!" she ordered. "Sensors along the perimeter of the property have been tripped."

"How do you know it's not an animal?" asked Paddy.

"Because the sensors know the difference between a biped and a quadruped! Now, the wands on the blinds work as you would expect them to, except when you press the button on the bottom of the wand and hold it for five seconds. Then, they activate borescopes fitted with wide-angle lenses embedded into the walls on the outside of the house. If you turn the wand while holding the button on the bottom, it rotates the camera. Through these, we can view the entire circumference of the cottage. Press the bottom of the wand another three seconds, and it activates the connected picture next to the window, which is a monitor that shows what the borescope sees. Got it?"

"The pictures are monitors?"

"Of course! Now get over there to the window and do what I said."

Paddy wondered whether Iain and Corryne were also spies, like Grandpa, or whether they just had some very sophisticated ways of protecting themselves from the SMITs.

He did as instructed, and the picture of a vase of flowers faded to reveal a wide-angle view of the entire side of the cottage. He could move the lens to different positions to see higher, lower, or to the sides. Corryne watched both her monitor and Paddy's.

"There, hold it," she whispered to Paddy.

"Uncle, look behind the tree on Paddy's monitor. It's Sean Geelan's son, Shane."

"Sean Geelan, isn't he the head of the SMITs? Why would his son be here?" asked Paddy nervously.

"He often spies on us to get in his father's good graces by bringing home bits of information. He's a soulless scum. I'm ashamed to share the same planet with him," hissed Corryne.

Iain sighed loudly and spun around, heading toward the door. He walked swiftly out of the cottage and around to the backyard, directly to where Shane was hiding. "Something I can help you with, Shane?"

Shane slowly revealed his position. His face was absent even the slightest expression, but something in his eyes reminded Paddy of a predator about to attack. Even in the morning mist, Paddy could see he was a good bit taller than Iain and had thick reddish hair. He wore an oversized sweater that made his stocky build even more imposing, and he held a thick walking stick that looked more like a club.

His voice was low and raspy. "Just out for some fresh air. You know how stuffy Dublin can be," he replied, trying to sound at ease.

"Fresh air isn't restricted to my land. What's your business?"

"No need to get huffy, Iain. I have news I think may interest you."

"What is it then?"

"Rumor has it, William Duncan has been pretty busy lately."

"How would you know?" retorted Iain.

"Oh, you know us. We've always got our finger on the pulse of the competition."

"Shane, I've learned by now that if I believe the opposite of whatever you say, I'm more likely to come closer to the truth."

"Well, there's no need to be unkind. I was just making a neighborly visit to inquire about William, and you have to get ugly."

"It's time for you to leave. You can have all of the fresh air you want on your way back to your car. Now get off my land." Iain turned and headed back to the cottage.

As Iain walked away, Shane called out after him, "Jaipur. William is in Jaipur. You should keep in better touch with your family!"

"I've known that for days! You mean you are just finding out? You're falling down on your spy work, Shane. I guess we're outfoxing you, as usual."

Iain turned and walked back to the cottage and immediately sat down, putting his head in his hands.

Corryne rushed over to put her hand on his shoulder. "Uncle! Forgive me, but was that wise? He could have hurt you! There could have been others . . ." She began to fix him a cup of tea as Paddy continued watching the monitors to be sure Shane left as instructed.

When he was sure Shane was gone, Paddy sat down. "Are you okay, Uncle? What did he want?"

Iain looked up, and Paddy could see strain and weariness in his eyes.

"I'm all right. Shane wanted what he always wants. To drop bits of information to keep us afraid—to make sure we know they always have the upper hand."

"You'd think they'd get a life and focus on something else!" anger dripped off Corryne's words.

"Did he say something about Grandpa? I couldn't hear it all."

"He said William is in Jaipur, as if we didn't know."

"Did you ask him how they know?" asked Paddy indignantly as he began to pace the floor.

"I'm going to tell Douglass that Shane was here. He should know," said Iain.

Corryne looked at him and cocked her head as if she were trying to say something without words.

"He was going to find out anyway, dear. If you all are going into the Manufactory, Paddy should know he has backup."

From where Paddy was seated in the kitchen, he saw Iain open a door in the hallway that he'd previously thought was a coat closet. The opened door revealed another door immediately behind it. There was a device above the doorknob that had a keypad, and Iain entered a long sequence of numbers before turning the doorknob. He descended a step on the stairway behind the door and turned to shut the two doors behind him.

"Where is he going? What's going on?" Paddy asked.

"To the lab downstairs, of course. Ireland is the base of operations for the entire Proteus network. Honestly, don't you know anything? Where did you think we kept everything?"

"Look, I get that you know a lot, but you don't have to snipe at me constantly."

Corryne slumped into the chair opposite Paddy and stared at him. "Frankly, I'm shocked that there's so much you don't know. I don't mean to be rude, but after all, you've grown up with the Master Keeper himself. I understand if you don't know about how we support our spies on missions, but honestly, it seems like you don't know anything sometimes."

"I know plenty! Did you ever consider that I might know things you don't? You act like I'm brainless!" He rose and went to his bedroom. As he walked down the hall he said, "I thought we were supposed to work together."

"What is your *problem*? You should know by now that I speak my mind," she called out after him. "Everyone needs to pull their weight, you know. I don't have time to fill you in every five minutes." She sat in the kitchen, thinking about what she'd said. After a while, she went to Paddy's room and knocked.

"Come in," came a barely audible reply.

She sat on the chair next to the bed. "Hey, um, I guess you can't help not knowing this stuff if no one ever explained it. That wasn't fair for me to speak to you like that. I'm sorry."

"Forget it."

"Hey, . . . would you like to come downstairs with me to the lab after Uncle comes back? We have to keep someone upstairs at all times in case there's trouble, but as soon as he's back, we can go."

"Yeah, sure. I wonder if it's anything like Grandpa's."

"Man, I would kill to see Uncle William's lab! He built the one downstairs, you know."

Paddy didn't know, but he didn't want to say so. "I imagine there are a lot of similarities."

"Hey, I was thinking about your suggestion to create an explosion or a fire. I think it could work," offered Corryne.

Paddy could see she was making an effort to include him, which was a nice change. When they heard Iain's footsteps coming up the stairs, Corryne asked, "Ready to go downstairs?"

"Sure," answered Paddy.

16

THE ATHENAEUM

"THINGS ARE NOT ALWAYS WHAT THEY SEEM;
OUTWARD FORM DECEIVES MANY; RARE IS THE
MIND THAT DISCERNS WHAT IS CAREFULLY
CONCEALED WITHIN." ~PHAEDRUS

Corryne and Paddy started to go through the doors leading downstairs. Iain sighed and said, "Paddy, please don't be angry with me."

Paddy looked at him, his expression questioning what Iain meant. Iain shook his head and waved him on to catch up with Corryne.

They descended the stairs, which were lit by lightbulbs covered with metal cages, like a bomb shelter. He calculated that the steps must be about ten inches tall and counted twenty steps, making the depth at the bottom around sixteen and a half feet. As his hand touched the tunnel wall, he thought about how Grandpa's hands had dug this tunnel. He wondered if he would ever do half the brave things Grandpa had done in his life. They came to another door, but before Corryne reached for the key, Paddy asked, "Wait, let me see if I can find it . . . please?"

She moved away from the door. "Sure, no problem."

He began to examine the door carefully. There was nothing on the bottom corner as with the door in Grandpa's tunnel. He continued to look slowly from top to bottom, sectioning off each area into rows so he wouldn't miss anything. The door was ornately carved mahogany with gardenias cut in relief on its surface. Finally, in the center of the door, about two feet from the bottom, he saw it. Along the edge of one of the flowers were tiny letters etched into the wood.

He read aloud as his fingers traced the letters: "What expresses that which cannot be put into words and that which cannot remain silent?" Paddy smiled to himself, relieved that he knew the answer. "Good old Hugo."

"Hugo, who?"

"Victor Hugo. It's one of my favorite quotes. Grandpa just turned it into a question. The answer is 'music.'"

"Cool! So, um . . . does that help you open the door?"

"Well, Grandpa always prefers to code words into numbers when it comes to unlocking something. 'Music' in the simplest, abecedarian, single-level decryption would be . . . thirteen, twenty-one, nineteen, nine, and three."

"How did you guess that?"

"There's no guessing. It's just the letters' positions in the alphabet. I'd suspect he would use more than one level of encryption, though. Single-level would be way too simple, but then Uncle Iain probably isn't a phron."

"A phron?"

"It's a calque from the Greek. The word *phrontistes* means 'a deep thinker,' or 'philosopher,' or something like that. We use *phron* as a nickname for someone who works with ciphers."

Paddy began counting the stones on the floor, starting at the one directly beneath the doorknob, as he had in Grandpa's tunnel at home. "Thirteen down, twenty-one to the right, nineteen down, nine to the right, and three down."

He smiled as he lifted the stone, revealing the key beneath.

"Oh my gosh! How did you know which direction to go?"

Paddy paused. The temptation to bask in Corryne's admiration was too strong, especially given how harsh she had been. "Sometimes you just know," he asserted with a satisfied smile.

"That's awesome!"

Paddy pushed on the door which, despite its heaviness, opened freely to reveal a large room that must have been at least thirty feet square. The ceiling was low, and several old-fashioned, bell-shaped lamps cast wide cones of light over fifteen wooden desks. Over the silence, he heard the squeal and sputter of radios.

"Everyone, this is Paddy, I mean, Patrick Duncan, William's grandson." Corryne announced to what seemed like an empty room.

Slowly, workers emerged from where they were crouching under their desks. Stares turned quickly into smiling faces, and the room soon hummed with kind regards, "Oh! what an honor . . ." "Glad to finally meet . . ." "Your mama was so special . . ." "Your grandpa and I go way back . . ." as each one came over and shook his hand. When everyone had returned to their desks, an elderly gentleman came from a glass booth that had a large microphone hanging from the ceiling. As he approached, Paddy did a double take. He looked almost exactly like Grandpa, and even walked like him. He stood in front of Paddy with Grandpa's twinkle in his eyes.

"My, oh my! Let me look at you. You certainly have grown into a fine young man."

"Are you Douglass? My grandpa's brother?"

Douglass smiled. "Ha! And a wise lad at that. Sorry for the tentative welcome. We aren't used to anyone needing to figure out how to open that door." He glanced at Corryne with a raised eyebrow.

She replied, "It was just a bit of fun. You should have seen him. He figured it out without any help!"

Douglass patted her shoulder and smiled. He whispered, "Next time, maybe let us know ahead of time?"

Douglass put his arm around Paddy's shoulders and led him over to a couch by the radio booth. "What a day this is! Well, we have some catching up to do."

One of the workers quickly approached Douglass. "Sir, I'm so sorry to interrupt, but we are getting a message from China."

"My apologies, Paddy. May I turn you back over to Corryne for a few minutes?" he asked as he headed for the radio.

"Follow me, Paddy. I'll show you the Athenaeum," ordered Corryne as she led the way down a little staircase into an enormous room that must have been forty feet long by eighteen feet wide with a twenty-foot ceiling. There were chairs and couches set in small groups. Along the perimeter of the room were long, glass-topped tables with recessed display areas. Paddy briefly glanced into one of the tables and saw a collection of different types of compasses that appeared to be quite old. Framed newspaper articles covered the walls of the room to the point that there was little more than a few inches of space between them. Paddy read some of the headlines. The entire room was an archive of articles about significant historical events.

"Whoa! These must be worth a fortune!" Paddy walked slowly around the room, examining books, pictures, and strange mechanical devices. Finally, he sunk into one of the soft couches. "What is this place? It looks like a museum!"

Corryne began to answer, but Paddy interrupted with a flood of questions as a realization hit him. "Hang on. All this time I've been here, there have been people working down here? Why didn't you tell me? I recognize Uncle Douglass, but who are the others and what are they doing?"

"We didn't want to overwhelm you. So much of this is new to you. Iain especially wanted to ease you in gently. Don't be upset, please? Remember, I'm the one who brought you down here."

"So, this is why Uncle asked me not to be angry with him," Paddy muttered. "Explain," he said, echoing Corryne's earlier demand.

"Let's see; where should I start . . ."

"You could start with who those people are in the next room and how they know me."

"Well, there's Douglass, of course; there's your Aunt Catriona; there's my mom, Susanna, who is our master of disguises; Uncle Iain's daughter, Mira; and your cousin, Caleb. Then there's the radio crew: Andy and Kieran; and last but not least, Luke, Clyde, Gavin, Kirk, Leah, Kirsty, Gillian, and Rhona, all translators. Each one speaks at least three languages fluently, and they support the individual portals, most especially when we have a mission in their country.

"Do they live down here?"

Corryne laughed. "Of course not! They go home at the end of the day, all except for one of us. We take turns on the night shift."

"Are they all Duncans?"

"Oh, goodness, no. Over the years, a lot of families have joined us either by marriage or friendship. Most of them know about you because your mom used to visit and send pictures regularly. Not to mention, Uncle William brags about you all the time."

Paddy heard a loud squawk from the radio, followed by someone speaking in a language he didn't recognize.

"Come, let me show you my domain."

Paddy followed her to the far end of the room, where there was a large bookshelf. Corryne reached up and pulled *Anna Karenina* off the shelf and pressed a recessed button on the wall. A portion of the bookshelf the size of a door slid aside, revealing a small room. On one side of the room were mirrors set above a long countertop, which had cabinets below. On the other side of the room, from floor to ceiling, was a bank of drawers and cabinets of different sizes. There were three chairs, the kind that could be raised and lowered like those found in a barbershop.

"Here is where I transform you into someone else. My great-great-great-great-great-grandfather made disguises for Angus himself."

Paddy opened some of the cabinets revealing makeup, wigs, and thin, skin-like masks. In the corner, a computer appeared to be searching as numbers flashed continuously across the screen. There was a printer, and a camera on a tripod as well.

"What's all this?"

"This is where we make alternate identities."

"Isn't that illegal?"

"Paddy, the good guys want us to be undercover."

"Do you like disguising people?"

"Yes. It's like having a superpower when you wear a disguise. It's served me well. I would never have escaped the Manufactory if it hadn't been for my disguise and Ashok's time off."

"Huh?"

"Ashok was a worker, perhaps still is, at the Manufactory when I was there. He moved here from India. We would talk at lunchtime in French so no one could understand us. He was always kind to me. One day he asked me if I was free to leave, and I just looked at him without answering. He must have known, but I never told him. Sean Geelan told me if I ever told anyone that I was there against my will, he would kill my parents. I used to watch the workers leave in the evening from my window in the dormitory. Every day when Ashok would turn in his quota card and go out the gate to go home, he would turn and look for me.

"One day at lunch, he told me he would be gone for about a week because he needed to travel back to Morocco to see a sick relative. When he left on his trip, I sneaked scraps of muslin and sewed them together to make a turban, like Ashok's. I managed to take some linen from the storehouse, and I made a tunic and a sash like the ones Ashok wore.

"On the fifth evening, I knew it was my last chance because Ashok was supposed to return the next day. I pretended to go to the restroom, but instead, I went to the dormitory and put on my disguise. I used black wax marking pencils, the kind the cutters use, to color my eyebrows, and I put my hair up in the turban. I even stuffed batting in my cheeks to make my jaws look wider.

"When all the workers filed out to turn in their quota cards, I joined the line. I almost didn't pull it off. Shane Geelan was checking everyone's cards, and when he saw me, he asked what I was doing there, thinking I was Ashok. I just looked at him, knowing if I spoke, it would give me away. Thank goodness Ashok is a man of few words! Shane just shrugged and said, 'I guess you like us so much you came back a day early!' and I just walked out the front gate."

"You must have been terrified!"

"I only wish I could have been there to see their reaction when they found out I was gone," she said, laughing.

Paddy was quiet as he tried to imagine it.

"I decided somewhere on the long walk between the Manufactory and home that standing up to the SMITs of this world is a way to make my life count. Someday, I hope I can travel and find ways to secure freedom for the thousands held in slavery in other countries. I experienced it for six months, and I don't want anyone else to have to live like that, even for a day."

"I'm sorry you had to go through that, and escaping . . . that was so brave! I don't know if I could have done it."

Paddy looked around the room at different headlines. He stood to read them more closely. "'April 10, 1919, Troopship Mongolia Carrying Boys of 26th Division—First Ship to Sink German Submarine,' 'Discovery of Stolen Art Taken by the Nazis,' 'King Haakon VII Escapes Norway Unharmed, as Germans Pursue.'" He looked at Corryne with wide eyes.

"Uncle Douglass likes keeping mementos. He comes in here when he needs encouragement."

"Did we have something to do with all of these?"

"That's why they are here."

"Oh my gosh! This is unbelievable!"

"That last one you read, about King Haakon, was a sad time. Your great-grandfather, James Duncan, went on a mission, and he took Uncle William along to train him. Your grandpa was only sixteen. They needed to get a message to King Haakon as he and his family fled north when Germany invaded Norway. Each time the king and his family thought they were safe, the Germans found out where they were hiding. James and Uncle William, disguised as Norwegian soldiers, delivered the message to the king that German planes had been dispatched and would soon be attacking where they were. The king and his family got out just in time and escaped to rule in exile until the war was over.

"James and Uncle William hiked back into the woods to passage back here when a German paratrooper began shooting at them. One shot hit James in the chest. Uncle William was able to passage back with him, but James died soon afterward. He died in your grandpa's arms."

Paddy was quiet for several moments. "He never told me about that. Wait, how could Grandpa passage together with his father?"

"We just link together using these." She held up her wrist to show an ornate medallion on a chain fastened to her wrist.

"What's that?"

"We call it a 'bridge.' Angus's grandson, Callum . . . let's see, he would be your great-great-great-grandfather, knew James Clerk

Maxwell, the famous scientist. I think it was around 1873. Callum approached Maxwell to discuss some questions about magnetism, and soon they were helping one another create the bridge to extend a magnetic field. Very simply, when someone puts on a cover, whoever touches them wearing a bridge is carried with them. The bridge extends and concentrates electrical forces within our bodies and connects them to the electromagnetic field created by the seals, which, as you know, connects to the earth's magnetic field. Oh, I almost forgot. I have one for you." She retrieved a bridge from the pocket of her jeans and handed it to Paddy. "Better put it on now. You never know when it might be needed."

Paddy put it on. "Cool."

"Don't get any bright ideas about starting a travel agency, okay?"

Paddy laughed and shook his head. "Don't worry."

It was strange how receiving such a simple thing had such an immediate effect on Paddy. Suddenly, he felt included, even welcomed.

Half joking, Paddy asked, "Have we overthrown any governments lately?"

Corryne's response was dead serious. "Earlier this year, we thwarted an effort to assassinate a democratic leader in Brazil. In February, we worked to get key leaders in Central America to see the benefit of a peace agreement, which was eventually signed by the rebels on the left and the leaders of the political right. Among other things, we are working behind the scenes with several countries to bring about a halt to the famine in Yemen."

Paddy was stunned. "Gosh, I had no idea. I'm trying to figure out what to do now that I've graduated. The problem is, I've lived my whole life with my father planning on me taking over his shop. I've never dared tell him that I'd like to do something else, at least for a little while first. It would break his heart. Don't get me wrong; I'm proud of my skills, and I enjoy the work. It's just the prospect of doing it forever in that tiny little shop. I'd like to do something exciting, something involving travel."

"Like what?"

The question startled him. "I'm not exactly sure, but whatever it is, I'd like to do it without feeling like I'm a disappointment to my dad. I want to do what's right for me, but I feel selfish around people like you who want to rid the world of evil. I'm not the hero type."

"Ha! I wish it were that dramatic! I think it's okay not to know exactly what you want to do. Plenty of people make a decision when they're young and realize in their fifties that it wasn't right for them. Then they feel it's too late for a new start. I think it's better if it's a process, like trying on shoes. We see a pair we think we love, and after we walk around in them a while, we realize they just don't fit right. We often have to try on lots of shoes before we find the perfect ones. What's wrong with trying on a few different things right here? We need help, and we can't exactly put an ad in the paper for someone willing to travel in the earth's magnetic field, now can we?" She smiled as she spoke, and the lightness of her tone made Paddy feel better despite his dilemma.

"You might learn some skills you'll use later in doing what you finally decide is a perfect fit. Plus, everyone here could probably learn a lot from you."

"Oh yeah, they could learn a lot from me all right," he mocked.

"The trouble with you, Paddy, is that you don't know what you know. The Master Keeper himself trained you! No one else grew up hearing all the stories about Uncle William's missions, and all you know about cryptography? I heard you speak a few languages too."

"Sure, I'm pretty good at cryptanalysis, and I speak a few languages, but . . ."

"Don't you get it? Do you think the average grandpa teaches his grandson those things for fun? No, they throw a baseball, they go fishing, they make a birdhouse. Here, we support missions. Sometimes, we do small missions ourselves, but even then, we are just following directions. You grew up with a mastermind! You have whole libraries of strategy in your head."

Paddy looked around again at the hundreds of news headlines hanging on the walls. Iain had tried to tell him the same thing, but it wasn't until that moment that he began to grasp it. The realization almost took his breath away. *What if it's true? What if Grandpa was teaching me so I could help others with these skills? What if I could help plan missions or even go on a mission and do something to make a difference?* He was quiet for some time as he pondered these thoughts.

Corryne finally said, "I'm going upstairs to get some of Uncle's cake before it's all gone. Want to come?"

"What kind of cake?"

"Irish tea cake with raspberries."

"Oh yeah! . . . with coffee!"

⚜ 17 ⚜

THE PLAN

"ACTIVITY BACK OF A VERY SMALL IDEA WILL
PRODUCE MORE THAN INACTIVITY AND THE
PLANNING OF GENIUS." -JAMES A. WORSHAM

The sound of a flurry of voices the next morning shook Paddy from his thoughts. He opened his bedroom door quietly and listened.

"Kieran, you stay behind and operate the radios. Remember the frequency we use on Fridays. Don't forget to check the schedule for the proper channels for each day."

"I always remember, Uncle Douglass."

"Gillian, your bridge should be tighter on your wrist. It looks like it's been a while since you passaged."

"Yes, sir."

Paddy could sense an urgency in Douglass's voice, and he suspected something was about to happen. He dressed quickly and hurried to the kitchen. Gathered in a circle was a group of strangers dressed in business attire.

Paddy looked at Iain as if to ask, "Who are these people?"

"Oh, Paddy. No worries. It's just the crew from downstairs in disguise."

"Wow! Very convincing!"

Corryne was focused. "Do they want you to take anything?"

Iain replied, "Our contact's message translated to 'Portuguese entourage needed to make presentation to political leaders by impersonating executives from the Liga de Saúde e Longevidade dos Recursos Brasileiros or the League for the Health and Longevity of Brazilian Resources.' They sent a handout and talking points, so we are all set. Douglass knows more, so he'll take the lead on this."

"Do you need any help?" Paddy asked.

"You and I have to work on the plan to get into the Manufactory," declared Corryne.

"You're going to Brazil?" asked Paddy.

Kirsty explained, "We are going to bring some gentle pressure on Brazilian leaders. We need them to convince the president that deforestation of the Amazon is affecting the rest of the world through climate change. The immediate crisis is that a diamond mining company from Africa wants to put a mine in the Amazon. If that wasn't bad enough, that company is known to use child labor."

Paddy remembered seeing her downstairs. She was tiny, probably no taller than five feet, and she had long blond hair, blue eyes, and freckles across her nose. Her quiet voice sounded kind, almost shy. She seemed out of place in the world of espionage.

Everyone except Paddy, Iain, Corryne, and Kieran formed a circle, and Paddy noticed each one was wearing a bridge identical to the one Corryne had given him. They all took hands except for Douglass. He held a cover that looked remarkably like the one Paddy had used.

"Everyone ready?" asked Uncle Douglass.

"Ready," replied each simultaneously as they all held hands.

The two standing on either side of Douglass, with one hand, held the cover by its shoulders behind him, with the armholes easily accessible, and with their other hand, they held the hand of the person next to them. With one amazingly swift motion, Douglass slipped his arms through the cover and grabbed the hands of the two standing on either side of him.

The next thing Paddy knew, he was on the floor feeling as though an electric charge had blasted through the kitchen, forcing him to the ground. He blinked several times, still seeing the reflection of the flash of light.

Iain helped Paddy to sit at the table. "Oh, sorry about that. Forgot to tell you to shut your eyes and brace yourself. There's a lot of power generated when you have that many passaging together."

After a few moments, Paddy remarked, "You do realize that this *isn't normal*, right? People disappearing and all . . ."

Iain and Corryne looked at each other and laughed. Iain responded, "What you need is a good hearty breakfast. Say, doesn't Clara feed you back home? You need some meat on those bones!"

Iain served Paddy a hearty plate of loin bacon, eggs with mushrooms and tomatoes, and a thick slice of fresh bread with butter and cinnamon sugar. He took a seat across from Paddy and sat quietly for a moment before he spoke.

"Son, when my mother sat me down and explained everything to me, at first, I thought she'd lost her mind. When I finally realized it was all real, it took a long time before I could fully accept it. I felt like an outsider looking in—like I wasn't a part of what everyone else accepted as normal."

"Yeah, that's putting it mildly," Paddy replied, still dazed.

"In a way, I felt betrayed. I was angry that my family had kept a secret from me. Later, when I told my mother how I felt, she cried. She told me how hard it was to raise me all those years, knowing that one day, she would have to tell me."

"How old were you?"

"Twelve."

"Well, there's a huge difference between twelve and eighteen! What I don't get is how in the world you live your life keeping what you do a secret? It's like I stepped into another world. Maybe it's easier to learn about it when you are younger."

"I imagine you are probably right."

"What made you decide to give so much to all this? I looked through the closet in the bedroom. You made those suits, didn't you?" He didn't wait for an answer. "Uncle Iain, you are amazingly talented! You could've been rich, not stuck here in this little cottage harassed by SMITs."

"Now, don't you worry about old Iain. Duncan Tailoring is one of the most profitable tailoring establishments there is, and every tailor is supported well. Besides, having a purpose that's more than just making money is what makes life worth living! That's what SMITs have never understood—that a handful of skill and love of quality is better than a bag of gold. We tailor for beauty and for the joy of knowing we've created a high-quality garment that will serve its owner well. A true tailor sees his creations not a whit differently than Leonardo da Vinci probably saw the *Mona Lisa*. SMITs have never understood that tailoring is far more art than craft. Don't worry about them. We triumphed in this war long ago because we have what will always remain out of their reach."

Paddy listened quietly. "You can say we triumphed, Uncle, but they have Duncans in there. That doesn't look like a triumph to me."

"I know, I know. We will get them out. I'm just trying to help you see the big picture. That's where we have to keep our focus."

"Can we get to planning now?" Corryne's anxiousness was evident. "I'm going out to get my notebook from my bike pack."

"What's Corryne's issue now?" asked Paddy, seeing her out the window.

"Be patient with her. What Corryne has in talent, she lacks in gentleness, to say nothing of tact. It's not that she's unkind, she's just afraid of getting too close to people. She doesn't want to risk getting hurt. Try to see her good points."

"She is pretty smart."

"That she is. You know, Paddy, we have a saying here in Ireland. 'You've got to do your own growing, no matter how tall your grandfather was.' It means that you have to make your own decisions about your future. You shouldn't be a part of anything if your heart isn't in it, and you should never be ashamed to follow your own path."

Paddy looked down at his plate. He appreciated Iain's understanding. It helped to know that others had felt just as confused as he was. He was beginning to see a little more clearly why Papa was so adamant about Paddy staying and running the shop. It was undoubtedly the safer choice. Paddy decided that he would stop being angry at Papa for not telling him about his family's *other life*.

Corryne returned and sat at the kitchen table. "So, I was thinking about Paddy's idea—that we need a diversion—and I think it could work if it were big enough that if we went in, no one would be suspicious."

"Like a fire?" asked Paddy.

"An actual fire or just triggering the fire alarm?" asked Iain.

"Do they have an alarm system?" asked Paddy.

"Of course. All employers of that size have to have alarms, so they comply with labor regulations. They have those red, pull-down switches by every door," replied Corryne.

"It would be so much easier if we knew one of the workers who might be willing to set off the alarm," suggested Paddy.

Corryne smiled. "Remember I told you about Ashok Anand? He is the friend I impersonated to escape. I think he would do it if I can reach him somehow. Hang on; I'll be right back. Let me go see what I can find on the computer."

Corryne returned to the kitchen about five minutes later, waving a small piece of paper. "I found his home address and phone number. I'm going to talk to him in person."

"Is it safe for you to go by yourself?" asked Iain.

"I doubt the SMITs would be watching his place. He's just a regular worker, but we need to figure out the rest of the plan before I go. We might want him to do something else for us."

"What do they do when they have fire drills?"

"I'd suspect they only have alarms because they have to. Knowing them, they would view a fire drill as a waste of work time."

"So, if they don't have fire drills, that could be a good thing because, if the alarm goes off, everyone will think there is a real fire," said Paddy, thinking aloud.

"Good point, Paddy," offered Iain.

"Okay, so we arrange for Ashok to pull the alarm at a set time, and as everyone exits the building, we'll go in and find her." Corryne paused, working the details out in her mind.

"What is it? I can see your wheels turning," observed Iain.

"We will disguise ourselves as firefighters," Corryne declared.

"What? No, we are not. Surely, that's a crime. I'm not impersonating a public servant," argued Paddy.

"Don't you see? I'll text a signal to Ashok, and he'll pull the alarm. The alarm will trigger the fire department to respond, and when they arrive, we'll slip in with them."

"What if the real firefighters realize we're not part of their crew?"

"They will assume we are part of the Manufactory's fire brigade, and the SMITs will assume we are with the fire department."

Paddy sighed slowly. "I just want it to be on the record that I am *not cool* with pretending to be a firefighter."

"Forgive me, but this lady needs us," snapped Corryne. "There is no risk-free way to get her out, so I'd rather do it while there are firefighters there than in the cover of night, when Sean Geelan wouldn't hesitate to shoot us. Plus, if all else fails, I know a way out behind the old compressor building where there's a loose section of fence."

Suddenly, Kieran burst through the doorway from downstairs with a look of panic.

"Someone shot Kirk!" he shouted.

Iain went to him and put his hands on his shoulders. "Tell us what you know. Where was he shot?"

"In Rio!" Kieran shouted, panicked.

"We can help more if we stay calm. We know where he is. Where on his body was he shot?"

"He took a bullet to the leg. Everyone is safe for the moment, but they are going to be back any second. We are going to need a doctor!"

"Paddy, call Rebekah and tell her we need her urgently. Her number is by the phone," ordered Iain.

Paddy dialed the number and said nervously, "Kirk has been shot in the leg. Iain asked that you come right away!"

"I'm at a farm nearby. I'll be there in five minutes," answered Rebekah.

"She said she'd be here in five minutes!"

The next second, there was a shockwave and a split-second flash of light. The first thing Paddy heard was Kirk crying out in pain. A tourniquet was already applied using someone's belt. Paddy brought a pillow from his room and helped Kirk prop himself up against the wall. Corryne grabbed a towel and began to put pressure on the wound.

"Do you know if it's through and through?" asked Iain.

"I . . . I think so. There is a lot of blood on the back of my pants."

"Hang in there. Rebekah is on her way."

"Yes, she said she's in the area at a nearby farm and will leave immediately and come."

Corryne brought some hot tea to Kirk, who was beginning to look pale.

Within minutes, the door opened, and Rebekah entered. "Where is he?"

She took one look at Kirk and said, "Help me lay him down." She started intravenous fluids, injecting something into the line for pain. "Okay, let's see here . . ." She cut away his pants leg and looked at the amount of blood. "Looks like it missed your femoral artery, you lucky boy. We'll get you patched up. Iain, I need more towels so I can irrigate this wound, and let's get him onto the kitchen table."

Everyone except Paddy, Douglass, Kieran, and Iain retreated downstairs to make room for Rebekah to work, while Corryne phoned Kirk's family to let them know what happened.

About an hour later, Rebekah was washing her hands and said to Kirk, "You should stay the night here. I'll come by tomorrow and bring you some crutches. Call me right away if there's any sign of any fever. Iain, do you have some pajamas Kirk can borrow?"

"Of course. Paddy, you and Kieran help him up and into the little room beside mine. There's a nice bed in there, and I can hear him if he needs anything in the night."

Once Kirk was settled and everything cleaned up, Rebekah sat at the kitchen table. Corryne made her a cup of strong coffee.

"Now, is someone going to tell me how this young man finds himself with a bullet through his leg, or am I not allowed to ask?" asked Rebekah.

Douglass explained, "We had just met with one of the Brazilian leaders, and we were headed over to another building to meet with another. That's when the president's motorcade drove by, and someone fired a shot. It missed the president's car and hit Kirk. We had a devil of a time getting to a secluded alley so we could passage back without being seen. It had nothing to do with us."

"How can you be sure?" asked Rebekah.

"They were all in disguise, Sister. It was a fluke accident," added Iain.

"I'll go sit with Kirk," offered Paddy as he walked to the bedroom. Paddy pulled an overstuffed chair over to the side of the bed and sat down. "Is the pain any better?"

Kirk pushed himself to a seated position and leaned back against the pillows. "It's subsiding now, though it hurt something fierce when she stitched it up."

"I heard her say the bullet grazed the bone. Amazing that you didn't have to go to the hospital," observed Paddy.

"Oh, Rebekah is used to this—not bullet wounds, mind you—it's just that several of us are accident-prone. She's amazing. Thankfully, she doesn't charge family."

"That was pretty scary. I'm glad it wasn't more serious."

"So, I heard you are William's grandson. What's that like?"

"What do you mean?"

"I mean, when did he start training you for missions? I can only imagine what you must know about cryptography. I could probably use your help decrypting some of the messages on my desk. I have several that have me stumped."

"Oh, he's been teaching me about codes since I was little, but all the rest of this is new to me."

"Oh, wow! I bet your head is spinning. Baptism by fire, huh?"

"Yeah, something like that."

"The rest of us began hearing about it from our parents at least by the time we were twelve or thirteen. 'Now, Son, you need to understand that our family is a *little different* . . . ,'" he mimicked and then laughed. "By the time we came of age, there was nothing we wanted more than to be a part of it all. Who would turn down travel, danger, and experiencing foreign cultures? A bit more exciting than tailoring!"

"Yeah, you get to do things that get you shot," added Paddy with a smile.

"Ah, well, you take one for the team now and then. No big deal."

Talking with Kirk lifted Paddy's spirits. He learned that Kirk's father, Benjamin, was a fisherman whose poor eyesight disqualified him from being a tailor. His family struggled financially, and by the time Kirk was eighteen, he was working on merchant ships going to Belgium, Cameroon, and Japan to help feed his family. Kirk was a trained radio operator, and he also went to school to learn languages. He spoke French, Dutch, and Japanese fluently.

Paddy shared with Kirk their plan to get into the Manufactory.

"Iain told us about William saying that four Duncans are there. It's a brave thing you and Corryne are doing. You get into any trouble, ring me up." He laughed, "I'll slug 'em in the head with my crutches!" They both laughed. "Well, I think I'd better try to get some sleep before this leg wakes me up hurting again."

Paddy brought the pain pills Rebekah had left and put them on the bedside table with a glass of water. "If you need anything at all, just call. Either Iain or I will come."

THE NEXT MORNING, PADDY WAS AWAKENED BY A LARK THAT landed on the edge of his bedroom window. He rose and looked out over the fields. A heavy mist was rising from the distant hills, and the sheep were already out grazing. The coolness of fall and the changing leaves energized him and reminded him of when Grandpa would take him camping in Mount Greylock State Reservation in Western Massachusetts. Closing his eyes, he could almost smell the coffee percolating on the camp stove. It was their secret that Grandpa would allow Paddy to have coffee with him when he was little. Drinking it with Grandpa made Paddy feel grown-up even though his coffee was half milk. As he reminisced, he realized how much he missed Grandpa.

He dressed quickly and went to check on Kirk, who was still sleeping. He placed a book of Robert Burns's poems that Iain had loaned him by Kirk's bedside, refilled his water glass, and shut the bedroom door quietly.

At nine thirty, Rebekah arrived to check on the patient. She brought a berry pie, cookies, shortbread, and crutches for Kirk.

"He's still sleeping. Would you like some tea?" offered Paddy.

"I'd love some coffee. Honestly, I'm practically an American when it comes to my fondness of that elixir. With my lack of sleep, it helps me focus. Let's see . . . Ah, here we go." She removed a small tin of coffee, which was almost full, evidence it was rarely used.

"I love coffee too," added Paddy.

"Ha! I suppose you got some help from William with that!"

Paddy smiled and nodded.

"I don't know what I'd do without coffee. I had twins to deliver at a farm last night about an hour from here. I was up all night. Couldn't have done it without coffee."

"Why not take the person to the hospital?"

"I don't suppose the hospital would allow the delivery there!" she chuckled.

"Why not?" asked Paddy.

"Delivering calves is kept to the barnyard in Ireland."

"Oh, are you a veterinarian too?"

"Not by profession, but I'm the backup when the real vet is busy with other emergencies. I suppose I'm better than no one at all."

Paddy poured her a cup of coffee and one for himself. He still liked it with lots of milk.

"Well, I guess I'll have to wake Kirk up, much as I hate to do that. Was he up in the night?"

"I never heard him, not even once. You'll have to ask Uncle whether he heard him."

"Where is that brother of mine?"

"I'm not sure. He's usually in the kitchen, no matter how early I get up."

Just then, Iain emerged from the basement door, still wearing his pajamas and robe.

"There you are," stated Rebekah.

"Morning, Sis. Apologies. They needed some help with a translation last night. We've been at it since two this morning."

Corryne walked into the kitchen, taking off her motorcycle helmet. "It's like a Scotch mist out there. I'll be right back. I have to check something on the computer downstairs."

Rebekah came from Kirk's room. "He has a low-grade temperature.

I'd guess his body is fighting off a possible infection. I'm going to need someone to check his temperature every hour and call me immediately if it goes up. I've left some antibiotics beside his bed. Make sure he takes one pill every four hours."

"I'll be here all day. I'd be happy to remind him," answered Paddy.

"Thanks, Paddy. I'll stop by at the end of my rounds. If Kirk has to go to the hospital, you folks better come up with a believable story about how he got that bullet wound." Rebekah lowered her head and gave Iain a disapproving look, picked up her bag, and headed out to her car.

Paddy grabbed a handful of cookies and a glass of milk and took them to Kirk's room. "Hey, Kirk, want some cookies?"

"That'd be great. I'm ravenous. Hey, thanks for the book on Robbie Burns. It helps to pass the time."

"Have you tried walking on the crutches?"

"Oh, it's a cinch. I've been on crutches a couple of times before. I'm sort of accident-prone, I guess."

"Well, I hardly think the bullet was your fault, but at least you'll have an impressive scar. Hey, if you are that hungry, how about some breakfast? Uncle Iain made enough for an army."

"That would be great!"

Kirk followed Paddy into the kitchen just as Corryne returned from downstairs, with a worried look on her face.

"Hey, Corryne, you want some breakfast?" offered Paddy.

"No, thanks. Well, I just hacked into the SMITs employee roster. I found out her name is Christine. The roster lists her 'absent due to illness,' and it looks like she's been that way for a while."

"How did you do that?" Paddy asked, surprised.

Corryne cocked her head to the side as if to say, "You need to ask?"

"Do we know anything about her? How sick is she? What if she can't walk?"

"No, there's no other info."

"You kids have the details all worked out yet?" asked Iain.

"Not yet," replied Paddy.

Iain invited Kirk to join them at the kitchen table to discuss the plan.

"If you guys want to have a reason to set off a fire alarm, I can let you have some plastic explosives that we use at the shipyard to bust off large pieces of barnacles from the ships. All your friend Ashok has to do is stick one of the mini bombs to a surface and detonate it with a remote. I can rig it so it won't do much damage. All you need is a bit of smoke to give him a legitimate reason to pull the alarm. I could even make two small ones, so it looks like there's a bigger fire."

Iain looked at Corryne. "Do you think he'll do it? How much information do you have to give him to get him to help us?"

Corryne thought for a moment. "I don't know, but I should go speak with him now before we count on him being the key to our plan. If he doesn't help, we'll have to regroup and do something else. I think he's probably home since it's the weekend."

"Be careful," warned Iain.

Corryne nodded and headed out to her motorcycle.

❧

CORRYNE DROVE BY ASHOK'S HOME SEVERAL TIMES BEFORE PARKING her motorcycle. Ashok was playing with his daughter and son in the backyard with a boomerang. Corryne waved, and Ashok walked quickly over to where she was standing.

"Corryne! My friend! How are you?"

She smiled, his warm welcome encouraging her. "I'm doing okay, Ashok. It's so good to see you. I hope you don't mind that I looked you up online. I didn't know how else to reach you."

"Mind? My goodness, no, of course not! I'm so glad you found me! Please, won't you come in and meet my wife? I told her about you when we worked together. She would love to meet you."

"Sure, I'd like to meet her as well."

"Naseema! We have a guest; come see!" Naseema came to the door, and Corryne couldn't help but stare. She was stunningly beautiful. Naseema's beauty was the type that would make most anyone stop and stare, yet everything in her demeanor showed that she was unaware of it. Long, thick eyelashes framed her green eyes, and her thick black hair had auburn strands that shone like copper in the sunlight.

"Oh, please forgive my appearance. I've been cooking." She smiled shyly, but she carried herself with confidence. Ashok looked at her lovingly and smiled.

"I'm so glad you came today. Naseema usually works on Saturdays at the hospital, but she has today off."

"Are you a nurse?" Corryne asked.

"No, I'm a doctor. I bring little ones into the world. Ashok told me you worked with him, and that you left when he was on vacation. Did you find another position?"

Corryne had no idea what to say. "I'm still looking," she replied haltingly.

"Ah, well, no worries," replied Naseema, touching her lightly on the arm. "You'll find something soon. I always say it's best to wait for the right job if you can. If you'll excuse me, I have some chicken in the tandoor. You two sit and visit, and I'll have Sabrina bring you some tea."

Ashok motioned for Corryne to sit down in the living room. "Are you okay, Corryne? You seem worried."

"Ashok, this may sound like an odd question, but why do you work at the Manufactory? Are you happy working there?"

"Several years ago, I decided to try my hand at tailoring. My father is a well-known tailor who has many shops throughout India. He also has a large company that dyes fabric. I learned some from him, but I still have a lot to learn. I want to become a master tailor someday. When Naseema got the job here at the hospital, the only tailoring job I could find was with the Manufactory. Still, as you know, they have me doing piecework month after month, and it's not professional tailoring, if you know what I mean. I'm thinking of leaving soon, but I need to find a place where I can truly learn the trade."

"What do you think of Sean Geelan and those who run the Manufactory?"

Ashok paused for a moment, wondering why Corryne was asking. "Honestly?"

"Yes, honestly."

"I do not find them to be good men. I find them to be cruel. They don't appreciate the art of fine tailoring, and they only focus on profit.

That makes them not value their workers at all. We have similar textile manufacturers in my country. People only work there because they need a job, not because they have a passion for what they do."

"Ashok, some people work for Sean Geelan because they need a job, and some have no choice."

"What do you mean—no choice? They have slavery here?"

"Sean has people working for him who can never leave, and they never receive payment. I suppose you could call it slavery."

"How do you know this?"

"Ashok, I consider you to be my friend. I trust you. I hope you trust me because what I'm going to share, you must please, please, promise me that you'll tell no one."

Ashok looked genuinely concerned for Corryne. "Are you in trouble? Can I help you?"

"Yes, you can help, but it's not me that's in trouble. You asked how I know that some people are held there against their will? I was one of them. They came in the night, kidnapped me, tied my hands behind my back, threw me in the trunk of a car, and brought me there. I don't know if you remember, but there was someone assigned to watch me most all the time when I first was taken."

"I remember. I thought they were just training you."

"They were guarding me to keep me from trying to get away."

Ashok's eyes grew wide. "Oh my gosh! So, you escaped? You escaped when I was on vacation! Right?"

"Exactly. I have to thank you because you provided me a way to get out. I disguised myself as you—turban and all—and when it was time to punch out for the day, I just joined the line and walked out the front gate."

"You were disguised as me? I can hardly believe this! They are terrible men—Sean Geelan and those who work for him!" He thought for a moment and looked up at Corryne. "Oh my gosh, now I feel terrible that I never knew you couldn't leave! I felt something was wrong, but I thought perhaps your parents wanted you to work there and you didn't like it. I am so sorry! Why did you not tell me? I could have called the police!"

"Unfortunately, we can't involve the police because Sean has officers he pays to look the other way. They make sure that any complaints are ignored."

Ashok looked at Corryne's face and tried to read her expression. "So, there's someone else there who is a slave?"

"Yes, you may have seen her. She's been very sick lately. She may have been staying in the dormitory or in the clinic instead of working. We have to rescue her. Her life depends on it."

"Someone must stop this! It's barbaric!"

"Ashok, please trust me when I say that I can't tell you everything because it would put you in danger. You are a dear friend, and I would die if anything happened to you or your family."

"Is this about human trafficking? Are they criminals?"

"All I can tell you is I consider them criminals. They hate my family because our tailors value quality above profit, and as a result, we've prospered. We have shops around the world. Gosh, this probably sounds like I'm making all this up. I've probably said too much . . ."

"No, my dear. I believe there is a knowing in the heart when one hears truth. I know what you are saying is true. I give you my word, which is more valuable than my name. I will tell no one what you have shared with me, but how can I help?"

"My family has a plan to rescue the lady who is sick, Christine. What we want you to do is plant a couple of small devices that will create some smoke, detonate them, and then pull the fire alarm. When the fire department arrives, the firefighters will first evacuate everyone. I and one other will pose as firefighters and help evacuate people, all the while looking for Christine. When we find her, we will escort her out and free her. Hopefully, no one will notice in the chaos."

"Gosh!" Ashok thought for a moment. "What if they catch you? They know what you look like."

A sick feeling coursed through Corryne at the mention of being caught, but she mustered her courage. "We won't be caught. We'll be in disguise, and either way, it's a chance we have to take."

"Is that all I need to do?"

"If you are willing, I'll bring you two small devices that you will secretly attach anywhere where it will do the least structural damage.

They are intended to create a little smoke and provide a reason to pull the alarm, no more. I'll also bring you a remote-control detonator that you'll hide in your pocket. I'll need your cell phone number. When I send you the text, 'Get milk,' you will press the button on the detonator. As soon as you detonate them and you see the smoke, yell 'Fire' and pull the fire alarm. You should wear gloves when you place the devices and when you handle the detonator, so your fingerprints aren't on them. Once you trigger the detonator, find a safe place to throw it away."

Ashok thought for several moments. "That poor woman. I saw her once before. She does not look well. The Geelans' cruelty makes me want to turn in my resignation this very moment."

"Please stay long enough for us to get her out. There are three more besides her. Right now, we have to focus on Christine. We'll go back for the others another time."

Ashok paused as if he were considering the possible ramifications of his involvement. Then he announced, "It will be an honor to help."

"Good. I'll bring the devices here and leave them in your mailbox. Please retrieve them immediately. Instructions will be inside the package. All you have to do is to place them, click the detonator, pull the fire alarm, and you are finished. Then evacuate with everyone else, and if Sean or Shane asks you any questions, just say that you saw smoke and assumed there was a fire."

"Got it."

"Thank you so much, Ashok."

"Corryne, you say you are from a family of tailors? What is the name of the company?"

"Duncan Tailoring."

Ashok's eyes grew wide. He whispered, "*The* Duncan Tailoring?" Corryne smiled and nodded.

"We even have Duncan Tailoring in India! They have locations all over the world. Perhaps when everything settles down, if you hear of an opening for an apprentice tailor in your company, you might let me know?"

"I absolutely will."

"I will say a prayer for your plan to go smoothly."
"Thank you again. Your help is so appreciated."
"Remember, I'll deliver the package tomorrow into your mailbox."
"Please be careful."

✿ 18 ✿

WHO RESCUED WHOM?

"WHEN TOLD THAT THE NUMBER OF PERSIANS WAS SO GREAT THAT THEIR ARCHERS' ARROWS WOULD DARKEN THE SKY, DIENEKES REPLIED, 'GOOD. THEN WE'LL HAVE OUR BATTLE IN THE SHADE.'" ~HERODOTUS, THE HISTORIES

It was almost dark when Corryne returned to the cottage. Voices led her to the backyard, where she found Kirk outside talking with Paddy. Iain was busy pulling weeds in the last of the sun's light.

Kirk saw her and waved. "Hey! I trust it went well?"

"Very well," she replied with a slight smile.

"I was just showing Paddy how we disguise the radio antennae to look like trees, and how we get into the Base the back way."

"It's ingenious!" exclaimed Paddy. "No one would ever guess a trap door in the potting shed led down there. I'll have to check Grandpa's Cave at home and see if there's a back entrance like this."

"His Cave?" asked Kirk with a laugh.

Paddy chuckled. "Oh, that's just what I call it. It's so far underground it may as well be a cave. Honestly, I think it could easily serve as a nuclear bomb shelter."

Iain approached with handfuls of weeds.

"I see you've been working hard," observed Corryne.

"Well, to quote Cicero, 'If you have a garden and a library, you have everything you need,'" replied Iain.

Paddy shook his head and chuckled. "Is there any apothegm you don't know, Uncle?"

"Ha! I'm sure there's many you know that I wish I knew. Let's go inside and Corryne can tell us how it went."

Iain served everyone a large helping of shepherd's pie and took a fresh loaf of bread from the oven. "Paddy, could you bring some strawberry-rhubarb jam from the press?"

"Sure. You know, I think I've gained five pounds since I got here." Paddy smiled as he patted his stomach. "I'm not complaining, though."

Corryne began, "Ashok agreed to help us, and I will deliver the explosive devices and then text him the message, 'Get milk' from a burner phone so it will look like a message his wife might send. He'll pull the alarm, and when the firefighters arrive, we'll slip in and find Christine."

"If anyone asks who you are, tell them you are volunteer firefighters in training. After all, in a way, you are!" offered Iain.

Paddy sighed. "It's not a bad plan, but it's rather stressful thinking we are just going to walk calmly out with her right under their noses."

"I agree it's a risk, but it seems to be the only way not to draw undue attention. It would look odd if you tried to sneak her out the back fence. You both will be in disguise, so that should help." Iain continued, "She may be too weak to walk. I assume you all know how to make a bench with your hands. It may be best, even if she can walk, for you to carry her out that way because it takes two. There's less chance you'll be called on to help with something else if you are both busy evacuating her. It would be good to get her directly into an ambulance if one is there. If not, ask them to request one. Be sure to take some water for her. When the ambulance takes her to the hospital, call me, and I'll meet you there. The hospital is a neutral place to stage the next step of our plan to get her to safety.

"When the SMITs see me at the hospital, it's going to put you both at risk. You can't leave your disguises on because they'd wonder why firefighters are waiting in the emergency room for her. If you've removed your disguises, that will create another set of problems. I think you both should make sure she gets to the hospital and then come home until I return."

"No way!" declared Paddy and Corryne in unison.

Corryne spoke first. "Sean Geelan's men will ambush you! Do you think they will stand by and let Christine go home with you? They are proud of how long they've held her. No, there's no way we are leaving you, and I, for one, don't care if they see me. I hope they do."

Paddy looked at Corryne, and a smile played at the corner of his mouth. He was glad to find someone willing to stand up to the SMITs. He remembered his conversation with Papa when he'd insisted *someone* needed to put a stop to the SMITs tactics once and for all. "I agree with Corryne," he announced confidently.

"All right, you two, but I hope you realize how dangerous this is. You are right; we'll have a better chance with three of us than if it's just me alone, though I shudder to think what will happen when they recognize either of you."

"It's just how it has to be," declared Paddy.

"Let 'em try something. I'll have my black belt soon. I could use the practice," growled Corryne.

"Corryne," reprimanded Iain with a warning tone.

"Okay, okay. I'll be over in the morning after I drop off the package at Ashok's so he has it before he goes to work. Then, I'll come and do our disguises, and we'll head out." She grabbed a piece of Iain's fresh bread and headed out the door. She turned to Paddy and responded in an unusually sympathetic tone, "It's all going to work out fine. You'll see."

Iain sighed deeply and looked at Paddy for several moments. "I suppose we're passing the torch to your generation now. I trust that you all will protect our secrets well."

IT WAS NO SURPRISE THAT CORRYNE WAS SEATED AT THE KITCHEN table at seven a.m. sharp. What surprised her was that Paddy was ready and had already had breakfast.

"Okay, let's review the plan," blurted Corryne, anxious to begin.

"May I ask a question first?"

"Go ahead."

"What, or rather who, will I look like in my disguise? No offense, but I don't want to feel like I have papier-mâché on my head when I need to be focused on the rescue." Paddy waited for her reprisal.

Corryne gave him a smirk. "Dying is even more uncomfortable. You want it to be convincing, right?"

"Yes, right. Of course."

"Oooh, I could make you into an older woman . . . ," she teased.

"You will not! Besides, if you put me in a dress, my hairy legs would give me away."

"Oh, we have ways of handling that." She grinned.

"What older woman would be firefighting? And in a dress?"

"Hey, these are modern times. Anything is possible!"

She laughed, and Paddy was glad she was trying to lighten the mood. "Don't worry; I have the perfect clean-cut fireman look for you, but you will have a full-face mask."

"Corryne, please let the crew know that if the SMITs show up here, and if an emergency exit is necessary, everyone is to take the long way," advised Iain.

"What's the long way?" asked Paddy.

Corryne answered hurriedly, "You saw the exit in the potting shed, right?"

"Yes."

"That's the short route. There's a longer one for emergencies. Right at the end of the tunnel, before you go up the stairs to the potting shed, there is a door on the left. That door leads directly west and ends in the woods, about a kilometer from here. When you reach the end, you go up a set of stairs, and you are inside an old hollowed-out tree. There's a makeshift door so that you can get out. We keep a van at the end of the route, so we have transportation."

"A kilometer! How in the world did they dig that far?"

Corryne paused and gave him a sideways smile. "One shovelful at a time."

Paddy shook his head. "Ha-ha."

"So, are you ready to become the most good-looking firefighter in all of Ireland? Sit down here while I close the curtains."

One hour later, Paddy was speechless as he looked in the mirror at his darker hair and firefighter's jacket. "Hey, I think you made me look taller!" The transformation was so convincing it was eerie. He waited for Corryne to finish her disguise downstairs in her lair, as she called it. When she came upstairs, Paddy could only stare. She was now a clean-cut firefighter with exceptional features. She had somehow padded her shoulders and arms to appear more muscular . . . *way* more muscular.

"Whoa, if I were Sean Geelan, I wouldn't mess with you. That is amazing!"

"Any chance I can take to intimidate them . . . So, are we ready then? Remember, we may have to take her to the hospital ourselves, but I'd rather not if we don't have to. There's a good chance the SMITs would follow us."

Paddy asked, "What time does your watch say? We need to synchronize."

Corryne looked at her watch. "Nine thirty-two, and twenty seconds."

"Got it. We're good," replied Paddy.

"I told Ashok we'd send the signal to detonate the explosives around ten thirty. So help me, if there weren't Duncans in there, I'd plant real explosives myself and destroy the entire place and all the SMITs with it."

Paddy wished for her courage. His biggest fear was that they'd fail and become the SMITs' prisoners, a thought that terrified him.

They drove on in silence. Corryne stopped about half a kilometer from the Manufactory and parked under some trees. At precisely 10:28, she started the car again and drove slowly until they were one block from the Manufactory. She put the car keys in her pocket and then reached into the glove box and handed Paddy a duplicate set of keys. "In case I don't make it out. Don't risk leaving her to come after me." She looked Paddy directly in the eyes and put her hand on his arm. "We are going to get her out. It's going to work. We just need to stay focused."

"Right. Stay focused," Paddy responded, and added, "We've got this." He was hoping to encourage her, but saying it out loud made him feel better.

He wondered if she was afraid to be going back into the Manufactory, or if her determination was stronger. Given what he knew of her, it was a wonder she hadn't torn the entire place apart trying to escape when she was held there. Corryne was not only brilliant, she was also strategic. She had what Grandpa called "the ability to play the chess game in your head."

Corryne sent the "Get milk" signal to Ashok at precisely ten thirty.

They both jumped when they heard the fire alarm sound. The fire trucks arrived in less than three minutes. It helped that the station was less than a half a kilometer away. As soon as the trucks arrived, Paddy and Corryne ran toward the Manufactory. They ducked behind a hedge close to the gate. The color faded from Corryne's face when she saw that the firefighters were wearing orange suits instead of yellow. She grabbed Paddy's arm and whispered, "Come this way!" Paddy followed her reluctantly, looking back at the front gate, which was now opening.

"Where are you going?" he whispered in return.

"Don't you see their suits? It's obvious we aren't with them! We are going to have to pose as the fire brigade. Now come on. We are going to the back fence."

They could hear sheer pandemonium inside as smoke began billowing out from the open windows. Corryne could hear Ashok's voice above the others, yelling, "Fire!"

"This way, this way!" yelled the firefighters as they directed workers to evacuate and began unrolling hoses.

Every few moments, Corryne could hear Sean Geelan's voice cursing and yelling at the workers. There was no doubt that he would blame his employees if any damage occurred. Corryne and Paddy squeezed through the break in the fence, and Corryne whispered, "We are going to have to split up."

"What? No! Iain said we need to stay—"

Corryne cut him off. "We have one chance, and we don't know if she's in the dormitory or the clinic. Whoever finds her first will text the letter Υ to the other. Then we'll get her out together. Go! You take the dormitory!"

Paddy looked panicked, and Corryne pointed to a door and said, "Fourth floor!" She ran behind the buildings around the perimeter until she reached the clinic. Paddy raced up the stairs two steps at a time and reached the fourth floor out of breath. He gingerly opened a door labeled "Women's Dormitory" and saw what must have been forty rusty antique iron beds lined up together along one wall. Only one bed had an occupant. Paddy ran over to a woman whose emaciated form left him wondering whether she was alive. Her eyes were closed and sunken, and what remained of her hair was in long, thin, gray wisps. Her clothes were filthy, her fingernails dirty, and she appeared to be unconscious. Above the bed on the wall was a greasy sign that said, "Bed 5," which Paddy remembered was the bed Grandpa had indicated in his message.

Paddy touched her hand and whispered, "Ma'am? Christine? I am Paddy Duncan. We have come to get you out of here; to take you home. Ma'am?" He waited for a response, but there was none. He grabbed his phone and texted Corryne. She arrived in less than a minute. Paddy said in a panicked voice, "She's not responding!"

Corryne's eyes filled with tears as she looked at Christine. She knelt down and felt for a pulse. Then her voice quavered, "I can't find a pulse! We are too late!" She took Christine's hand in both of hers and began to sob.

"Corryne! Maybe her pulse is only weak. Look! There's an ambulance here now! Let's get her downstairs. Come on! Let's lift her with the bedsheets." They rolled the edges of the sheets and made a sling, lifting Christine gently. Paddy could hardly believe how light she was. They made it down the stairs, and Paddy kicked the door open so hard it banged against the brick building, drawing the attention of everyone outside. Paddy shouted directly at the firefighters, "Looks like we *forgot* one upstairs! She needs to get to the hospital *now!*" His tone was so commanding that firefighters and EMTs immediately rushed over to help, and an EMT raced to get a gurney. Within seconds, the siren sounded, and the ambulance was off to the hospital. Shane Geelan and his father stood outside the smoking building with looks of pure rage.

Thankfully, the fire chief called them back into the building as the smoke subsided. "Come with me. I'll show you the sources of the smoke," he said.

After the ambulance left, Corryne stood in the middle of the street, looking dazed. Paddy took her arm and began to run toward the car. He led her around to the passenger seat and then ran around and jumped behind the wheel.

"How about I drive this time? I need you to give me directions to the hospital, though." Corryne had begun to cry again, so she pointed where Paddy needed to turn. He parked and began to take off his disguise.

Corryne stared at him for several moments and said, "Thanks for taking over back there. I don't know if we reached her in time. I guess I just wasn't expecting that."

"I understand. We have to hope and pray that we did make it in time."

Corryne called Iain. "It's done. She's at the hospital." Her voice faltered. "I don't know if she's alive. I couldn't find a pulse."

"My dear, you all did the best you could. I've been waiting. I'm just a block away."

Corryne sighed. "Good. Please hurry and get inside before Sean and his others get here. We'll hang back a few minutes in the parking lot and watch for them. They know something is up. A firefighter showed the Geelans the source of the smoke. I would go ahead and evacuate the crew and put the cottage on lockdown now. I have a feeling they know we set the explosives."

"Of course, they know. Did you expect otherwise? Now be calm, child. Let's stay on our toes."

Corryne and Paddy watched as Iain parked and pressed through the cold wind to get inside. He had forgotten to hang up his phone, and Paddy and Corryne could hear loud voices shouting as he entered the emergency room.

"She's going into arrest! We need a crash cart in E-1!" The voices faded, and Paddy could see Iain slump into a chair through the large windows in the waiting room.

"Oh my gosh, she's alive!" yelled Paddy.

Corryne squeezed her eyes tight and whispered, "Please, God, please!"

Corryne stared silently ahead at the doors to the ER, with a glazed look as if she were lost in thought. Paddy noticed a blue panel truck enter the parking lot, and seven men in dark overcoats began to walk quickly toward the hospital. Though Corryne seemed to be looking straight at them, she didn't move.

Paddy asked, "Should we be concerned about those men going into the hospital? Do you think they are SMITs?"

"Oh, crumb!" whispered Corryne. She grabbed a pocketknife from the console of her car and ran toward the hospital.

Paddy grabbed the car keys and ran after her. He had no idea what Corryne was capable of, especially in her present state.

When they entered the waiting room, Corryne took a seat one chair away from Iain, her body tense as a jaguar ready to pounce. The men stood together in a group. Paddy recognized one of the men as Shane Geelan. Shane sauntered up to the desk and began speaking with the receptionist. Paddy took a seat by the door and pulled the hood of his windbreaker up over his head and kept his head down, pretending to read a magazine.

When he overheard Shane identifying himself as "Mrs. Duncan's kin," he had to intervene. He walked quickly to the "employee only" entrance and put his head inside. Paddy motioned for the receptionist to come to the door. She scowled at him, but Paddy persisted.

"It's urgent, ma'am."

She asked Shane to wait a moment and walked to the door. Paddy whispered, "I know you have no reason to believe me, but these men mean to harm the lady, Christine Duncan, who just came in by ambulance. They want you to release Mrs. Duncan to them, but they are not related to her, and any so-called proof they might provide to you is fraudulent. Her true relatives are that gentleman over by the window and the young lady sitting beside him. Please! You must protect this patient. She is in great danger! These men kidnapped her, and they can be violent!"

The young woman had apparently been trained to respond to such situations. She answered with a simple, "Thank you, sir," and returned to her chair. As she did, her left thumb imperceptibly pressed a silent alarm. Within seconds several armed security officers were present. The receptionist walked over to speak with them privately, and then one officer called Paddy to a corner to talk with him.

Another went over to speak to Shane, who was now standing with his cronies. "Good day, sir! My name is Senior Officer Neil Wood. May I know the reason for your visit to the hospital today?" he said in a singsongy Scottish brogue.

"You may. We are kin of the old, I mean, elderly lady, Mrs. Duncan, who was just brought in by ambulance. We wanted to ask about her condition. She hates hospitals, and we'd like to bring her home as soon as possible."

"You say she's your kin?"

"Aye."

Paddy overheard the questioning. Corryne looked as if she were about to launch from her chair. He was afraid of what might happen, so he boldly interrupted, "Officer, I'm sure we can clear this up if we see some documentation. The patient is Christine Duncan, and these men are not Duncans at all. If you look at their driver's licenses, I'm sure you'll see . . ."

Paddy's voice trailed off as he saw each of the men pull out driver's licenses from their pockets and hold them out. The officer walked down the line of men and read them aloud, "Peter Duncan, Sean Duncan, John Duncan, Matthew Duncan, and Daniel Duncan, Phillip Duncan, and Patrick Duncan." As he finished reading the names, he looked at Paddy and then called him aside.

Paddy was seething. "Sir, those . . . licenses . . . are . . . *fake*! The one over there with the scar on his face? His name is Sean Geelan! He's probably in your criminal database. If you don't believe me, make them go down to the police station and show their birth certificates. They tried to kill her!" Paddy trembled in anger.

Officer Wood spoke in a gentle, steady voice. "You are right, my boy. Now you just leave this to old Neil. They may have the police in their pocket, but security at this hospital is another thing. You rest easy here while I ha'e a bit o' fun w'em." He strode confidently over to Shane and his group. "Well, gentlemen, we can make a day of this down at the police station and charge ye all for falsifying identification, not to mention your true motive for being here, or, ye can leave now, and I can go eat me bangers in peace. What'll it be?" Officer Wood was so cheerful, and the men were so confident in their deception, they appeared not to know whether to hold to their story or leave. Officer

Wood held his billy club high, as though he were about to strike Shane, and boomed, "Shane Geelan, get your scoundrel hide out of my hospital and take these reprobates with ya!"

The entire group rushed out of the waiting room and into the parking lot. Officer Wood didn't leave the sidewalk outside until the men got into their van and left. Paddy breathed a sigh of relief.

A nurse called from the door leading to the treatment rooms, "The family of Bridget Duncan? You can come and see her now, but only for a few minutes."

Paddy looked at Iain and Corryne. "Does she mean Christine? Why did she call her Bridget? Is she talking about a different patient?"

Iain closed his eyes and shook his head. He stood and put a hand on Paddy's shoulder and tried to speak but couldn't. A tear rolled down his cheek as his chin quivered. Corryne just stared at Paddy with a worried look.

Paddy replied, "What? Who is *Bridget* Duncan?" As the words left his lips, suddenly, the realization hit him like a tsunami. The force of it made his knees buckle, and he fell into the nearest chair. He sat, mouth open, staring at Iain and Corryne, saying nothing for what seemed like an eternity. He whispered, "It's not possible. It can't be . . ."

Iain sat beside him, putting his arm around Paddy's shoulders. "It's okay, Son. It has to be a shock. Give yourself time."

Tears began to course down Paddy's cheeks, and he could hardly speak. "But how . . . ?" He was confused, not wanting to believe something that couldn't possibly be true. His emotions were so wrenching; his stomach felt as if it were in knots as he tried to reason how the person they had rescued was, in fact, his mother, Bridget. He distinctly remembered being at her funeral thirteen years ago. Then, he remembered that Papa had told him recently that they had buried an empty casket.

Iain said gently, "Please don't be angry with us for not telling you. We haven't known long ourselves, and we thought it best to focus on rescuing her." Iain took Paddy's hand with both of his and, through his own tearful emotion, whispered, "Today is a day to celebrate, not to be sad, eh?"

Paddy was in shock. All his strength drained out of him as his mind raced. Iain took him into his arms, and Paddy began to cry in muffled sobs that shook him to his core. He cried for all the years she'd missed being home and being loved. He cried for Papa's pain and sadness, and he cried for the love he needed growing up. Most of all, he cried for the horror to which she had been subjected.

Finally, Iain held Paddy at arm's length and said, "She is back with us again, thanks to you and Corryne."

Paddy looked at Corryne. She tried to contain her emotion and looked down when Paddy's eyes met hers. Now Paddy understood why Corryne was so emotional when she'd seen Mama's condition.

"But, how long *have* you known?" asked Paddy, still trying to grasp the truth.

"Not long at all. Your grandpa let us know just as you were finalizing plans for the rescue."

Paddy thought for several moments about all that had transpired. Grandpa must have known while he and Paddy were still in Weymouth that she was alive. He must have hidden the blueprint at Monasterboice on his last trip. *But why would he trust me with something like this?* Then, the last lines of the riddle Grandpa had written in the note hidden at the church came back to him: "In its heart is a treasure sown, with ample pow'r to heal thine own." As he thought about the moment he'd looked at Mama at the Manufactory, the color drained from his face. He whispered, "I didn't even recognize her. My own mother . . ."

Corryne's reply was firm but unusually kind. "You need time, Paddy. You were only five. Just go back there and sit with her and hold her hand. Look in her eyes and think about how happy she'll be to see you." Her voice broke, and she finished haltingly, "We'll wait here and join you in a few minutes."

Paddy's emotion made it hard to speak. "Does Papa know?"

"We've tried to reach him, but he was out. I left a message on the home number and his mobile asking him to call any of us as soon as possible. So, if he calls you, you're the lucky one that gets to tell him," answered Iain with a smile.

Paddy thought for a moment. "This will change everything. Papa can be happy again." He turned and walked slowly through the doors. Fresh tears streamed down his cheeks, but he didn't feel them. He was unaware of most everything, even that his feet were touching the linoleum floor of the hospital corridor. He also didn't realize that he was smiling, even as tears flowed. He was aware of only one thing. His beloved Mama, who was dead, was now alive.

⊗⊗⊗

SHANE GEELAN AND HIS MEN HAD ONLY DRIVEN A FEW BLOCKS AWAY from the hospital after being so unceremoniously routed. Shane dispatched the others to the Manufactory and kept only Max and Bruno with him. Now they were planning their return to the hospital over steaming baskets of fish-and-chips.

"I say we just blast in there and take out anyone who gets in the way," offered Max.

"That's why you have a rap sheet!" snapped Shane in reply. "These things have to be done delicately."

"We could try the ol' delivery trick," suggested Bruno. "You know, pretend one of us is delivering flowers or something."

"Just be quiet and let me think," ordered Shane, still feeling the sting of being forced to leave the hospital. He'd felt confident that the forged identification they made years ago to impersonate Duncans would fool the hospital staff, and he had planned to be back at the Manufactory with Bridget by now. His father had tried calling him four times already, and he'd let it go to voicemail. If Shane didn't return with Bridget tonight, his father would view him as a failure, and he couldn't let that happen . . . again.

He clenched his teeth in anger. They needed a foolproof plan to get her back. Keeping Bridget at the Manufactory was the tangible proof that they were superior to all Duncans.

☙ 19 ☙

JUSTICE

"...THOU KNOWEST NOT THE HEART OF
WOMAN... NOT IN THY FIERCEST BATTLES
HAST THOU DISPLAYED MORE OF THY
VAUNTED COURAGE THAN HAS BEEN SHOWN
BY WOMAN WHEN CALLED UPON TO SUFFER
BY AFFECTION OR DUTY." ~SIR WALTER SCOTT

When Paddy entered the room, he was again struck by how thin and frail Mama was. Anger churned within him toward the SMITs as he saw the IV line, EKG leads, and various machines connected to her that were evidence of her critical condition. He thought for a moment how he would file suit against the SMITs for abuse and neglect, to say nothing of kidnapping—though no punishment could ever atone for the years lost.

What he wanted most was to hear her voice. Paddy sat quietly by her bed, and ever-so-gently took her fragile hand. He had flashes of memories—one here, another there. He remembered when he was little, that she and Papa would take him on walks in the park. They would sing together, and each would take one of his arms and swing him high as they walked along. He was lost in thought and didn't notice she was looking at him and smiling.

He spoke haltingly, "Mama? It's me, Paddy. Um . . . how are you feeling?"

In a soft quavering voice, she replied, "Oh, let me look at you! How did you get to be all grown up?" She reached to put her hand on the side of his face and then asked him to stand. "Look how tall you are! My little boy is all grown up."

They talked for a while before Iain and Corryne joined them. They all reminisced for a little while, avoiding any conversation about the SMITs or the Manufactory, which wasn't easy.

Then, Nurse McCleary instructed that Mama needed to rest. "You'll likely be spending at least a few days with us before going home. You are severely dehydrated. I have some medications for you before you go to sleep. I'll be back in a few minutes, and then we'll move you upstairs."

After Nurse McCleary left, Iain whispered to Bridget, "What did you tell the doctors about how you got in this condition? Did you tell them they held you against your will?"

"I was too weak to answer."

Iain replied, "The SMITs have always retaliated when we've reported them, but the way they treated you!"

"Others have suffered worse. I'll hold off answering them. Ask William. I don't want anyone else harmed."

"Sounds good, my dear. William will know what to do."

An orderly came, and he and Nurse McCleary wheeled Mama upstairs and got her settled in her room. Iain, Corryne, and Paddy followed behind.

"You'll sleep well tonight," noted Iain. "I'll see you tomorrow, sweetie. Corryne and Paddy will stay the night with you."

"Oh, there's no need . . ."

"Ha! A thousand wild horses couldn't tear them away, I'm afraid." Iain didn't mention that they had already tangled with Sean Geelan's men in the emergency room.

"Oh, Iain, does Malcolm know?" asked Bridget.

"We've been trying to reach him. I reached Graham, and he said Malcolm is away at the Sheep and Wool Festival. Unfortunately, he tends to leave his cell phone on silent. We did leave several messages. Don't worry; I'll have you both chatting on the phone together soon. Now, you rest, and soak up all this good care and attention," he said with a smile as he kissed her forehead. "I'll bring you some fresh bread first thing in the morning."

"Oh, your bread, Iain. I'd almost forgotten."

"Now, my girl, it's your recipe, remember? Pinch of cinnamon? Ol'

Iain didn't forget!" He smiled and tapped his temple.

"Thanks ever so much," Bridget whispered. She appeared exhausted from talking. Corryne encouraged her to close her eyes and rest.

"Absolutely not," announced the nurse after hearing that Corryne and Paddy wanted to stay the night with Bridget. "We do not permit visitors after eight o'clock for *any* reason. Patients need their rest, and those are the rules. We do not break the rules on my watch."

A voice boomed from the hallway in a thick, Scottish accent, with exaggerated trilling *r*'s. Officer Wood came around the corner. "Absolutely, never, ever, brrrroken, but occasionally bent, with approval, of course, and this would be one of those bending times, Nurse McCleary." Neil sauntered confidently into the room, giving the nurse a sideways look over the top of his glasses, raising his bushy red eyebrows. "The CEO has decided that Mrs. Duncan needs special protection, so we are going to consider her a celebrity to keep her identity confidential," Neil announced. "Nurse McCleary, I believe you are familiar with the celebrity policy?"

"I wrrrote the policy!" replied Nurse McCleary, mocking Officer Wood's accent.

"Good! Good! Then you know that the rules for visiting do not apply in cases like these. We shall be referring to Mrs. Duncan with the code name 'Zymo,' and we need to delete all references to Bridget Duncan from the computer in all its forms."

Nurse McCleary was visibly upset about Officer Wood taking charge on her ward.

"My officers and I will be guarding the room in shifts around the clock. We have additional officers stationed around the perimeter of the hospital for added safety.

"Corryne and Paddy? Let me find you both a recliner for the room that will let you get some shut-eye tonight."

Nurse McCleary followed Officer Wood down the hall for a few steps, her brow wrinkled into a scowl, and her lips pursed so tightly that she looked like a triggerfish. "Why don't you just take over the entire nursing wing since you have everything so righty tidy!" she called after him in a loud whisper. She stomped off down the hall, the sound of her footsteps muffled by her padded nursing shoes, except for one little squeak coming from her left shoe.

Officer Wood returned with two reclining chairs. "There, now! If there's anything else you need, just ask the officer outside the door. I'm on first shift, and another will replace me at two o'clock."

Paddy and Corryne settled in their recliners, one on either side of Bridget's bed. Paddy knew he wouldn't sleep. He couldn't stop thinking of all that had happened.

⊗⚬⊗

AT TWO FIFTEEN, THERE WAS A NOISE IN THE HALLWAY. PADDY woke and saw that Mama's eyes were open, and she'd pushed herself up on her elbows. There was a muffled yell and then a scraping sound, followed by the closing of a metal door. Paddy rose to lock the door just as three men in ski masks burst into the room. In moments, Corryne, Paddy, and Mama had duct tape over their mouths, and plastic fasteners were tightly binding their hands and feet. The men yanked the IV line from Mama's arm and commanded her to get into a canvas laundry bag, but Mama was too weak. The men grabbed her and shoved her tiny frame into the bag.

Paddy and Corryne were frantically struggling to get free, but they couldn't do anything to help her. One of the men came over and used another fastener to tie Paddy's hands *to his feet*, so he was forced into a bent-over position. Still, he kept his head up, watching Mama.

They pulled the opening of the bag over her head and tightened the drawstrings. Every muscle and nerve in Paddy's body was straining to allow him to keep looking at her, but the SMITs tied the drawstrings and grabbed the bag by the two leather handles on the sides, carrying it out into the hallway.

Paddy began to feel dizzy as if he needed more air. He looked at Corryne, who had managed to get her knife from her jeans pocket and was desperately trying to cut the ties around her wrists. Paddy's heart was pounding so loudly, it sounded audible to him.

Finally, Corryne broke free from the ties that bound her wrists and ankles. She freed Paddy and motioned to him not to speak, in case the

SMITs were still in the hallway. She whispered in his ear, "I think I know where they've gone, but we should split up just in case." They checked the hallway, and Paddy gestured toward the nurses' station as though asking if they should be alerted. Corryne's look indicated a definite "no." Though Paddy didn't understand, this was no time to argue.

"Do you think they took her to the laundry area?"

"I'm not sure, but I have a hunch they took the service elevators, and these closest to the room say they go to the kitchen. Why don't you take the shortcut to the laundry this way? I checked it out earlier."

She led him through a door marked "Staff Only," which had a large laundry chute on one wall. Paddy didn't hesitate. He jumped in, hoping the added momentum would help him reach the bottom more quickly. He hadn't quite thought through the effect of falling so far in a stainless-steel tube when you are *not* a sack of laundry. He landed with a thud in a huge bin of laundry bags, with a bewildered laundry worker staring at him. "Sorry, I guess that wasn't the elevator. Have you seen three men carrying a laundry bag?" The worker shook his head no. Paddy jumped from the laundry bin and headed toward the kitchen, looking for any sign of the SMITs.

MAX KICKED THE LAUNDRY BAG AS THEY WENT DOWN IN THE service elevator. "That was a stupid thing you did, letting those idiots bring you here."

"Shut up! Don't talk to her!" rebuked Bruno.

"I can't believe you two are the best my father can come up with to help me," snapped Shane. "Here's how it's going to go down. We'll walk through the kitchen to the exit and then make our way to the van. Take your masks off now. We don't want to look like kidnappers. Just pretend we are the new laundry service, and we got lost on our first nightly pickup. Here we are."

The elevator doors opened, and the three stepped out. They were immediately face-to-face with the kitchen's night supervisor, Axel. He stood six feet, eight inches tall and weighed 269 pounds. He was wearing jeans and a T-shirt that was stretched tight across his bulging chest and arm muscles, and he had on an apron covered in blood from cutting meat. A tattoo on his right forearm read, "Axel" above a hand holding a large meat cleaver. Another tattoo on his left arm read, "Pump iron, or die." He had a receding hairline, but his remaining long gray hair was thick and tied back in a braid. A bolt pierced his right earlobe, and he had a long scar from his right temple to his chin. He looked suspiciously through squinted eyes at the three men. Since Axel blocked the only exit, they all just stood staring at each other.

"May I help you?" Axel asked gruffly. Just as he spoke, an old familiar feeling of danger set his senses on edge, and none too soon. Out of the corner of one eye, he saw Shane slowly reach inside his coat, while simultaneously he saw the glint of a knife as Bruno pulled one from a leather sheath at his waist. Axel pivoted on one foot and reached up to where a large granite cutting board was hanging on the wall, and he scooped a handful of knives into his enormous hand just before ducking behind a food preparation table.

He yelled for his team to evacuate the kitchen with one code word, and in seconds, his staff scattered to a safe area to notify the authorities. From where he was crouched, Axel was horrified to see that the laundry bag was moving slightly. He remembered that the hospital had a patient whose identity was protected, and he immediately realized this was a kidnapping.

Shane, Bruno, and Max left the bag for a moment when they realized that Axel was armed, and they hid behind some nearby shelves stacked with baking supplies. As they did, a large tin of baking powder fell off a shelf and spilled all over the tile floor.

Axel's brow furrowed as he set his jaw, and his body tensed. He put the rope handle of the cutting board around his neck as a makeshift shield, freeing each hand to hold a cleaver. The other knives he put into the large pocket of his apron. He uttered a low growl that rose in volume to a roar as he jumped on top of a stainless-steel table. His heavy boots made a sound like thunder as he jumped from one table to the next, moving closer to where the men were hiding. His only thought was to position himself between the intruders and the patient.

At that very same moment, the service elevator doors opened, and

Corryne stood warily looking out, not knowing what to expect. She saw the bag with Bridget lying about five feet from the elevator. Then she saw Axel with a knife in each hand. Corryne realized that he must be trying to defend Bridget, which meant that Shane and his men must be nearby. She put her hand up to hold the elevator doors open so she could pull the laundry bag back inside. Just as she was about to reach for the bag, Bruno swung his body from around the corner, pushing his face into hers. She recognized him from the Manufactory, and all the courage she had melted away.

"You!" He stabbed her hand with his huge knife. It seemed to Corryne as if everything happened in slow motion. The blade pierced the top of her hand and went all the way through into the crack where the elevator door was recessed. The pain burned through her and over-flowed in a loud, anguish-filled scream.

When Axel saw Corryne attacked, he realized she wasn't party to the kidnapping. He threw one of his cleavers at Bruno, cutting off his ear and a large section of his cheek. Bruno ran screaming toward the exit door and out to the loading dock, a trail of blood following behind him. Shane remained where he was. It was now two against two, and Corryne was wounded.

Shane fired his gun haphazardly at the kitchen lights, apparently oblivious to the fact that darkness only made his position more precarious.

Corryne worked the knife free and wrapped her hand tightly in a dish towel. She was losing blood quickly and bent over with pain. Axel motioned to Corryne to try to pull the laundry bag into the elevator and leave.

She gently eased the bag into the elevator with her uninjured hand and pushed the button for the door to close. Just before the doors closed, Paddy came rushing in from a side hallway, having made his way to the kitchen. He caught a glimpse of Corryne and shouted, "Did you find Mama?"

Shane caught sight of Paddy and jumped out from where he was hiding, grabbing Paddy from behind, placing his arm tightly around his throat. Then he put his gun to Paddy's head. From where Shane was standing, he couldn't see that Corryne had taken Bridget. He pushed

Paddy toward Axel and growled, "Either we are going to leave here with that bag, or lots of people will get hurt. What'll it be, huh?"

There was a standoff for almost a full minute. Paddy kept hearing Grandpa's voice, as he had so many times when a problem stumped him, "Make a plan, and step-by-step, you'll solve it." Axel noticed Paddy's eyes. Paddy was repeatedly looking downward toward his hand and then back up at Axel. Paddy's hand was slowly making the sign of one, two, three with his fingers. On three, Paddy jammed his elbow into Shane's side, breaking his hold, and simultaneously ducked down away from the gun and out of Shane's grip.

Shane fired his gun, and the bullet shattered a pastry case. Axel defended himself and Paddy with the only weapon he had and threw his cleaver at Shane. It landed deeply embedded in the left side of Shane's chest. Shane staggered and fell backward onto a table, dropping the gun and gasping loudly for breath. His expression seemed almost to convey surprise that this might be his end. He tried to pull the cleaver with both hands as if he thought he might be able to remove it. Max emerged slowly from his hiding place, took one look at Shane, turned, and ran out the exit.

Paddy stared at Shane's body with wide eyes, his heart pounding. He had never seen anyone killed before.

Axel's hands were shaking as he called the emergency room. "We need a crash cart to the kitchen. Hurry!" There was no way that anyone could live with a blade that size straight into the heart. The emergency room staff entered the kitchen and assessed Shane as deceased within moments.

Axel then called the police. "Sir, please send a unit to the hospital kitchen. This is the supervisor, Axel. I didn't mean to, but I have killed someone. Please come right away. I'll be waiting for you." Axel looked at Paddy. "No sense delaying it."

"But it was self-defense! They were kidnapping my mom. You saved my life!"

Axel replied, "Or maybe you saved mine. That was some quick thinking you did. Hey, you better go make sure your mom is okay."

"I'll be upstairs if anyone needs to talk to me." He ran to the elevator and realized he wasn't sure where Corryne had taken Mama.

He texted her with shaking hands and received the reply, "26." As the elevator rose, adrenaline flooded Paddy's brain, making his thoughts tumble over and over. One moment he was sure they would blame him as well as Axel for Shane's death, and the next, he thought of Sean Geelan and what terrible fury he would now unleash on them all now that his son was dead.

❧

WHEN CORRYNE DRAGGED THE LAUNDRY BAG WITH BRIDGET back inside the elevator, she took her to the twenty-sixth floor to get as far away from Shane and his men as she could. When the elevator doors opened, the police were waiting and immediately radioed their counterparts stationed at elevators on every other level that they had recovered Zymo. The nurses immediately began paging doctors for Bridget. She was surrounded by nurses and aides checking her vital signs, reconnecting her IV, and trying to assess what had happened.

In the commotion, Corryne went to a corner and slumped down onto the floor. The towel was now completely soaked in blood, and a pool was forming beneath it. It was a few minutes before the nurse at the desk saw the pool of blood growing under her hand and shouted for assistance. The medical staff rushed Corryne into surgery.

Security officers immediately stopped Paddy when he arrived on the twenty-sixth floor.

He put his hands up. "It was self-defense! I swear!"

"Who are you? Show some identification!" barked an officer. Just then, Officer Wood came from the hallway, where he had been checking on Bridget.

"Paddy, my boy! Where have you been? It's all right, gentlemen. Paddy here is Zymo's son!" Officer Wood led Paddy to Mama's room, which was accessible only through three guarded and locked doors.

❧

SEVERAL HOURS LATER, CORRYNE CAME OUT OF SURGERY. MAX'S large knife had cut a two-inch gash through the middle of her hand, severing nerves and blood vessels and fracturing a bone. They placed Corryne in the same room with Bridget and brought in cots for Iain and Paddy to stay the night.

Before Officer Wood left, Paddy asked, "This will sound strange, but I have reason to believe that members of my extended family may be in danger from those men who tried to kidnap my mom. Is there anyone you know who could go check on them?"

Officer Wood was so outraged by the fact that, as he put it, "the ranks were breached" by what had happened to Bridget and Corryne, that he put his hands on Paddy's shoulders and announced, "I'll take care of that perrrsonally."

Paddy sent a text to Uncle Douglass asking if they'd evacuated or if they were still at the Base. He replied, "Yes, we are all still here. We're anxious to know what happened."

"Well, we have a lot to tell you, but my mom is safe." He fought tears as he typed the words. "Officer Wood, from security here at the hospital, is sending an officer to watch the cottage tonight, so don't be alarmed if you see someone."

Later, Paddy learned that Officer Wood had called the entire Thistle o' the Wood Scottish Pipe and Drum Corps, ex-military friends, and asked them to camp out on Iain's lawn.

Kirk later told Paddy that the crew used earplugs to sleep because the Corps practiced their repertoire all night long. "But, I don't think a SMIT would have dared come on the property. You should see the size of some of these guys!"

In the morning, they all woke to Nurse McCleary's knock at seven thirty. "Time for breakfast and a surprise," she announced. A cart rolled in, pushed by none other than Axel himself.

Paddy was so surprised, he practically shouted, "Mama, this is the man that saved us!"

The footage of the security camera completely exonerated Axel. He was dubbed the hospital hero, and was rewarded with a bonus and complete freedom to cook whatever he wanted for "Zymo and her family." When he entered the room, he checked with Corryne to be sure she was all right.

She replied her usual, "Right as rain."

Then, he lowered himself onto his knees so Bridget wouldn't have to look up at him. He ever-so-gently cupped her hand in both of his and asked, "Are you feeling all right, ma'am?" It was the most tender sight, seeing Axel holding Bridget's hand as tenderly as if it were the petal of a rose.

Bridget placed her other hand on top of his. "I am doing well, thanks to you! You risked your life for all of us yesterday. Words are not enough to express our gratitude."

Axel replied, "Aww, well, it was the right thing to do. Now, I have a little breakfast here for you all." He had made four different breakfasts so that everyone could choose. Each was so sumptuous that they all shared everything.

The police came by several times during the week, asking questions about Bridget's condition and who was responsible. Iain still hadn't heard anything from William as to how much they should say. Bridget tried to stall because she knew that as much as everyone wanted her to tell the police all the horrific acts the SMITs had committed, the welfare of the remaining Duncans still held inside the Manufactory was paramount.

Nurse McCleary guided Bridget through signing the discharge paperwork.

"Almost finished?" asked Paddy.

"I am. This sweet lady is such a great help. She's become a good friend." Bridget reached out and squeezed Nurse McCleary's hand.

Iain and Paddy gathered up all the cards and flowers Bridget and Corryne had received, when one of the nursing assistants entered with a dozen brilliant white roses. "Delivery for you, ma'am."

"Oh, will you look at those. My favorites." Bridget opened the note, and her smile faded. She looked up at Paddy. "Son, would you mind finding me a pencil and paper?" Paddy was curious to read the note but went to ask the nurses for what Mama needed. He returned, and she began to jot down letters into a grid so quickly he could scarcely believe his eyes. The note was in code, and to Paddy's utter amazement, she appeared to be deciphering the code without any key. A couple of minutes later, she stopped and sighed.

"Paddy, would you mind calling Officer Ashe back? He was just here." She answered Paddy's inquisitive look with, "It's okay. It's just a note from your grandpa."

It didn't take long for Paddy to locate Officer Ashe. When he arrived, Bridget said, "I'm so sorry, Officer Ashe, but some details have finally come back to me. Is it possible that through all this, I had amnesia of some kind?"

"It's entirely possible. Just tell me what you clearly remember." Bridget asked that Paddy close the door. "Paddy, maybe you and Corryne should wait outside?"

Corryne started to leave, and Paddy replied, "I want to hear it. I want to know what they did. I'm not afraid of them, Mama." Mama hesitated and then nodded her agreement for them both to stay.

She told the officer everything: how they had kidnapped her, how they never let her contact her family, and how she worked twelve-hour days and was constantly harassed—even in the middle of the night. She explained that when she got sick, they left her in the clinic building for days with no food and with no one tending to her. She told how she had to wash her bedding and clothing in the bathroom sink if she wanted them cleaned.

Paddy was silent, but his agony at hearing these details was evident. At one point, he got up and went and stood in the corner of the room and cried silently, his grief, pain, and rage seeking an outlet. *They stole her from me!* He realized he needed to process this at another time. He didn't want to disturb Mama lest she stop telling the details to the officer.

Paddy realized that Grandpa must have told Mama in the message to tell the police the details, but he wondered what had changed. Several times Corryne and Paddy looked at each other, both wondering whether Mama's confession would put the other Duncans in jeopardy. Corryne suddenly began texting frantically, and Paddy assumed she was asking Grandpa what happened.

Officer Ashe asked all his questions with stoic professionalism, but from time to time, it was evident that he was taken aback by what he was hearing. When he finished, he placed his hand on Bridget's. "It's okay that you were afraid to tell it. I can't begin to imagine what that must have been like to suffer that many years. You've done the right thing today. You've done a courageous thing." Mama dropped her head, and for the first time in all the ordeal, Paddy saw her eyes fill with tears. She closed her eyes, more tears spilling freely down her cheeks onto the pin tucks of the pretty floral-print dress Iain had bought for her.

She'd remained silent and obedient to her captors for the sole reason of protecting her family and other Duncans all these years. For now, there seemed nothing more right than being able to report what had happened, in the hope of finding justice.

The officer left and said he would provide an escort as soon as Bridget and Corryne were packed and ready to go. They all made their way to the elevator and down to the lobby, led by Officer Wood. Just as they were exiting the front doors, Bridget asked, "Could you please wait a moment?" as she turned her head back toward the elevators.

"What is it, Mama?" asked Paddy. Several seconds passed, and finally, the elevator opened. Axel emerged, smiling, with a wrapped parcel of special treats he'd made especially for them all.

Bridget laughed. "I was so hoping I'd get to see you before we left. Now you take good care of yourself!"

Axel smiled, but his eyes brimmed with tears. "I sure will. You take care too, Mama!" He gave a thumbs-up to Paddy and Corryne. Mama asked Iain for a white rose from the bouquet William had sent, and she gave it to Axel.

Taking his big hand in both of hers, she answered softly, "I will never forget you. You remember that! If you ever want to come to visit us in America, you contact Iain here."

Axel pursed his lips together to keep his emotions in check and stepped back and waved.

Officer Ashe had a caravan of nine police cruisers waiting. Paddy, Corryne, Bridget, and Iain were each placed in different vehicles in the middle of the group. Paddy asked an officer, "Are you sure we need all this?"

"Just following orders. Our captain is taking this case very seriously."

The trip home was uneventful except that Officer Ashe confided in Paddy that the police and a SWAT team would be storming the

Manufactory that afternoon to take the SMITs into custody. He explained they had enough evidence, but they would be questioning the workers to corroborate the information they had. He recommended that they all remain home at Iain's cottage for the remainder of the day.

"Sir, no offense, but rumor has it that Sean Geelan had paid the police to look the other way if they received complaints about the Manufactory. I appreciate the police helping us, but is there a risk of any officers tipping off the Geelans? I don't mean any offense. It's just what I've heard."

"No offense taken. The emergency room is required to report cases of abuse. When they provided pictures of your mom's condition, and she provided corroboration of what happened, well, the short answer is that as of right now, those officers are no longer with the Department. In fact, they'll never work on the force again. Suffice it to say that some top brass are pretty upset that this has been going on under our noses for this long."

◈

THE BEST PART OF ARRIVING AT IAIN'S WAS WATCHING EVERYONE'S faces light up when they saw Bridget. Even younger members of the crew were joyful, even though they only knew her from pictures. It took ten minutes to get inside.

A surprise awaited Paddy when he walked into the kitchen, for sitting there, larger than life, was Grandpa himself. He gave Paddy a giant bear hug.

"Grandpa!" Paddy yelled as he bounded over to hug him. "You're here! What are you doing hiding inside?"

"I didn't want to steal any of the welcome away from your mama!" He held Paddy at arm's length, looking him in the eyes. "I was sure you could do it. I knew it all along. I never doubted for one minute."

"If it wasn't for Corryne . . ."

"She's a great one to have on your team, isn't she?"

To Paddy, the whole ordeal had seemed, at best, haphazard, and at worst, dangerous to the point of near failure. It hadn't quite sunk in yet that their plan had succeeded, but the thought was certainly a welcome one.

Grandpa turned to Bridget and carefully hugged her tiny frame. He helped her to a comfortable chair in the living room by the fire. "William, look at you! You haven't aged a day."

"Ho! My dear, I wish I felt that way!"

Paddy leaned over to Corryne and asked, "Do you think Ashok got out before the police got there?"

"I texted him to get out fast when we were in the hospital and your mom started telling the officer what happened. I thought they might send police to check it out if they could find any honest ones."

"Officer Ashe told me that they would be sending a SWAT team out this afternoon. He asked that we all stay here today. He also told me that all those officers who were being paid by Sean Geelan are out of a job. When they saw pictures of Mama's condition, they put two and two together. I still don't know how they figured out that some of the officers were protecting the SMITs."

Corryne was speechless. She just looked at Paddy and smiled and sighed. "Gosh, I wonder if we'll get a bit of rest from them for a while. Then again, with Shane dead, it could get worse."

Iain laid out a feast of shepherd's pie, hot bread and butter, and enough side dishes to look like a meal competing for a prize at the annual fair. Everyone made a plate and found a place to sit and eat since the kitchen table couldn't fit everyone. Iain set out five different pies and the biggest carrot cake Paddy had ever seen. It was a feast worthy of the celebration.

Corryne showed Paddy her phone. "Look, Ashok just texted me. He says, 'Home safe. Many rats in cage . . . but not all. Be careful.'"

"You need to tell Grandpa," answered Paddy.

"I know. I'm just waiting for the right time. I want to find a way to meet up with Ashok and get more details if I can."

"Corryne, the officer said not to leave here today, and if that text refers to the SMITs as rats, I think it means some escaped the police. Just talk to Grandpa."

Kirsty said to Paddy, "I haven't seen Luke for over an hour. Have you?"

Paddy replied, "No, I haven't either. That's weird. Wait, isn't that his car that just drove up? Someone is with him."

Luke had a smile from ear to ear as he came in the door. "Everyone, I found these gentlemen on the road, making their way here on foot." One by one, three men dressed in ragged, dirty clothes filed into the living room. Bridget put her hand over her mouth.

"What is it, Mama?"

"They are from the Manufactory."

William recognized the three men and rushed over to hug each one. "Everyone," he announced, "this is Klaus Donnachaidh, our portal for Poland, and this is Lucas Duncan, a key contact of mine from France and assistant portal there. Last, but not in any way least, is Richard Falmouth, a former SMIT who has devoted himself to our cause for many years. Welcome home, gentlemen!"

"Oh my gosh, Paddy! It's the other three!" whispered Corryne.

Luke explained, "Yeah, so I was out trying to find some flowers for Mrs. Duncan's homecoming, and I guess I just got curious. I drove by the Manufactory and what a sight! SMITs lined up with their hands against the wall, being arrested by the police. One officer opened the gate and let all the workers go. I saw these three leaving on foot, so I asked if they needed a lift. Do you know what they asked me? They wanted to know if I knew Iain Duncan!" Everyone laughed.

Mama noted with a sadness in her voice, "I recognize you all from the Manufactory. I'm sorry, but I never knew you were our tailors."

Corryne whispered to Paddy, "That's because the Geelans never let Duncans speak to one another."

"I'm so sorry about what happened to you, Corryne. It must have been terrible," replied Paddy.

"Thanks. You know, I heard that they tortured Richard Falmouth for two years straight because of his dedication to us. I never saw him when I was there. I thought he was dead."

"Well, the SMITs are in jail now," added Paddy.

"But, for how long? Sorry, it's hard for me to believe it will ever be over."

Bridget looked up at Iain, her eyes speaking her request. Iain put up his hand. "No need to ask, my dear." He assigned a member of the crew to each of the tailors to help them get cleaned up, to find clean clothes, and to phone their families.

The best part of the day was that Papa finally returned Iain's call. Everyone gathered around, listening as Iain put the call on speaker. He tried to prepare him gently. "Malcolm, if you had one wish, just one thing that you could have on this earth, what would it be?"

"That's an odd question. Are you feeling all right, Iain?" Tears filled Mama's eyes as she heard his voice.

"Come on, Malcolm; it's an easy question."

"Well, you know there's only one thing in the whole universe I would want; that would be to see my Bridget again." Every eye in the room glistened. Someone handed Mama a handkerchief. She closed her eyes as if trying hard to hold on to her emotions.

Iain and William were both worried that the news might be too much for Papa since his heart had grown much weaker in recent years. There was no way to ease into it more gently, so Iain spoke in a serious tone.

"Malcolm, we all thought Bridget was gone. We buried an empty coffin. But all this time she has been at the Manufactory. William found out she was there, and Paddy and Corryne rescued her."

He paused, and it seemed like an eternity before Malcolm responded haltingly, "Iain, Iain, y-you would never play a joke on me like this." His voice was trembling, and Paddy's heart ached for all the years Papa had spent without her. Corryne put her arm around Paddy's shoulders to steady him. Seconds felt like minutes, and finally, Malcolm answered with hesitation, "Can it be true?"

Before handing the phone to Mama, Iain reassured him. "Malcolm, you are right, I would never joke about that. And yes, it is true, and she is sitting right here in my living room waiting to talk with you. Malcolm, all is as it should be again, and we will have her home with you very soon." Muffled sobs could be heard from the speaker as Iain handed the phone to Bridget and then turned off the speaker so they could talk privately. Everyone went either downstairs or out into the backyard to give Mama privacy. They were all so overcome that no one could speak.

Mama began, "Sweetheart? I have missed you so! I'll be home

soon." She could only hear Malcolm crying. "Now, you rest, dear, and I'll call you tomorrow, and we'll talk some more. I know this is so hard over the phone. I never thought I would hear your voice again. I love you, sweetheart. I love you so."

"Oh my . . . Bridget, my Bridget! It's you!" Malcolm's voice was trembling.

"Yes!" She chuckled. "It's me, and it's all because of William and Paddy and Corryne, with a lot of help from Iain, I'm sure."

"Oh! Bridget! My Bridget! Oh, I cannot wait to see you. Are you all right? You tell William to hurry up and get you home!"

"I'm okay, and I expect I'll be home very soon. How are Clara and Graham?"

"They are just fine. Oh! They are not going to believe me when I tell them the news!" The call ended with promises to call first thing in the morning.

Paddy smiled at the thought that back home in Weymouth, Papa had probably already closed the shop, and the entire house would be all abuzz with preparations for Mama's homecoming.

<hr />

"WILLIAM, COULD YOU COME DOWNSTAIRS FOR A MOMENT? CORRYNE and I need to chat with you," called Douglass through the doorway that led downstairs. Grandpa waved for Paddy to come along, and Douglass led the way to the Athenaeum.

"Coffee?" offered Corryne as they all sat down.

"Love some," answered William and Paddy simultaneously.

Douglass began, "We received some unusual information regarding what happened today at the Manufactory after the police arrived. They arrested ten of the SMITs, but they didn't get all of them."

Corryne added, "While we were still at the hospital, I texted Ashok, the worker who helped us by setting the explosives, and told him to get out before the police arrived. He later sent me a cryptic message that read, 'Home safe. Many rats in cage . . . but not all. Be careful.'"

Douglass continued, "Depending on who did not get picked up by the police, I have some serious concerns about our safety, especially with what happened to Shane. And, as long as Bridget is here . . ."

William replied, "I'm not comfortable with the Base remaining here. We can't just sit here thinking there will be no retaliation. Douglass, please draw up a plan to move to Rebekah's in Tullyallen as soon as possible. Let her know it's only temporary—six months or so, until things quiet down."

William turned to Corryne. "Do you think Ashok may know more than what was in his text?"

Corryne shrugged. "I don't know. Do you want me to try to make contact with him?"

"Do you trust him?" asked William.

"Implicitly," replied Corryne.

"Why?" asked William.

"He looked out for me when I was captive there. He brought food to me when he saw that they were limiting my rations. When I asked him to set the bombs, he agreed, and he welcomed me in his home to meet his wife and family." Corryne got frustrated, realizing that nothing she offered lent itself to be a reason to trust Ashok per se. "I can't tell you in words why I trust him. It's a gut feeling."

"I appreciate your honesty, sweetheart. My concern is that he is, or at least was, an officer of the Indian Intelligence Bureau."

Corryne's eyes grew wide. "Are you sure?"

"He worked in a unit specifically tasked with monitoring terrorist activity through coded radio broadcasts about ten years ago. It could be just a job he held when he lived there, or it could be he's here on some assignment. I don't know, but I'm sure it's him. When we set up our portal in Jaipur, we had to get our radio license, and he came to the site to see our setup."

"But . . . how do you know it's the same person?" asked Corryne.

"I never forget a face. I remember he had a healthy suspicion that we were not simply amateur radio operators. That may mean he has good instincts, or it may mean we were under surveillance. Then again, that was many years ago."

"He's a good man. I can easily see him just wanting to protect his country that way," defended Corryne.

"Try to make contact with him and see if he knows anything more. Just take care not to be seen."

"Yessir, I'll be careful."

Corryne went upstairs and then slipped quietly outside, her breath making smokelike clouds in the moonlight as she pushed her motorcycle away from the cottage so she wouldn't make noise. She knew William didn't expect her to go out tonight, especially when it wasn't safe, but she wouldn't be able to sleep unless she tried to contact Ashok.

"Evening, Miss Corryne," greeted Ernie, as he tipped his cap. He was just inside the fence of the pasture across the lane. "Just came out to fetch ol' Betsy here. She won't come in with the others anymore, poor gal. It's her bum leg. Plus, she knows I'll fetch and carry her in every night. Well, I'll bid you a good night."

"Good night, Ernie. Take good care of Betsy. You know she's my favorite."

"Yes, ma'am, I know. Hard not to like sweet Betsy."

Corryne started her motorcycle gingerly, trying to avoid the pain in her hand, and rode to the edge of Ashok's neighborhood. She sent him a text that read, "Okay to come over to talk tonight?"

A message came right back. "Yes."

Corryne responded, "Back door." She pushed her motorcycle into a hedge and went to the back door and knocked.

Naseema answered. Corryne asked if they could talk in the dining room, where there were no windows. Then, she explained what had happened at the hospital.

"Oh my! Shane Geelan was killed?" asked Ashok in disbelief.

"Yes, one of the hospital employees defended us. Shane was shooting, and he had Max and Bruno with him. It was pretty amazing that the rest of us made it out alive."

"What happened to your hand?" asked Naseema.

"Bruno put his knife through it," she replied matter-of-factly.

"You must have needed surgery!"

"Yes."

"Thank goodness you and your friends are all right! That must have been a terrifying ordeal," said Naseema, astounded.

Ashok added, "I'm so happy that you got your friend out of the Manufactory. The thought that they had been holding her there, keeping her from her family all those years; there are just no words . . ."

"Is her condition stable now?" asked Naseema.

"Yes, thank you. She is recovering slowly and gaining strength."

"Ashok, I hope you realize that we could never have done this without you. Thank you for your courage." Corryne felt herself getting choked up and quickly changed the subject. "But what about your job? They've shut the Manufactory down, right?"

"Yes. I don't know when it will reopen, but it's okay. Naseema and I already agreed that even if they open again, I cannot work for such people. With what you have told me and what I have seen for myself, working there would be like being part of a criminal enterprise. I cannot continue there. Truthfully, I feel free, like a weight has lifted off my shoulders."

"Ashok, your message made it sound like some did not get arrested. Do you know why?"

"Tunnels. They escaped through the tunnels. I saw Shane Geelan move a bookcase once and descend a hidden staircase. I knew there was at least a room or basement beneath the main building. Because I was in charge of inventory, I had access to different buildings and sections of the main factory where other workers did not go. My training in the Intelligence Bureau in my country taught me many things, and I recognized the false walls that covered the access doors. There are five in all. One day, when the Geelans were out, I opened one and found that it led into a tunnel. I went through the tunnel, and it ended in the back of a poor workman's house, not far away. He was so afraid when he saw me; he just kept saying, 'I keep the tunnel clean! I do the work for the money you give me. I do!' It was clear that Sean paid him to keep the tunnel clear of debris, and in exchange, the Geelans and their cohorts had a temporary safe house in case they needed to escape. I saw several other entrance points, so I deduced there could be other tunnels."

"They are like rats," added Corryne.

"When I got your page that the police were coming, I went home and got my binoculars and then drove to the top of the hill overlooking the Manufactory to a place where I could see the whole compound from above. The police stormed in, and they lined up the supervisors against the wall and put them in handcuffs. Some tried to pretend they were workers, but the tailors pointed out the Geelans, Warwicks, and Falmouths for the police to arrest. Everyone else was released, and the police put a chain and lock on the gate. Then I watched to see if there was movement around where I thought the other tunnels might end. Since I knew where one ended, I assumed the others might be about the same length. Then, I saw a vehicle make a circuit to three nearby houses and then head toward downtown Dublin, so I decided to follow at a distance. I could see five people in the car, and one of them was clearly Sean Geelan. I followed them to the pier, where they boarded the ferry going to the Isle of Man."

"That was brave!" Corryne was shocked that Ashok had so much information.

"Or foolish," chided Naseema, shaking her head. "Corryne, would you like some tea?"

"Oh, no, thank you. I have to be going."

"If you don't mind my asking, how long have these people troubled your family?" asked Naseema.

"It all started in Scotland in 1774. They tried to steal our reputation by claiming their work was performed by Duncan tailors." Corryne sighed. Whenever she spoke of it, she felt an ache in her heart.

Naseema's eyes narrowed, and she cocked her head to the side as if she had not heard correctly. "Since 1774? You can't be serious."

Corryne forced a weak smile. "I'm sorry, I have to be going. It's not safe for you if I stay here."

"Please take care of yourself," Naseema said as she hugged Corryne.

"And let us know if we can do anything," offered Ashok.

"You have done so much already. If you find yourself in danger, please call or text me, and either I or someone from my family will try to come and help. Take care." She turned as she was leaving. "I don't want to alarm you, but until things calm down, please keep your children close, very close. It may not be a good idea for them to play alone outside for a while."

❧ 20 ❧

PASSAGED

"I BEG YOU TAKE COURAGE; THE BRAVE SOUL
CAN MEND EVEN DISASTER."
-CATHERINE THE GREAT

The next morning was unusually warm for so late in the fall, and the dew on the pasture reflected sunlight like a million tiny stars. Ernie was working Jennah, practicing for a herding competition.

Paddy had watched him for several mornings. "Do you think the sheep really know their names?"

"No doubt about it," mused Iain as he puffed lightly on his pipe. "I've watched him call them out one at a time from a group. Darn things are more like dogs than sheep. If there was ever a sheep whisperer, it's Ernie. Most gentle soul on the earth. Those sheep trust him."

"Do you suppose he's content? I mean, does he like being a shepherd?" asked Paddy, wondering aloud.

"I'd wager you'd get the best answer if you asked the sheep," replied Iain, a thin line of smoke from his pipe making a circle above his head.

William and Bridget emerged from the two separate hallways simultaneously. "Good morning, Bridget! You are up bright and early. Sit down, and let me get you some tea," offered William cheerfully as he pulled out a chair from the kitchen table for her. "How about one of Susanna's ginger scones?"

"Oh, that would be lovely. Thank you."

Corryne added, "Mom made them fresh this morning."

"My goodness, and she's already downstairs working? Your mom was always such a hard worker," replied Bridget with a smile.

"I only wish she wasn't such an early riser. Now she's got me waking up by five o'clock."

"'Early to bed, early to rise,'" Iain quipped.

"Corryne, could you call downstairs for everyone to come up for a quick stand-up meeting?" asked William. "I promise it won't be more than five minutes."

In a few minutes, everyone was assembled in the kitchen, with some spilling into the living room. They lowered the blinds as a precaution, so no one could see that so many people were there.

William began, "Sorry to interrupt; I'll make this short. The latest report on the Manufactory is that the police closed it down. We have reason to believe that the Geelans and other supervisors escaped and took the ferry to the Isle of Man. We have lookouts stationed on the island and some at the ferry dock. At some point, they will regroup, but we don't know where or when. I'm also concerned about the fact that Shane is dead, and they will likely retaliate at some point. I don't say this to scare anyone; I just want you to know the whole situation. This is a time for cool heads, steadiness, and not taking any chances.

"This isn't the first time something like this has happened, where we've had to consider moving operations away for a time, and we think it's wise to do so again. So, today, we will move the contents of the Base to Rebekah's in Tullyallen. We have a contingency plan to move it back to Dundee, if necessary. Still, I want to avoid that if possible because that would mean our radios would be down for several days, and I don't know how many of you would be able to relocate that far away.

"Now, I know being in Tullyallen will be hard because your homes are here. For those of you who weren't here when we moved last time, suffice it to say that when I built the basement at Rebekah's, I made it a bit larger than the one here. There are some small rooms with bunk beds, so you may choose to stay there and not make the commute every day. If you do commute, don't travel alone. We'll begin packing immediately. Our portals are depending on us. For that reason, we need to be quick, but methodical so that when we get to Rebekah's, we can unpack and set up with minimal downtime."

Mira, Iain's daughter, asked, "Dad, do I stay at Aunt Rebekah's or come back home?"

"Take your things and stay there, sweetie. I don't want you driving back here. This place is now probably a target."

William continued, "Corryne has brought an ample supply of boxes and tape in her van outside. I'd prefer that no more than four people at a time are outside loading up the cars. If you hear anything suspicious, come back inside and engage full lockdown procedures. We've all drilled many times, but just a reminder, the doors going downstairs and at the end of the tunnels are to be double locked. Hopefully, we won't be interrupted.

"Luke, Clyde, Gavin, and Kirk, you'll take down the radio antennas, and the rest of us will load boxes. Douglass, you'll need to get on the radio before they dismantle everything and contact each portal. Let them know they'll have radio silence for about twenty hours or so. Tell them also to begin precaution protocols. We have no idea what the SMITs may try next."

Paddy looked at Grandpa. "How can I help?"

"Ah, you and Corryne can help pack, but when we leave, you both will transport Bridget. Until Bridget gets the all-clear from Rebekah, we can't risk passaging her back in her weakened condition. Hopefully, it will be soon," he added as he smiled at Bridget.

"I understand, William. It's enough for now that I can speak to Malcolm by phone every day and write to him."

"I know this is a bit unusual, but I've asked our friend Neil Wood to come along with his piper friends and accompany us to Tullyallen." The quizzical looks made William put up his hand. "Let me explain. They are coming with us for some added protection. They may be a pipe-and-drum corps, but they are also members of a private militia, and all of them are former military. Also, most of their members are champions of the Scottish games. I would venture that a SMIT wouldn't want to tangle with them."

Kirk raised his hand. "Will they be armed?"

"I didn't ask, and I don't want to know, but I wouldn't be surprised." William looked at the faces around him. There was more uncertainty than confidence in their expressions. "I'll grant you, it's not the Royal Regiment of Scotland, but we don't exactly have a cause we can shout from the rooftops, now do we? Neil and his friends will remain in their vehicles, and they won't get out unless there is a need."

"How many vehicles will they have?" asked Paddy.

"Four. One van in front and one in back of each of our two groups. Corryne, Paddy, and Bridget will be in one group with two other cars driven by Clyde and Susanna, and the second group will be the remainder of the vehicles. Each group will go by a different route."

"What about Uncle Iain?" asked Paddy.

"Iain will secure the covers that remain here by passaging to our safe house in Dundee. We cannot risk trying to transport them locally, but there are three exceptions. The Dublin cover will go with Douglass to Tullyallen. Iain will take its match to Dundee, so that he can return to Rebekah's later. Paddy, you will take the covers for Virginia and Weymouth . . ."

"The Weymouth cover isn't here, Grandpa."

"It is now. I sent for it through our couriers. So, should anything go wrong, Paddy, you'll have to passage yourself and Bridget home to Weymouth early, and we'll have to pray that she makes the trip okay. But that is only in case of an emergency. You'll also take the cover to Virginia in case you both get separated, and you have to passage Bridget to Weymouth ahead of you. Then you can follow later to Martin's in Virginia and make your way home by bus. Now, if there are no more questions, we've got a busy day ahead of us."

The thought of passaging again made Paddy feel uneasy. He had only done it once, and he couldn't imagine ever getting used to the feeling.

Catriona and Kirsty affirmed in unison with a high five, "Yesss! Let's do this!"

"That's the spirit, girls!" whispered Bridget.

The packing took most of the day. Finally, around five thirty, the moving truck and cars were loaded and ready. William called Neil, who had the members of the Corps on standby. They arrived about twenty minutes later in four white vans marked "Thistle o' the Wood Pipe & Drum Corps." William joined Neil on the front porch to confirm the plan and then called into the cottage, "Everyone ready?"

Kirk commented to Corryne, "Look at the size of those guys! I don't know about you, but I'm glad they are coming along!"

"They aren't all guys. There are three women, and they are members of the Royal Marines," announced Corryne proudly.

"Really? You almost sound a little jealous. Maybe you should think about joining?"

"I would if I didn't have a problem taking orders."

"Whatever. You have the grit; that's all I know," added Kirk.

Iain said goodbye, promising to see everyone soon. "When will you go to Dundee?" asked Paddy.

"Oh, I'll be leaving in a few minutes. I don't have any notion about hanging around here alone. Ernie will keep an eye on the cottage for me. He has my number, and he will call if anything looks suspicious."

Ernie waved as the vehicles filed out of the driveway. Half the group turned left at the corner, and the other half continued straight. After seeing the size and strength of the members of Neil's group, the entire crew was more than glad they were accompanying them to Tullyallen, especially as darkness began to fall.

Paddy's group took back roads but mainly followed a more easterly course north toward Balbriggan. The other group took mostly highways. Traffic was heavy, and Paddy's group took about an hour and a half to reach the area near Balbriggan. Bridget was beginning to look weary.

"Aunt Bridget, are you feeling all right?" asked Corryne.

"Just tired, my dear."

"It shouldn't be much longer. Tullyallen is not far." Bridget closed her eyes and leaned her head against the window. Corryne gave Paddy a look that told him she was concerned.

Paddy pulled a thermos from his backpack and poured some hot tea for Bridget. Paddy could see that her hand was trembling. "Here, let me help you," he offered. After a few sips, she'd had enough, and she leaned against the window again to rest. Paddy pulled a blanket around her to keep her warm.

"I'm worried about her," whispered Corryne.

"I know. We just need to get her to Aunt Rebekah's . . . fast."

Leaving Balbriggan, they continued north until they came to a police barricade. Each driver ahead of them pulled off, and an officer appeared to ask a question and quickly wave them on. The pipers' van and Susanna's car passed through, and both pulled over a few yards up the road on the shoulder to wait for Corryne's van and the rest of their caravan.

When it came Corryne's turn, she rolled down her window. The officer, who was wearing a windbreaker with the hood pulled over his hat, leaned down and asked, "Where are you headed?"

"Just headed north to see the countryside—" Corryne gasped. It was Bruno. He still had stitches in his face from the fight in Axel's kitchen.

He looked uncomfortable in his too-tight policeman's uniform, and when he recognized Corryne, he placed his hand on his gun. He leaned down to see who else was in the vehicle, and then hissed, "Well, well, look who's here. An escapee! Maybe we can overlook the loss of one sick Duncan when we have two more in exchange." He called Max. "We've got them in the bag. Move the cruiser, and then take down the barricade. Call in reinforcements."

Paddy looked in the backseat at Mama. She had put the blanket over her head and was lying across the backseat.

Bruno began to reach into the car as if he was going to take Corryne by the throat and then stopped. Then, in a mocking tone said, "Ma'am, if you'd be so kind as to move your vehicle over to the side here, we have a few questions for you and your . . . boyfriend."

The barricade was close to a twelve-foot fence, and now Max had moved the police cruiser so that if Corryne had wanted to go around Bruno, she would have to either knock down the fence or hit the police car.

Corryne began to do as Bruno asked.

Paddy panicked. "You will not! We are not giving Mama back to them!"

"Paddy, he has a gun! If I try to drive out of here, at best, he will shoot out our tires, and we'll still be his prisoners. At worst, he could shoot us. Now, you can work against me, or you can work with me, and we can try to outsmart them."

Paddy heard a tiny voice from the backseat. "Listen to her."

It was everything he could do to try to keep control as his memory flashed scenes from what happened in the hospital. Then, he got an idea. He released his seat belt and slipped between the front seats, sitting next to Mama, who was now sitting up, as Corryne drove slowly to where Bruno had designated. Paddy spoke quickly as he pulled the Weymouth cover from his backpack. His hands were shaking from fear that she would refuse. "Mama, please do this. Just put on the cover, and you'll be with Papa in a moment. I promise we'll be okay, but you . . . you have to do this. Corryne and I can't bridge with you now because we can't let the boxes in the back fall into their hands. I can't let them take you back. Mama, do this for me, please? I beg you."

Corryne interrupted, "Paddy! How do you know she's strong enough?"

Mama smiled at Paddy. She put one arm into the cover, pulled Paddy close, and kissed him on the cheek. "Be careful, Son. I love you so much!" she said.

In the next second, she slipped on the other sleeve and was gone. Paddy sucked in his breath and held his hand over his mouth. His hair stood on end for a moment from the static electricity generated by the cover. He wasn't sure whether to be happy Mama was safe, or worried he had caused her harm.

"Get back up here!" whispered Corryne as she brought the van to a stop. "Quick, code a message to Uncle William."

"What should I say?" asked Paddy.

"Here he comes! Just type 'SOS Balbriggan.' Hurry!"

"Won't the others come to help us?"

"Just do it!"

Paddy had just sent the message when Max opened his door and dragged him out of the van and pushed him down to the ground.

Paddy landed on his hands and knees, and Max pulled his leg back to kick Paddy in the stomach. Paddy saw what was coming and grabbed Max's foot, holding it tight to his chest, and then rolled completely over, twisting Max's leg in the process and knocking him to the ground. There was a loud popping sound, and Max screamed and fell to the ground holding his knee. Paddy was on his feet instantly, in a position that looked as if he were ready to take on the next opponent. He was surprised that his old wrestling training from high school had instinctively come back to him. When he looked up, Bruno had Corryne backed up against the van. He was holding his gun to her head while he glared at Paddy, daring him to move closer.

"I have a mind to end you both here and now," Bruno shouted. He said through gritted teeth, "It's your fault Shane is dead! You think we are gonna let that go? Someone has to pay!" Bruno backed away from Corryne, keeping the gun pointed at her, and moved toward Paddy. Paddy moved slowly away from him, getting between him and Corryne. Suddenly, Bruno took out his billy club and ran at Paddy using the club to push him by the neck back against the van until he was next to Corryne.

"Just who do you think you are stealing our workers? Where is she? Tell me!"

Corryne could tell Paddy was about to respond, and she knew that was the worst thing he could do. She reached over and took his hand and squeezed it, pain from her surgery searing up her arm.

"You don't want to share anything with Bruno? Maybe you need a little persuasion!" Bruno reached back with his billy club and hit Paddy on his legs, numbing them instantly and doubling him over in pain.

"Now, one of you is going to talk. I want to know where she is!"

Max, being an incorrigible thief, had managed somehow to hobble over to the other side of the van and was rummaging through Paddy's backpack.

"Oh, ho! Look what I found!" he said in a mocking voice to Bruno. "It's a new Duncan-made coat, and hand-stitched at that! We can get a pretty penny for this."

Bruno shouted, "Put that down! Anything we find, we take to Sean."

Max ignored him and continued in his mocking tone, "I'm just looking at it! Come to think of it, there's no harm in trying it on . . . just to see what it's like to dress like a real gentleman."

Corryne shrieked so loudly that Paddy thought Bruno had shot her. She immediately slid sideways under Bruno's arm and ran around the back of the van toward Max. Knowing Max had picked up the cover, she had to stop him. If he put it on, their world, and over two hundred years of successfully protecting the covers, would end. Worse, if the SMITs had the covers—and they would have a pair if Max passaged to Virginia—they could use them to do horrible things.

Paddy punched Bruno in the chest so hard that it knocked the air out of his lungs. He fell to the ground, gasping for breath, and Paddy wrestled the gun from him before running to Corryne. It was too late. Max was gone. Corryne crumpled on the ground screaming, "No!" over and over. Paddy's first instinct was to try to console her, but the magnitude of what had just happened froze him where he stood.

All he could think about was what might be happening in Williamsburg right now in Martin's house. Max would arrive terrified, not knowing what happened. Traveling through the passages wasn't like anything one experiences on earth. There was simply nothing to compare with it. Paddy shook himself into action, took his phone from his pocket, and texted Grandpa in their private code. The message read, "One C taken, call Martin NOW. Sent M home."

"What have you done with Max?" boomed Bruno, having recovered somewhat. Paddy backed away from him but kept himself between Bruno and Corryne. Bruno grabbed for the gun, but Paddy pulled it away. Just then, Paddy remembered one of Grandpa's sayings. "When faced with the unexpected, always improvise."

Paddy began haltingly, "Max? Oh, you're looking for Max! Well, you won't be seeing him again anytime soon. You see, this is what we do when people mistreat us, take our property, or kidnap our relatives! We send them into . . . outer darkness! Let's see, Corryne, what should I do to Bruno here? I should send him somewhere very cold to match the coldness of his soul. How about we give him fifty years to think about what he's done?" Paddy didn't believe that Bruno would buy his act, but he was stalling for time, hoping the others would soon arrive or would call the police.

What Paddy didn't realize was that Bruno had been watching Max through the windows of the van the moment he had disappeared, so Paddy's threat, however absurd, struck fear in Bruno's confused mind. He held up his hands and backed up as he spoke. "You don't need to do nothin' to me, nothin', I'm *leaving,* see? I'm going right now." Bruno spun around and ran only two steps before he hit the chest of the biggest member of the Corps, a piper named Kyle. Everyone from the other vehicles gathered and surrounded them.

"Not today you're not," Kyle said as he reached for the handcuffs in Bruno's back pocket. He put Bruno in the police cruiser and hand-cuffed his hands to the steering wheel, locked the keys in the trunk, and proceeded to call the police.

"Officer? I was driving north on Drogheda Street, leaving Balbriggan and, I know this sounds odd, but a police officer seems to be in distress on the side of the road. He appears to be handcuffed to his steering wheel. You'll check it out right away? Oh, thank you, sir."

"I'm sorry we didn't get here sooner, Paddy," explained Steven, another Corps member. "Those goons figured out we were with you and detained us. We took care of them, but it took a few minutes. Let's just say they will have a very long walk home."

Paddy replied, "We have to get out of here before the police arrive. We can't do anything about what has happened here. Let's get to Tullyallen. Can I get someone else to drive the van? I don't trust my American driving. And, can someone help Corryne into the van?"

Paddy was trying to be sensitive to Corryne because she was so overcome, but she yelled, "I do not *need* help! This is all *your* fault! One of our most prized possessions and you leave it in your open backpack for the world to see? Some grandson of the Master Keeper you are! Have you any idea what you've done? It's over! You've ruined everything!"

Susanna took charge, speaking to her daughter first. "Corryne! That's enough. Get in the van. No one is going to blame you or Paddy. Now is a time for your problem-solving skills, not for finger-pointing or giving up. Paddy, you ride in the car with us. I think Corryne needs some time alone right now. Come on, everyone, let's get to Tullyallen before we run into any more trouble."

❧

MARTIN WAS AWAY GIVING A LOOM-WEAVING DEMONSTRATION IN Williamsburg when his phone showed a coded text from William saying that a SMIT named Max had used the cover to Virginia and was likely in his house. Martin hurriedly finished and went home. He slowly entered the house and crept into the back bedroom, where the closet was located, and listened.

"Hello?" Martin called out softly. "Is anybody there?" There was only silence.

"Let me out of here!" came an anguished cry from inside the closet.

"Who are you, and how did you come here?"

"I am Max Sullivan." The voice was timid at first, followed by panicked shouting, "I don't know how I got here or where I am, but I'm not supposed to be here! I need to get back to where I was! Let me out!"

"Well, Max, that must have been pretty scary, and I want to make sure you are okay and that you get back where you belong. Now, I can open the door, but it's a small door, so if you are wearing a coat or anything bulky, you should take it off first. Can you do that for me?"

"I took it off! It must be a hundred degrees in here! Let me out, or I'm gonna lose the rag!"

Martin unlocked the door, and Max jumped out while shading his eyes from the light. "Where am I? Was I knocked out? What happened? I thought I'd gone away with the fairies!" Max's eyes grew large as he looked at Martin dressed in his period costume from the demonstration he'd given earlier.

"A-am I off me trolley? Have I gone back in time?"

"Martin followed Max's gaze. "Oh, these clothes! No, no, I work in an old village here in Virginia, where we dress as they did in the seventeenth and eighteenth centuries just for historical purposes. It's like a uniform. You haven't traveled back in time."

"Virginia? In County Cavan? How'd I get here . . . and in your closet?"

At that moment, a relatively large gathering of historic Williamsburg's village workers passed by in full costume, having just held a skit of a typical political rally for visitors. Max caught sight of the group through the window. "What about all those people?" asked Max with a terrified look.

"Yes, they all work here too."

Max began to rush to every window, and it just so happened that at that particular moment, there was only costumed staff visible. They were working, laughing, and engaging with one another as if they were conducting activities of everyday life—seventeenth-century life. A horse-drawn carriage went by, and a costumed worker with a border collie drove a small flock of sheep down the lane. There wasn't an automobile anywhere.

Max's eyes grew wider, and beads of sweat covered his forehead. He turned and glared at Martin. "You lied to me! I'm not in some make-believe village! I have gone back in time! I've seen shows on television about this! Send me back!"

Martin tried speaking in a calm voice. "Max, I didn't lie to you. If you go out and speak to those people, they will tell you they dress up to play a part, just like I do. When they finish work, they get in their cars and drive home. They have phones, they ride in airplanes, and they have computers. It only looks like it did years ago. Come, we'll go together, and we'll both ask them."

"You liar!" shouted Max as he picked up an iron candelabra from the dining table and swung it at Martin. At first, he missed, but he was younger and quicker than Martin and lunged toward him, striking him on the side of the head. Martin fell to the floor, unconscious and bleeding badly.

Max dropped the candelabra where he stood. There was blood splattered on the walls and over his shirt. "What do I do? What do I do?" he asked, terrified. He ran outside, in a zigzag pattern down Duke of Gloucester Street, looking desperately for any sign of something he might recognize.

A man dressed as a seventeenth-century politician was giving a speech to a crowd and spotted Max. "Sir? What say ye to this abominable tariff? Are we to condone a further fourpence deduction on every pound of indigo we ship to the king? What say ye?"

In his bewildered state, he ignored the man and continued stumbling through backyards, avoiding the main street. A woman dressed in period attire came out of one cottage and asked him if he needed any help, but Max ran away. The blood on his shirt and Max's terrified look led her to call the police. "You know your business . . . but you just might want to bring along someone with psychiatric training," she suggested.

When the police arrived, Max had wandered farther up the street through various backyards and was almost to the edge of the historic section of the village. From where he now was, Max could see tourists in modern dress visiting different shops, and cars in the parking lot. He could see the ticket booth for the historic village. He wandered away toward Lake Matoaka and hid under a canoe lying upside down on the shore.

At about the same time, the police surrounded Martin's home. EMTs wheeled Martin on a stretcher to a waiting ambulance. He had regained consciousness but had a severe concussion. His head had a large bandage covering the wound. A young man was speaking to a police officer outside.

"I'm Captain Murphy. May I ask you a few questions?"

"Yes, sir; I am a student at the college here. Martin Duncan is a physics professor, and I'm his lab assistant. I came by to drop off some research materials for him a few minutes ago, and that's when I found him. This is so horrible. Is he going to be all right?"

"Did you notice anything unusual or out of place?"

"Um, well . . . the door was open, so I leaned in and called for Dr. Duncan. That's when I saw the bloody candlestick on the floor. Oh, and one other thing. It's probably not important, but I could see a coat on the floor in the bedroom. I didn't go in there. I just saw it from where I was kneeling to check on the Professor while I was calling you guys. The only reason I mention it is that Professor Duncan is a neat freak. He would never leave a coat on the floor like that. Also, I've known him for four years, and he's only ever worn black coats. It's a thing with him. He has one black raincoat and one black wool coat he wears in the winter. That coat on the floor is tan colored. I'm not saying it isn't his. It's just odd. It was on the floor, and it's not one I've ever seen him wear. I just wondered if it might belong to the person who did this to him."

"You didn't see anything else unusual?"

"No, sir."

"All right, you are free to go, but we may need you to come down to the station later on, so don't leave town."

"Yes, sir. You have my phone number. Please call me if I can do anything."

The officer called to his assistant, "Hey, Fraley, bag that coat in the bedroom and take it into evidence . . . just in case."

"On it, Boss."

"We need to get this wrapped up. It looks like a robbery gone bad. The old guy is pretty lucky. They are saying it looks like he'll make it after all."

Back at the police station, Officer Fraley checked the items gathered at the scene into the evidence room. Zelda, the clerk on duty, checked the pockets and noticed the coat was hand-sewn. A seamstress herself, Zelda examined the cover, marveling at the handwork.

"Hey, Fraley, look at this button on the hem. It looks like a kind of label. See? You can turn it over. Oh my gosh, look! Little gears are moving inside!"

Officer Fraley looked closely at the glass back of the seal. "Well, would you look at that. Hey, look at the engraving. It has a number, and it says, 'Duncan Tailoring.' I've heard of them. My father had a suit made by them once for my sister's wedding. He had to travel out of state to get fitted. Why don't you check online and see where their nearest shop is? Maybe they can tell you whose coat this is. Meanwhile, let's get forensics to check it over for hair or anything else that might tell us who tried to hurt the professor."

Zelda found the phone number of Malcolm's shop in Weymouth online and called him. William had already called Malcolm to tell him of the missing cover. When he got the call from the police station, he tried to remain calm.

"Yes, this is Malcolm Duncan. Yes, that coat belongs to our company. It's a display sample. Martin Duncan is supposed to have it. He is one of our tailors. Is Martin all right?"

Zelda asked Malcolm to hold, and she checked with Officer Fraley on Martin's condition. "Mr. Duncan, I've just been told that Martin Duncan was taken to the hospital in Williamsburg with a serious injury to the head, but they expect him to recover."

"Oh, my gosh!"

"Sir, you are certain this coat belongs to Martin Duncan? It has an interesting button on the hem."

Malcolm thought quickly. "Oh yes, it's just a device by which we keep track of each of our display models. That coat is an example of the fine handwork we do, and it is extremely valuable. Thank you for letting me know that you found it."

"Yes, sir. No problem. Should we return it to Mr. Duncan or you?"

"Given what has just happened, I'd prefer to send someone to come get it for safekeeping. When will we be able to pick it up?"

"After our forensics department finishes with it, I'd expect."

"Very well, then. May I call back to check on the status of the investigation?"

"Certainly."

"Thank you so much."

Malcolm phoned William and told him that Martin was in the hospital, and one of the Virginia covers was at the Williamsburg Police Department.

"Are you sure Bridget is okay?" asked William.

Malcolm replied that she was weak from the passage, but not harmed. "Dr. Foster is going to stop by and see her today. I expect that he thinks I've lost my mind since I called him and said Bridget is here. I wonder if there's such a thing as a reversal of a death certificate."

"What a wonderful problem to have. If you do get one, we'll have to frame it and hang it on the wall!" They both chuckled.

"I wonder what happened to the guy who took the cover," said Malcolm. There was a long silence on the phone as they both contemplated the gravity of the situation.

"I have to go there and get the covers," replied William. We cannot risk either of them falling into someone else's hands, least of all a SMIT. But I don't have a cover to get me there. There's nothing left to do but go the old-fashioned way. You take care of Bridget, and Paddy and I will fly to Newport News and drive to Williamsburg tomorrow. Hopefully, we can get a flight out early. By the way, you can thank your quick-thinking son for getting Bridget back to you. Wait until you hear the story. You will be so proud."

Malcolm's voice grew quiet. "I've been so hard on him. What he's become is more because of you than me. I guess I gave up when Bridget disappeared. Having her back feels like a second chance. Dad, she is just as beautiful as ever. Thank you for finding her."

"I'm so happy for you both, Son. I'll call you tomorrow with an update. Once we get the covers, Paddy and I will head home. All right then, talk with you soon."

⬥

REBEKAH ROSE AT FIVE IN THE MORNING AND COOKED A FULL IRISH breakfast, putting it on warming trays so the crew could serve themselves. She left a note saying she had patients to visit and would be back by early afternoon.

The note had a postscript that read, "P.S. The post for Iain now comes here by forwarding order. You might want to call him to let him know he received the attached." The envelope had no return address. Kirk called Iain, who instructed him to have William open it.

Inside was a note from Sean Geelan that read, "We know you have taken Max. Unless you want to pay a heavy price, return him to the Manufactory. You have twenty-four hours. ~ S. Geelan."

Grandpa stoically read the note and then handed it to Paddy, who read it aloud to the crew. Everyone was silent. Paddy felt responsible for Max having taken the cover in the first place, so he mustered the courage to take charge.

"I'm writing him back. We are not going to live in fear of them anymore." Paddy took a page from a notepad by Rebekah's phone and began to write, reading aloud as he did. "You and yours have taken countless members of our family and sabotaged our livelihood for generations. Never touch another unless you want to pay a *heavier* price. It ends here." Paddy signed it, "Patrick Duncan."

He looked around the room. "Everyone okay with it?" Each of them looked at Grandpa and Douglass.

"I'll stand behind it," said Grandpa.

"Aye," said Douglass, folding his big strong arms across his chest.

"In my opinion, it sounds like we are squaring off with them—like we are lowering ourselves to play by their tactics," observed Corryne.

Paddy started to defend what he wrote, but Grandpa intervened. "I agree with you, Corryne. It may infer that we would reciprocate according to their schemes, but it doesn't say exactly what price they will pay. We did not take Max, and I don't see any harm in using the situation to let them think that we used a little muscle of our own. Who knows? Perhaps it will send a message. Besides, the shorter our reply, the better. No good comes of dialogue with SMITs, as we have learned the hard way."

❧

The next day, William and Paddy flew to Newport News and took a smaller plane to Williamsburg. They rented a car and drove straight to the police station. Grandpa took off a device that hung from a chain around his neck under his shirt and handed it to Paddy. "Put this on. It's called a . . ."

"NOVA?"

"Good, I see Iain has already filled you in. There's a tiny lever on the back. Once you activate it, you'll be invisible. Go inside and find the cover. Oh, you may feel a slight buzzing while you are in parallel time. I'll explain later."

"Are you sure you want me to go?"

"And why not? You passaged to Ireland, you rescued your mom, and you outwitted the SMITs. I have complete confidence in you."

"Couldn't we get in trouble for this? Didn't Papa say the police would return it when they finish with it?"

"Paddy, the technology in that little seal is what we are protecting. We can't let some curious person tear it off and keep it as a souvenir."

Paddy took a deep breath and put the NOVA over his head and under his shirt.

"Be sure to keep it centered over your heart, and when you find the cover, you'll have to turn off the NOVA for a second so you can pick it up. Then turn it back on," added Grandpa.

Paddy slid the lever and immediately recognized the feeling he'd had when he passaged to Dublin—as if a million tiny objects were touching all of his exposed skin. He began walking to the door of the station. The door opened, and an officer came running straight toward him. Paddy froze where he stood. The officer ran right through him. Paddy turned to see the officer jump into his cruiser and speed out of the parking lot, his siren blaring. Paddy was stunned that he felt nothing. It was as if he were a ghost.

He tried to open the door, but his hand went through the handle. He inched forward, holding out his hand, which went *through* the door. He continued inch by inch until his whole body was inside. "Whoa! This thing is awesome!" he said to himself.

He saw a sign pointing in the direction of the evidence room. A sign on the door said the officer was on break and would return in five minutes. Once again, he inched his way through the door. It took some time to find the correct evidence box, but once he located it, he turned off the NOVA and grabbed the cover, making sure the seal was still attached. He quickly turned the NOVA back on and exited the building. Back inside the car, Paddy turned off the NOVA, and handed it back to Grandpa, sighing in relief.

William smiled and patted Paddy on the shoulder as he drove to the hospital. "Now, I'm going to go get the twin cover at Martin's. You go inside and check on Martin. I'll be along shortly. Oh, every portal is assigned a set of phrases we memorize and use to identify ourselves. It doesn't matter if you know someone by sight or not because it could always be the enemy in disguise. So, for Martin to trust you, you'll have to enter his room and say that you need to order a tuxedo in Italian piqué with side vents and a four-button sleeve. He will ask, 'Is that to be with a five-eighths grosgrain leg stripe?' You will answer, 'Only one-half inch will do.' Then he'll ask, 'Notched lapel?' and you respond, 'Shawl lapel, please.'"

"Italian piqué, side vents, four-button sleeve, one-half inch stripe, shawl lapel. Got it."

William said, "See you soon."

⳼⳼⳼

MARTIN WAS CONSCIOUS, BUT THE BLOW HE'D SUSTAINED HAD LEFT him weak and dizzy. After Paddy proved who he was, Martin said, "My, how you've grown! I haven't seen you since you were a little boy."

"I'm so glad you are okay. Do you remember what happened?"

Martin winced as he turned to see Paddy better. "I received William's text and went directly home. A man was in my closet."

"Yes, I'm acquainted with Max. That must have been scary."

"I called out to see if he would answer. He told me his name was Max Sullivan. He was desperate to get out of the closet. Terrified is a better word. Poor guy had no idea what happened to him."

"Did you get any sense that he knew the cover was what transported him?"

"I don't think so, but then he saw me dressed in my period gear, and he convinced himself he'd been sent back in time. The chap was so afraid, he thought I was lying to him."

"Uncle Martin, he is a dangerous man. You are lucky you weren't hurt worse."

"Did they find him?" asked Martin.

"Not to my knowledge. When will they discharge you?"

"Oh, in a day or two, they said. I'll stay with my daughter for a bit. She lives nearby. The police suggested I not go back home until they've found him."

"So, you'll have someone to take care of you then? We won't leave unless . . ."

"Yes, yes. Between my daughter and her family, I'll be fine. Ha! This isn't the first time I've tangled with a SMIT! Hey, I hear you have quite the homecoming awaiting you!"

"How did you know?"

"Ha! Iain and I are thick as thieves! He told me about what you did to rescue your mom. Pretty impressive to take on the SMITs like that.

Quite the buzz among all the portals, you know. Some are saying this is the greatest victory against the SMITs ever!"

"The portals know?"

"Of course! News this big had to be shared, especially the fact that you and Corryne walked right into their lair! Why, it was nothing short of brilliant! Iain said the fire ruse was your idea. Well, you are William's grandson, no mistake about that," he said with a chuckle.

"I'm just glad it worked. It almost didn't. The SMITs tried to kidnap Mama from the hospital." Paddy could see that Martin was getting sleepy, but he had one burning question he wanted to ask. "Sir? I was wondering, is it true that a group of students meets regularly here at William & Mary, and their discussions are like the original Lunar Society?"

Martin smiled knowingly. "Do you have a piece of paper and a pen?" Paddy found a pen and notepad by the phone.

It took Martin about thirty seconds to write his reply in code. He handed the note to Paddy. "You are welcome anytime. It would be an honor to have you. Just follow these instructions." Paddy looked at the note, and though it was in code, he felt sure that it was the date, time, and location of the next meeting.

"Thank you, sir."

William finally arrived, and they spoke with Martin a little longer. They decided to leave when his daughter and family came to visit him.

They drove all night long and arrived in Weymouth midmorning the next day. When they reached their neighborhood, Grandpa woke Paddy.

"We are almost home. I bet you didn't think you could miss it so much."

"That's for sure!"

"Well, I'd say you had quite a productive trip, considering you went there accidentally." Grandpa glanced at Paddy and smiled. "I don't know for sure, but I'd guess that the hardest thing you faced wasn't saving your mom or going up against the SMITs. It was your willingness to allow your courage to overcome your fear. Am I right?"

"Grandpa, you are always right," Paddy replied with a smile.

"Few people realize that you can have courage and fear at the same time. What matters is which one we let speak the loudest."

Paddy reflected on all he'd learned since he'd discovered Grandpa's Cave. "So, this is what the stories were for, right? Introducing me to the *interesting* side of the family?" he asked with a smile.

"I don't know what you mean. I'm your grandpa. Aren't grandpas famous for interesting bedtime stories?" They both chuckled.

❧ 21 ❧

THE MASTER KEEPER

"THERE IS NOTHING NOBLE IN BEING SUPERIOR TO YOUR FELLOW MAN; TRUE NOBILITY IS BEING SUPERIOR TO YOUR FORMER SELF." ~ERNEST HEMINGWAY

Fresh snow had fallen overnight, and the whole town looked wrapped in clean, puffy whiteness. It was a dry snow, the kind that crunches beneath boots and blows over everyday objects, transforming them into mysterious shapes. The town of Weymouth had Christmas wreaths with bright red bows on every lamppost, and virtually every home had decorations out to embrace the season. There was something magical about the approach of the holidays in Weymouth that made Paddy feel warm inside. Best of all, this was Mama's favorite time of year, and she was home.

As they rounded the corner, Paddy looked to see if Papa had put wreaths on the shop windows. What he saw made him sit up taller and lean forward. Since he was fourteen, it had fallen to Paddy to hang the Christmas wreaths on the windows. They hadn't bothered with garland and lights since Mama had gone. But there, just as if it were a perfect painting in a book, was the shop, decked in fluffy garland and fresh wreaths accented with bright red bows and little white lights. A lump formed in his throat, and he felt silly for being emotional. Grandpa put his hand on Paddy's shoulder and slowed his driving as they approached.

"Isn't it beautiful? A fitting welcome for Bridget." Paddy smiled. No words were sufficient. It was as if the shop itself beamed with joy to have Mama home.

So many thoughts and emotions swirled in Paddy's mind. When he was last home, he had wanted nothing more than to go away, but now that he'd gone, he couldn't think of any place he'd rather be right now. They made their way inside, and it must have been almost an hour before everyone settled down from hugs and answering questions about their adventures. For Paddy, the best part was seeing Mama sitting in her old chair. Papa had moved his chair close to hers so they could hold hands whenever they wanted. Mama was feeling better, and the color was returning to her cheeks.

Clara brought her some embroidery, which she loved to do, and Papa was treating her like a queen. He found a personal shopper to buy Mama some warm clothes, and he hired a florist to bring a bouquet of fresh flowers once a week. When Mama objected, Papa just took her hands and looked in her eyes and declared unabashedly, "Oh, my dear, I have to make up for lost time!"

Grandpa and Paddy took naps since they had driven all night long, and in the afternoon, Grandpa asked Paddy to come with him to the cottage. Paddy was surprised to see that everything had been put back into place.

"Graham must have tidied things up after the break-in," guessed Paddy.

"Now, sit down here. I need you to listen to me carefully. The day before I left, I promised I would explain everything to you. There's no question you've learned a lot on your own. You figured out my riddles, and you found your way into my office downstairs. This proves to me that you are using the knowledge I've tried to pass on to you. You also showed your leadership in Dublin, and that you're not afraid to challenge the status quo. Your reply to Sean Geelan's note showed courage and wisdom. Your split-second decision to crawl in the backseat and send your mom home when you did no doubt saved her life."

"Wait, how did you know the details . . . ?"

"Corryne told me."

"She told you? Gosh, I didn't think she'd ever mention my name again, not after the cover was lost."

"She said to tell you she was sorry for what she said. She also said to tell you, 'You are the Master Keeper's grandson,' though I'm not sure why she needed to say that."

"I know what she meant. Does she know you got the covers back?"

"Yes. I let her know. We all take our mission to protect the covers and the thread very seriously, but to Corryne, well, this life is all she knows.

"What we deal with is fulfilling, but it's serious and often dangerous. And, it's always unpredictable because we never know when the next assignment will come."

"Grandpa, you knew Mama was at the Manufactory. I don't understand why you didn't get her out using the NOVA. Why did you leave the riddles for me to find?"

"The NOVA only makes the person wearing it disappear. If the SMITs found out someone was attempting to get her out, I was afraid they would take her life. I also knew that if you knew it was your mom you were rescuing, it would seem impossible to you because she's been gone so long. It was complicated by the fact that the police were in the Geelans' pocket, but I felt certain that if I presented you a problem, that, just like any cryptography challenge, you would come up with a plan, and it would work."

"You had no reason to put that kind of trust in me, Grandpa."

"Paddy, I started out like you. School didn't give me the tools I use to help others. I had to be curious and find ways around obstacles. I know you well enough to know that you are made of the same stuff I am. That's why I trust you. You've proven yourself to me a thousand times."

"Now, I wish I didn't have to tell you this, but I'm going on another mission tomorrow."

"Grandpa! You just got home."

William put up his hand. "Now, listen. I didn't even know I was going until an hour ago. I've been waiting for this particular door to open in this country for many years."

"Where?"

"China."

"Do you have to go now? What if I go for you?"

William smiled. "It brings me joy just knowing that you are willing, but no, I have to go. I've worked with the contacts for so long; I'm the only one they trust. I need you to do something for me, though. I need you to decide, at least for now, if you think you want to take over for me.

"Now, I don't want to get in trouble with your parents—they are just glad to have you home after what you just encountered with the SMITs. But, when it's all said and done, it has to be your decision. No one can make up your mind for you, and that includes me. Sometimes, it can take years to find the thing that feels like it fits you, so there's nothing wrong with giving different things a try. After all, how else will you know? And if you don't like something, you can always change your mind and do something else."

"Papa doesn't want me to leave and mess up my apprenticeship. He says if I keep at it, I could become one of the youngest master tailors in the United States. While it's great to be home, especially with Mama back, I honestly think I'd go crazy if I had to spend several more years here. I want to do what you do, Grandpa. I don't need time to think about it."

"If you are interested in traveling for fabric purchasing as I do, I think it could be a good experience, and it might just give you a needed break without taking you totally out of tailoring."

"I wish I could come with you to China."

Grandpa looked at Paddy with a nervous look in his eyes. "Could you do me a favor? I don't want to have to explain this trip to Malcolm. I especially don't want him to know what I'm about to tell you because he will worry, and that's not good for his heart."

Paddy's face showed his fear.

Grandpa sighed. His eyes had a pleading look as if he were begging Paddy to believe what he was about to say. It struck Paddy at that moment how very lonely it must be to have so few people with whom to discuss the incredibly weighty secrets that Grandpa guarded.

"I've been experimenting with what I believe are layers of time." Grandpa spoke slowly and distinctly, and his eyes lit up as he explained, "I've seen them when I passage."

"What do you mean, *layers*? How can you see anything? You're traveling too fast."

"I've been able to slow my travel speed down."

"How?"

"You are *not* to try this on your own. I've been traveling through the passages for most of my life, but if you must know, I . . . " He hesitated. "I turn on the NOVA while I'm going through."

"Grandpa! Isn't that dangerous? I mean, do we even understand what's happening with the NOVA?"

Grandpa waited for Paddy to grasp the impact of what he had said. A little smile played at the corners of his mouth.

"What have you seen?" Paddy asked, leaning forward, eyes wide.

"If I tell you what I saw, will you believe me? I don't think I could bear it if you didn't."

"Grandpa, I've never doubted anything you've ever told me."

William looked him squarely in the eyes and said, "What I need to tell you is that there are *layers* of time and space. As best I can tell, each one represents a day. They look like the pages of a book, or a stack of fabric when you see it from the edges, and they surround the earth. I believe every day adds another layer closest to the earth, and it pushes the other layers out by a tiny fraction of space. I think this phenomenon, if it's true in other galaxies, could be the reason the universe is expanding as it ages. I've been slowing my travel to see the layers for the last fifteen years, and I've seen some amazing history. I was able to look into one day in Birmingham when the Lunar Society was actually gathering for a meeting."

"You can see people?" Paddy's eyes opened even wider.

"You see everything that happened at the same time you are traveling, just however many days or years or centuries ago. The layers parallel their locations on the earth, so over Birmingham, I can see the Lunar Society meeting in one layer, and in another layer, I can see bombs falling on the city in World War II."

"What happens when that day ends?"

"It never ends, Paddy. It is time suspended in space but traveling with the earth. The layer holds the events of that day, and you see what was happening on that day at the same time you are traveling. My theory is that every twenty-four hours, the earth sheds one layer and starts a new one. I suppose if you could stop and watch a single one long enough, it would seem as if the day repeated itself over and over.

"If you could visit one, and then travel to another, and then another, say, for research, you would be able to watch what happened on any given series of days. Can you imagine that in your arsenal, if your job were to solve crimes? Just think of it! What we know of history is from textbooks, but how do we know it happened that way? What if I could travel back and observe the explosion that changed the lodestone that night at the Lunar Society?"

Grandpa waited a moment, unsure if he should say what was coming next. "I'm going to try to travel to the layer when the explosion happened."

"Grandpa, no! You can't! This is crazy!"

"You must understand, Paddy. I'm old now, and I have been searching for this information all my life. It's always been out of reach. If I can learn more about the stone and communicate it back to you or the Base somehow, it would be the most important thing I've ever done. Something happened to the stone once; it could happen again."

"Why would anyone want it to happen again? Look at all the trouble caused by what happened that day!"

"I am proud of how our family has guarded this secret, but do you think it's right for us to keep it all to ourselves forever? We have learned a lot, but there is so much more to learn."

"What if you can't find the right layer of time?"

"I've come very close several times."

"And, if you do find it, you can't go into it. It's the past. To enter it would be to alter it, and you can't change the past, right?"

"But I can enter it and be invisible with the NOVA, and I can observe what happened. Just imagine it, Paddy!"

"You know what the magnetic field does to bodies! It's a miracle we're in one piece when we land, and you want to slow it down to stop and look at something? I'm sorry, Grandpa. It's not that I *don't* believe you. The trouble is that I *do* believe you, and I worry you won't make it."

Grandpa put his hand on Paddy's. "I'm not speaking to Paddy, the boy. I'm speaking to Paddy, the man. I'm not concerned about making it back alive. If I do, great. I'll hopefully have information that will help your generation keep the search going. If I'm unsuccessful, well, I can't think of a better way to go."

Paddy sat there looking at him, thinking that these moments might be the last he would ever spend with him. He knew there was no talking him out of leaving. "You are going to do this after your mission in China?"

"That's the plan. There is something you can do for me, though."

"Anything." Paddy felt a hard knot in his throat.

William smiled and got up from his chair. He pulled a book from his library shelf and said, "On page . . ."

Paddy interrupted and finished his sentence, "Twenty-one. On page 21, you've written the scrambled name of the country and the year when you started using that book for encrypting and decrypting that country's messages. Some countries have more than one book because you were worried that the code might get broken."

"Well, well, I am impressed."

"Don't be. That's all I figured out."

"You need to keep these books close, Paddy. At least once a month, I go to check on a portal somewhere. Any news or messages I have for them, I write out in code before I leave. You'll need the right book combined with the cipher for that day to encrypt them. Be sure to always date your messages, so the portal will know which cipher to use to decrypt the message. Twelve of the portals are spies themselves. Some of them have been tracked down by the SMITs, for no other reason than to limit the reach of Duncan Tailoring.

"Your cover will be as the owner of our company, and you'll visit our offices to take fabric samples and supplies of things they can't get in their home countries. Those tailors who are spies will tell you if there is a need for a mission in their country."

"But, I'm not the owner of Duncan Tailoring."

"As of tonight, you are."

Paddy was stunned. "But that's not possible. There's Papa, and there's Uncle Douglass, and there's Uncle Iain . . ."

"Now, I should think you'd know the genealogy of your own family a little better. Well, maybe it's not your fault. You see, the ownership passes through the line that directly comes from Angus. I'll spare you the details, but suffice it to say that Iain and Douglass aren't direct enough in that line, and your papa has already told me that he doesn't have any interest in managing it. If you don't want it, I'll make a trip to Tullyallen to see if the person who is next in line is interested."

"Grandpa, I don't have any idea how to run this company. What if I mess it up?"

"Do you think I would hand it over to you and leave you to figure it all out on your own? Everything is in the able hands of our accountants and our general managers in New York and Glasgow. But your name has been placed on the ownership documents as my beneficiary, unless you don't want it. If you don't, I'll call them in the morning and let them know."

"What are my responsibilities?"

"If you choose to take it on, you will work to ensure the profitability of our various worldwide locations. You do that by visiting with them about their needs and keeping your ear to the ground about current trends, fabrics, and techniques. You decide when and if we should agree to negotiate contracts, and you are the final decision on content for ads that we run in major magazines. It involves quite a bit of travel. Just like you wanted."

"Well, yes, that's what I want, but I wanted to be doing it with you."

"You don't need me! Goodness, you sure proved that."

"Grandpa, that was sheer dumb luck how that all worked out!"

"Most of the time, Paddy, that's all I have. You'll be just fine, and you have the crew at the Base to help you."

"Now, I'm going to China in the morning. I'm going to leave the cover for China there, so you'll have to fly to our portal in China next time and retrieve the cover. I'm also taking a cover no one uses anymore. Its mate is in Birmingham. Hopefully, I'll get to watch what happened the night of the explosion. Let's hope I don't get deposited in the Middle Ages."

"Grandpa, I don't think you should joke about that."

"Aww, come on, Paddy, let an old man decide how he goes. You'll be my age one day, and I bet you'll be a lot more daring."

Paddy shook his head and smiled, still finding it hard to believe he was going along with Grandpa's plan.

"I've already advised the organizations I work with that I have a new assistant. I have given them the phone number associated with this phone." Grandpa showed him a new cell phone. "It's got my voice on the voicemail for now because callers will be more comfortable if they think they are calling me. You'll reply as my assistant—at least for the transition period. Remember, never give your real name. Whoever calls will know to transmit messages in code. I'll leave you a key, so you'll know which cipher to use to decrypt the message."

"What organizations will call? NSA? CIA? Foreign governments?"

"Yes. Don't worry; contact Douglass if you have questions. He'll walk you through it. Just remember to text him in code. If you need to do any extensive planning, buzz over to Tullyallen."

Paddy felt utterly inadequate to take over for Grandpa. "Is there anything else you need to tell me?"

"Probably, but I'll write it down as I pack and leave it for you here on the table. It's getting late, so I'd better start." They stood and embraced one another. "Please tell your mama and papa that I love them both with all my heart. They will not understand, especially your papa."

Grandpa held Paddy at arm's length. "Never, ever forget that I love you."

Paddy couldn't speak except to say, "I love you too."

Paddy reluctantly left, stopping several times to turn and fix the image of the cottage in his mind as it was—warm and welcoming, with Grandpa still there. It would be cold and silent after tomorrow morning. He finally went inside and quietly climbed the stairs to his room. He sat on a chair by the window and looked down on the cottage at the window with the brightest lamplight. He was afraid to take his eyes off the light. He stayed up all night thinking until the early morning, when he dozed off for a few seconds, his head resting on the side of the window frame. He woke with a jump. Looking at the cottage again, he saw the light was off. He crept softly but quickly down the stairs and ran into the cottage.

"Grandpa? Grandpa!" He checked each room. He glanced at the table and saw an envelope with his name on it. He picked it up and sat down to open it, but emotion overcame him. Grandpa was gone—probably forever. He buried his face in a pillow and cried, "Why did you have to leave? I need you!" When he finally looked up, Papa was standing in the doorway. Paddy discreetly slid the envelope between the couch cushions.

"Paddy? What happened?"

Paddy tried to compose himself. "He's gone, Papa . . . He had to go. He said he had an urgent mission; that the door would only be open a short time, and that he had waited a long time for the opportunity. He said he wouldn't be returning . . ." His voice trembled, and he had a knot in his throat.

"What? Why?"

Paddy could hardly speak.

Papa sat down. "He told you this?"

Paddy nodded.

"But, how did he know he wouldn't be coming home?"

"He has to do something very dangerous. I don't fully understand, but that's what we talked about so late last night. I tried to stop him, but he had made up his mind."

"Did he say anything else?"

"He doesn't want to grow old and die lying around, feeling useless."

Papa's shoulders dropped as if someone had placed a heavy blanket over him. A look of understanding came over him. "So that's what it is. He's afraid to die. He's going to put himself in harm's way so that his life ends quickly, so he won't have to suffer." Papa looked back at Paddy. "I suppose there's no harm in telling you now. Grandpa has been battling bone cancer for two years now. He made me promise not to tell you. He refused to undergo any treatment."

Paddy was dumbstruck. His mind raced back through all that had happened in Dublin. Paddy couldn't think of one instance when he'd shown any sign of weakness.

Papa continued, "He's spent his life doing for others. I don't think he'd be able to stand it if he had to be fussed over and waited on if he wasn't able to do things for himself. I can understand why he'd want to do this. It's odd, you know. Of all the Master Keepers, Grandpa was most like Angus—always wanting to discover something new about the covers and the stone. I don't know if I ever told you, but Angus had bone cancer too. Doctors never could understand why he lived so long after he was diagnosed."

"Why do you think he lived so long?"

"I don't know. Apparently, he claimed it was rising early, eating a hearty breakfast, and spending time out there." Papa pointed upward. "He swore the magnetic field had something to do with slowing the growth of his cancer. Did your grandpa say anything else?"

"He asked me to tell you and Mama that he loves you both with all his heart."

Papa got misty-eyed. "He and I didn't always see eye to eye, you know. I felt I let him down. He wanted to pass it all to me, but I was never Master Keeper material. I sure will miss him, though." Then as if he didn't want to believe it, his tone changed. "Oh, you know Grandpa! He's probably still got a few miles left in him. He'll get his second wind and be back in a few weeks."

"Papa, if you don't mind, I think I'll stay here today. Please tell Mama I'll see you all at dinner."

"Sure. I understand if you need some time alone."

Papa walked slowly up to the shop, wondering how he would tell Bridget. She was especially fond of William.

PADDY TOOK THE ENVELOPE, DESCENDED INTO THE TUNNEL, AND opened the door to Grandpa's Cave. He lit the lantern and went straight to the secret compartment in the wall and opened the door to the inner office. He had wanted to come back here with Grandpa—to go through all the decades of memories and relive his adventures. Now, he had no guide to help him understand what things were souvenirs and what were tools that would still be useful for future missions.

"So, you found your grandpa's 'sanctuary within the sanctuary' all on your own. I'm so proud of you, Son."

Paddy whirled around to see Mama standing behind him.

"You knew about this? All this?" he said as he gestured in a sweeping motion to indicate the room.

"Yes, honey. I'm the portal for North America. My code name is Cassiopeia. After I was taken, William never stopped looking for me, and when he entered the dormitory in the Manufactory a few months ago with the NOVA, somehow I knew he was there and that he'd send someone for me. I just never dreamed it would be you!" She reached out her thin arms and drew him close for a hug. "I am so thankful for you!"

"Mama? So . . . you . . . you are a spy too?"

"Yes, Son. Your grandmother Agnes taught me everything I know. She was a well-known cryptanalyst at Bletchley Park during World War II. That's where she and your grandpa met. As you go through your grandpa's things in here, everything will start to make sense little by little. Let me know if you need help." She smiled.

"I'll leave you alone now. I imagine he left you a list." She winked. "He always does." She touched his cheek and then turned and made her way back up the tunnel.

Paddy sat in Grandpa's chair at his desk and opened the envelope. Inside was a letter with a list of things Grandpa needed him to know. Also in the envelope was the phone that Grandpa had shown him. Thankfully, the note was in the code that he and Grandpa had invented together years ago. They combined the characteristics of three different types of ciphers and used three different types of characters: numbers, letters, and symbols. Paddy was proud that none of Grandpa's friends or even Douglass could crack their code. In about twenty-five minutes, he had deciphered it. The list read:

1. Remember to visit the portals once a quarter, at least. Take Kirk with you sometimes to check their radios. Douglass has the coded list of phrases you'll need for each one so they can identify you, just like you used with Martin.

2. Brush up on your languages and check the international news daily.

3. Joe at the CIA can be tough, but he's been a friend for twenty-five years. He won't steer you needlessly into danger. Trust him.

4. I do code-breaking for many sources, apart from missions. I believe you can do it too. My code name is Scrydan for all such work and missions. Enlist the Base for help if needed.

5. Make time soon to go speak to Martin once he's recovered. He can tell you all about what the Ørsted League has learned about the stone. He has a duplicate of the NOVA that I have and plans to give it to you when you visit. You are going to need it.

6. The SMITs potentially know about the covers now. Speak with the Base and take all necessary precautions.

7. Corryne may seem like a fortress, but she is fragile. You'll need her skills, and she needs to contribute. Perhaps it will be your friendship that will coax her to trust others again. She's decided to join Proteus. Her code name is Artemis. She will now be the portal for Ireland. Iain is retiring . . . so he says.

8. Don't be afraid to take the reins. Your empathy is not a weakness. It's part of what qualifies you to lead.

9. I have known for a while that this time would come. I have discovered properties of the lodestone that I've shared with the portals. I have split up the information among each of them, and they know to share it only with you. Each one knows only the piece they have, and they will not give it up easily. They will test you to be sure you are not an imposter. Only you can retrieve each piece and put together what I have learned. Once you have them all, I hope you'll be able to carry on this work far beyond what I have done. If you write any of it down, never store any piece together with others.

10. It falls to us to protect mankind from himself. I would rather it all remains lost forever, than that what we hold dear should be destroyed or used unwisely. I pray a day will come when it is safe to share what we know with the world. The secrets of the universe give themselves willingly to those who will not exploit them.

11. Look inside the puzzle box in the Japanese step tansu. You'll need its contents.

12. I believe you have a greater ability to do this than I. If it's what you choose, there will be setbacks. There always are, no matter what

path we forge in life. Never forget our task—*Orbis Terrarum Relevetur ut Unum ad Tempus Consuo*—and never forget I'm out there cheering you on!

~ Grandpa

Paddy found the puzzle box and soon had it open. Inside was a rolled-up map with a symbol over the location of each portal. The symbol looked like a tiny dragon. There was a separate list of the current works of literature assigned to each country for deciphering coded messages, and a device with sliding tabs used to determine which cipher to use, depending on the specific day of each specific month.

He noticed that while the map was old, there was newer writing in pencil over some of the locations. It appeared that there was a code name assigned to the portal at each location: Ursa, Orion, Pyxis, Caelum, Aquila, Vela, Carina, Perseus, Lynx, Cygnus, Pegasus, and one newly penciled in over Dublin—Artemis . . . twelve in all. *No, wait. There's another.* A line through the name Cassiopeia over the state of Massachusetts had recently been erased.

Paddy stared at her name—Cassiopeia. *Did Grandpa know that guiding me to save Mama would also rescue me from my internal war of what to do with my life?* Though he believed that taking over Grandpa's role was his purpose, Paddy was bewildered about how to begin. *"Begin at the beginning," Grandpa would say.*

"These are all the people I need to visit," he said as he looked again at the map. "That's where I'll start." Somehow Paddy knew that this time when he told Papa he wanted to travel, he would understand.

He could hear the wind picking up outside by the sound of the iron clasp hitting the flagpole down by the beach. This time, it didn't sound like a warning. It sounded like a bell tolling, telling the entire town of a glorious victory.

He felt overcome with exhaustion from emotion and lack of sleep. He had just put his head down on his arms on the desk for a few minutes when he was jolted awake by the ringing of the phone Grandpa had left him. He was afraid to answer but then wondered if it might be Grandpa calling. Finally, he reluctantly answered, "Hello?"

The reply came in a gruff voice in Italian, "It's been a long time, eh, Scrydan? Are you free for another assignment?"

Definitely *not* The End.

I hope you enjoyed this introduction to Paddy's life, and how he first came to learn about the secrets closely guarded by his family. Be sure to look for the next book that will chronicle Paddy's own grand adventure as he follows in Grandpa's footsteps. If you'd like me to send you an email about future books or free supplements to books in *The Cover Stories* series, please sign up on www.lauriedouglass.com. Let's keep in touch!

Glossary

◊ abecedarian – arranged alphabetically.
◊ apothegm – a short, pithy, and instructive saying or formulation; an aphorism or adage.
◊ astrolabe – a compact instrument used to observe and calculate the position of celestial bodies (and one's position on earth in relation to them) before the invention of the sextant.
◊ benysoun – an ancient Scottish term meaning blessing.
◊ borescope – an optical device (such as a prism or optical fiber) used to inspect a space not usually accessible with the naked eye.
◊ calque – a loan translation of a word or words. A form of borrowing from one language to another where components of a word are literally translated into their equivalents in the borrowing language. English superman, for example, is a loan translation from German Übermensch.
◊ *Cé tusa?* – "Who are you?" in Irish Gaelic.
◊ *Conas atá tu?* – "How are you?" in Irish Gaelic.
◊ cryptanalysis – the solving of cryptograms.

◊ Enigma (Machine) – an encryption device with a rotor mechanism used to protect commercial, diplomatic and military communication. It was used extensively by the Nazis during World War II. At one time, it was considered able to create unbreakable code.

◊ Floccinaucinihilipilification - [flok-*suh*-naw-*suh*- nahy-hil-*uh*-pil-*uh*-fi-**key**-sh*uh* n] (rare) the estimation of something as valueless, as in, "To Paddy, all Papa's history lessons were a floccinaucinihilipilification."

◊ gnomon – an object that by the position or length of its shadow serves as an indicator of the hour of the day, such as the pin of a sundial or a column or shaft erected perpendicular to the horizon.

◊ Lunar Society – a group of intellectuals, philosophers, and scientists who met for discussions in Birmingham, England between 1765 and 1813. The group included: Joseph Priestley, Erasmus Darwin, Josiah Wedgwood, James Watt, Matthew Boulton, James Keir, Benjamin Franklin, and William Small, among others.

◊ Maquis – a term used during World War II to describe guerrilla fighters in the French underground. Some use the term maquisard to refer to an individual within the Maquis.

◊ *Milice française* – French paramilitary group sympathetic to the German forces during World War II. Singular: *milicien.*

◊ mnemonic – a device (such as a rhyme, acronym, ditty, or song) intended to assist memory.

◊ *phrontistes* – a philosopher or profound thinker.

◊ quinate – arranged in, or composed of sets of five.

◊ rashers – a thin slice of bacon or ham, broiled or fried.

◊ tandoor – a cylindrical clay oven in which food is cooked over charcoal.

◊ the jacks – an Irish slang term meaning the toilet.

◊ transit – a telescope that is mounted at right angles to a horizontal east–west axis on which it revolves. The device has many uses, including surveying land and in observing the duration of movement of a celestial body over a certain point.

Sources: www.merriam-webster.com and www.wikipedia.org.

ACKNOWLEDGMENTS

I owe so much to those who were willing to join me on this adventure. Each, through such inspiring talent and insight, helped make the world of Paddy Duncan clearer. Fiona McLaren, for your ability to see the big picture and patience to see which pieces were essential. My writing will benefit for years to come from your patience to teach through the process. Hampton Lamoureaux, for listening so patiently and managing somehow to create the exact cover that I saw in my mind's eye, and for paying attention to every tiny detail. Lynn Post, for such keen eyes and insightful suggestions. I learned so much from you. I hope we will be working together again soon!

Mark Frary, your book, *DE/CIPHER*, is my favorite historical chronology of codes. It continues to water my love of hidden messages and reveal a deep well I have yet to plumb. It is also now one of Paddy's favorite tomes. Thank you to all my kind beta readers and those who never tired of my questions—especially Sarah, Katherine, and Andreea. It takes a special devotion to be a beta-beta, and I am deeply grateful.

Thanks to all my friends and family whose encouragement was nothing short of faith. I am especially thankful for Tim, my husband,

and my best friend. This book wouldn't exist if not for you. I hope you know it's true, and how much I love you. Most of all, thank you, Heavenly Father, for filling my mornings and unexpected moments with sweet surprises—ideas I could never have thought of on my own.

ABOUT THE AUTHOR

Laurie Douglass is a fiction and poetry writer. She loves to inspire young and young-at-heart readers through storytelling that stretches the imagination and inspires curiosity. She prefers themes that touch on geoscience, culture, cryptography, and classic literature, always liberally woven with the unexpected.

Besides writing, Laurie enjoys discovering wonders in nature, day trips to the mountains (any mountains!), baking bread, and quilting. She has lived in South and Central America, throughout the US, and now makes her home in Maryland with her husband and their goofy dog, Grant.